AT FIRST SIGHT

AT FIRST SIGHT

Jodie Larsen

HAWK Publishing Group

Published in the United States by HAWK Publishing Group.

HAWK and colophon are trademarks belonging to the
HAWK Publishing Group.

Printed in the United States of America.

Library of Congress Cataloging in Publication Data
    Larsen, Jodie
        At First Sight/Jodie Larsen–HAWK Publishing ed.
        p.   cm.
        Hardcover edition: ISBN 1-930709-33-1
        Trade paperback edition: ISBN 1-930709-39-0
        1.Fiction–Oklahoma
        I. Title
    [PS3563.I42145R4 2000]
    813'.54   80-52413
                                          CIP

HAWK Publishing web address: www.hawkpub.com

H987654321

for Ellen

CHAPTER **1**

Her blood had a life of its own, long after I was sure she was dead. Oozing down one side of my face, it reached out to touch the corner of my lip. The taste of death was warm, salty, metallic. Everything I expected, yet much, much more . . .

Kaycee Miller turned the handwriting sample over, touching the indentations of the words as she consciously pushed aside the startling mental image they conveyed. Focusing only on the slant, the strokes, the intensity of the flow, the hidden message beneath the words quickly began to emerge.

Allowing her gaze to dart from one unfamiliar face to the next, she hesitated on each set of eyes only a fraction of a second. In spite of their encouraging nods, the men and women seated at the conference table couldn't hide the truth. They shared some secret, some cryptic knowledge that dragged down their spirits like a treacherous undertow. Instinct screamed for her to leave, but her practical side knew that earning the respect of another parole board would be a huge step toward gaining the acceptance of her peers.

To most of the psychiatric profession, graphology was on the controversial fringe of their science—an interesting marriage of art and knowledge that was still far too subjective to be taken seriously. There were plenty of vocal opponents who vehemently claimed that the ability to connect handwriting with human behavior was nothing more than a cheap carnival trick. Only a handful of her colleagues had taken the time to study the results of her groundbreaking research, to see the evolution of a valuable, exciting new technique.

Kaycee's work had already impressed several parole boards in Oklahoma, but she couldn't shake the feeling that this board meeting was far from normal. Was the New Mexico board really only testing her, making certain she could work under pressure? Or was she just being paranoid because so much was at stake, not only professionally, but personally?

Kaycee nervously ran a finger over the page as she stated, "This is a well educated man in his early forties. He put a great deal of effort into copying someone else's style, pressing much harder than normal, but there are still marks of his own personality. He's persistent, tenacious, coldly calculating, and too often lets his emotional side rule his actions."

A slight pinging in an overhead duct accompanied the prolonged silence before Kaycee finally asked, "Well, was I right?" Suddenly, it dawned on her. With a sly smile, she added, "It's one of you, isn't it? The emotional message was meant to cloud my judgment, make me assume we were dealing with a killer."

The tall, blond man at the head of the conference table grinned. "It's mine. And for the most part, you were right on target."

Returning his smile, she asked, "For the most part? I take it that means you disagree with at least one point, Mr. Palmer. I'm sure it isn't that you're persistent, tenacious, or quite bright, so it must be that you occasionally let emotion cloud your judgment."

Bob Palmer nodded, apparently unwilling to meet the challenge in her eye with the board watching. Wisely moving on, he said, "Ms. Miller, we realize that if you agreed to do contract work with us, you'd primarily be conducting more complicated tests. As we explained earlier, we think there are certain prisoners whose progress should be carefully tracked the entire time they're under our authority. I think I can speak for everyone when I say that your combination of psychology and graphology is quite intriguing. In fact, so far, you've done an excellent job."

"Thank you. Will you be contacting me soon?" she asked, starting to stand.

"Our decision should be made in the next two days. If you don't mind, we have one last set of writing samples we'd like you to examine."

Kaycee nodded. Settling back in her seat, she felt her confidence climb a notch. Total silence fell in the room as six pieces of paper were placed on the table in front of her. First she sensed, then witnessed, the people in the room tense—arms suddenly crossed, jaws stiffened, eyes focused elsewhere. She sighed. *So, they saved it for last. This is it. The real test.*

Looking down at the six slips of paper at her fingertips, she knew it didn't matter. For years she had lived and breathed graphology, studied how the mind and body blend to create the personal portrait that each person's writing was of their soul. From the first glance, she knew that these samples were unique, far different from the others they had presented. The difference was shocking, so shocking, in fact, that she instinctively cringed.

Taking her time, she studied the writing until she was as sure about her analysis as she had ever been of anything in her life. Clearing her throat, she pushed one slip of paper toward the center of the table. "This isn't his writing, but it's a pretty good forgery." She didn't miss the triumphant glance that passed from Bob Palmer to the woman at the end of the table, who didn't bother to hide her irritation.

Carefully lining up the remaining five pieces of paper, Kaycee continued, "These were all penned by the same person. A man. A very violent man. Most likely they were penned over a period of several months in the order I've arranged them. As you can see, they're all dark, heavy writing, but the pressure is steadily increasing. This man is getting tired of waiting."

Leaning forward, Palmer nodded. "That's right, Ms. Miller. What else can you tell us about him?"

Kaycee slowly turned the pages over, piece by piece, running manicured fingers along the impressions left by the ink pen before she spoke. On the back of each page the initials W.T. had been lightly penciled in the corner, along with a date. With pride she noted that the dates were in perfect sequential order.

Her voice conveyed her growing confidence. "He's prone to over-reacting, and has no regard for authority or rules." Picking up one of the samples, she stared at it. "This one shows the control he's capable of, and the intelligence that fuels it. Obviously, he knew he was being watched, felt the constraint of the test, the need to perform. The pressure on him is intense, trying to follow rules that he doesn't buy into. But even when he tries to obey, he doesn't quite succeed. Notice how the last letter of each word is a printed capital? That's just a glimpse of the violent nature shown in the other samples. And these—" she pointed to several cursive *t*'s "—these splinted *t*'s with heavy, descending crossings indicate that he's overly suspicious with a tendency to be cruel. I'd bet he's a loner who holds little value for human life, even his own."

The skeptical woman cleared her throat. "How dangerous do you think this man could be?"

Kaycee looked her right in the eye. "To be honest, I've never personally analyzed anyone who's so intelligent, yet so deeply disturbed. He's society's worst nightmare—a brilliant psychopath."

With a forced smile, the woman stated, "Ms. Miller, we really appreciate you traveling so far to demonstrate the merit of your work. One of the guards outside the door will see you safely back to your car. Thank you again for coming. Your presentation was very informative and educational. As Mr. Palmer said, we'll be in touch with you very soon."

Kaycee shoved her papers into her briefcase, nodding and smiling to hide her frustration at being so curtly dismissed. As she followed the armed guard outside, she realized that any one of the prisoners glaring at her could have written those frightening samples. Shivering, she quickened the pace.

•   •   •   •   •

Bob Palmer waited until the echo of the heavy metal door died before demanding, "Why did you cut her off like that, Susan? She was just getting to the interesting part."

"Because, thanks to you, it's too late," she snapped.

"Releasing Thornton wasn't just *my* idea. We all agreed that there wasn't enough to warrant keeping him here."

Susan bristled, "We didn't *all* agree. His case was practically shoved down our throats. And now we have confirmation that he may be a homicidal maniac. I don't care what Dr. Frank said, anyone who fries an entire litter of his neighbor's kittens in the microwave is never going to be a model citizen, no matter how much we try to rehabilitate him. I don't know about the rest of you, but right now I'm not very proud to be a part of this board."

Palmer slowly nodded, nailing her with an unwavering stare. "We all know this case is more complex than most. What about his other abilities? He's been a perfect prisoner since day one, so it's tough to deny the doctor's findings. Willy Thornton grew up bored and without proper constraints. Yes, microwaving cats for a science experiment was a danger sign, but it could also have been a call for help that was ignored. Dr. Frank claims his intellect is in control now that he's matured. Besides, you know we can't base our decision on an inmate's ancient history. We made the best decision we could based on the evidence we had at the time. Second-guessing ourselves isn't going to do anyone any good. Thornton may well be as dangerous as Ms. Miller just suggested, but we had no choice. If the doctor was wrong, I'm sure he'll break parole and be right back here where he belongs in no time at all."

"For all our sakes, let's hope he doesn't do it by killing a few hundred people," Susan muttered as she turned to leave.

• • • • •

Levi Crane's deep cough rattled through the darkness. Holding his breath, he waited for the rumble that meant Mother Earth was finally going to swallow them alive. He was sure they were half-way down her throat, where a simple gulp would hurl them the rest of the way to hell.

Another warning shower of tiny rocks fell, coating his lungs with even more dust and debris. The tap on the bottom of his boot kindled the growing sense of panic he'd fought all day.

"Levi, why don't you just light the way with a stick of dynamite?"

Levi's answer was little more than a hoarse whisper. "Sorry, Willy. This place gives me the creeps." He started to inch along again, crawling on his knees as he carefully moved the larger chunks of fallen rock to one side. Never before in his life had he felt such an overwhelming sense of dread. Being surrounded by tons of unstable ground was only a small part of the problem. It was Willy Thornton, the man behind him, who made his skin crawl. Once before he'd seen that glazed look in his eyes—the night he'd told him about killing that waitress.

Willy stayed a few feet behind Levi. Forced to pull his six-foot-five-inch frame along on his elbows and knees, it was harder for him to squeeze through the narrow opening of what had once been a spacious mine shaft. At least it was still wide, with plenty of room to turn around if necessary. Willy's voice was as low as his body, and even more stony than the rock-hard ground. "I can't believe the ceiling caved in. So many years without a hitch and then this. . ."

"At least it isn't totally blocked." Levi cringed, sorry he had ever let that jerk on the parole board convince him to keep an eye on Willy for a few days. Without thinking, his hand touched the wad of money folded inside his shirt pocket. A thousand dollars. *Easy money, my ass!* he thought. *If I get out of this hellhole alive, I'm gonna run like crazy and never look back!*

"Guess that makes me pretty lucky," Willy finally mumbled. "The tunnel should meet the cave real soon."

The flashlight beam bobbed through the dusty shaft ahead. "Looks like the chamber opens up in about twenty feet, but between here and there it might be too narrow for us to pass."

"Sure it is."

Levi didn't miss the edge of sarcasm in Willy's voice. A nervous little laugh fluttered from his lips as he pressed his body against the rocks and glanced back at his ex-cellmate. Shoving the flashlight back toward Willy, he offered, "See for yourself."

Just after the light left his hand, Levi glimpsed Willy's face in the fringe of the beam. Demonic eyes floated above chiseled, skeletal cheeks. He caught the smiling curl of a sneer the moment before the light snapped off. Silence haunted the darkness, coiling around his face like a suffocating mask until he found himself coughing more out of fear than from the musty air. "Wh. . .What's goin' on?" Levi managed to ask.

"You're planning to steal it."

The accusation barely had time to slice the air before Levi swore, "No way! It's your stash, Willy. I'd never. . ."

"But now you know where it is. And you know about the explosives I've got rigged."

"So? You asked me to come help you move it. You said the box was heavy, remember?"

Willy shook his head. "Sometimes I'm not too bright."

A single burst of light ripped through the still, stale air. The subsonic ammo and silencer on the .45 Colt semi-automatic minimized the sound of discharging the weapon, but Willy should have thought about the screams. They echoed through the shaft, vibrating like the fine whine of a tuning fork until Levi's last breath was finally spent.

Willy laid his head on outstretched arms and waited for the rocks to stop falling. Patience was something he had learned in his years in prison. Patience and strength. When combined, they were unstoppable. Once the filth settled, he snapped on the flashlight and aimed it past Levi's unseeing eyes. Although it was still more than wide enough, the opening was far too narrow for him to crawl through. Stretching his arm as high as he could, he aimed the beam down into the space ahead. Sure enough, at the side of the opening he spotted the edge of the box and grinned.

Not a hint of regret or sorrow nagged Willy, although it did occur to him how odd Levi looked. His head lolled at a peculiar angle, as if he were peering at some puzzling creature in the distance. A fresh layer of dirt covered him from head to toe, except where it was sliced by the crimson stream dripping onto his shoulder.

With a shrug, Willy plucked the wallet out of his friend's jeans, then patted his pockets. Laying down the flashlight, he extracted the wad of bills and counted it twice. Laughing aloud, he began to crawl backwards. By the time he reached the area where the shaft was still open, a smile had settled in his eyes. He knew exactly who was small enough to help dig out the opening of the cave. It would be hard, she was probably just a puny kid, scared of her own shadow. He was sure that stupid mother of hers was filling her little head with fear: fear that would ruin her, if he didn't teach her the real way life worked.

It's time Maggie met her Daddy.

The granite angel stood in the corner. Her graceful face looked past the cold pane of glass into the world, seeming to search the steel grey clouds for even the tiniest glimpse of warming sunlight. In reply, the first flakes of snow drifted carelessly down, coaxed by the wind before settling on the frozen land.

Kaycee stared at the statue she had fallen in love with just last year, staggered by how much her life had changed in the course of those twelve short months. Where she had seen beauty and happiness before, she now saw pain and suffering. The intricate details of the angel's flowing gown and delicate wings were lost in the intense gaze of her exquisitely carved eyes. Kaycee wondered if those angelic eyes, the same almond shape as her own, held the power to open the gates of heaven—or maybe they had unlocked the gates of hell. A shudder stopped her breath. *Stone eyes. Dead eyes. The streak of bad luck started the day that statue was unveiled.*

Turning away, Kaycee tried to warm herself by rubbing her hands along the sleeves of the soft burgundy sweater she wore. Her life—no, *she*—had changed so much. Fate kept dispensing bad news like sharp little slaps—stinging blows that were ripping the fight from her soul. "Why the hell haven't they called?" she whispered.

The granite angel, a creation of her sister's raw, God-given talent, mocked her with its innocent irony. Purity and love locked inside rock—paralyzed for eternity, frozen in time. For years she had fought for the life she wanted—and in the end, she had won. At least, that was how it seemed until a few weeks ago when her doctor had shattered every dream with five simple words : *There's nothing I can do.*

It wasn't her nature to passively accept such devastating news. She'd pulled every string in the book to get an appointment with one of the world's leading specialists, and she had no intention of missing it. Glancing at her watch, she knew she had to get going soon, whether the parole board called or not.

Distancing herself from the taunting work of art, she pushed down the familiar flood of white-hot anger, trying to gain control of the runaway roller-coaster ride her life had become. Across the room her sister was watching television. She knew she should just tell her, tell *someone*, but she just couldn't. Not yet. Not until she was sure there was no hope.

"It's time!" her excited voice called.

The news snapped Kaycee out of her dark mood as the television sparked to life in the corner. After a deep, calming breath, she watched and listened with her heart to the story she knew all too well. . .

Beauty and silence filled the television screen for the first few moments. A cascade of glistening black curls surrounded a face with such delicate features that it seemed to defy its own somber expression.

"I'm thirty-one years old, and I'll probably be in this wheelchair the rest of my life." The words were spoken with great care, as if forming each syllable required utter concentration.

The camera zoomed in on bright, intent eyes—passionate blue eyes that craved the ability to change just one moment in time. As the shot held a steady closeup, the woman's frail voice wavered, then grew stronger. "I was a downhill skier. An artist. Last year some friends threw me a thirtieth birthday party. A *friend* convinced me that my life had become boring, that I should try something new, something exciting. That *friend* gave me a line of cocaine. Told me it would change my life forever. I tried it. Once. One line. She was right. My whole life changed."

A different camera angle showed her head tilt slightly down as she gathered strength. Casting a disgusted look at her nearly useless legs, with great effort she raised her curled left hand, finally managing to extend one shaky finger. "One time. I used cocaine one time and had a massive stroke. I'm lucky I can still speak. My art is on hold for now. Chances are I might never walk again. Chances are—it could happen to you."

The screen faded to black as the logo for the national anti-drug campaign glowed for five seconds. Kaycee snapped off the television with the remote control and squeezed her sister's hand. "I'm so proud of you, Niki," she declared.

"It's good, isn't it?"

"No. It's absolutely brilliant. Anyone who isn't moved by that commercial has the brains of a tree frog."

"So you're saying it won't stop most teenagers from trying drugs?"

Kaycee laughed. "If they've evolved past the croaking stage, it'll scare the hell out of them. Besides, if it stops just one person. . ."

Niki lightly tugged on the cross that dangled from the gold chain around Kaycee's neck, searching her sister's troubled face. "Stop worrying about me. I'm going to be all right. I really do get better every day, and now that I have the special van I can go anywhere I like, all by myself."

Sucking in a long, deep breath, Kaycee fought the urge to tell her the real reason she was so distraught, but the words wouldn't come. Niki had enough problems without worrying about her.

After a long, quiet moment, Kaycee finally replied, "I'm very proud of how you've handled this. Then again, Dad always said the Miller girls were strong as bears." Tapping the wheelchair, she added, "You're going to break out of this iron cocoon and float down those mountains again like a butterfly. You just have to give it time. Time, energy, and the Miller fighting will."

Niki snapped, "Considering my state of mind, I'd prefer to buzz down the hill like a wasp. I can think of a few people I'd love to sting."

"Such as?"

"The *friend* who talked me into this mess."

Relieved to see a spark in her sister again, Kaycee flashed a genuine smile. The phone rang, and the two women exchanged a nervous glance. Picking it up, Kaycee nodded to let her sister know it was the call she'd been waiting for all day.

Five minutes later, Kaycee cradled the receiver.

"Well?" Niki asked anxiously.

"Remember that creepy handwriting sample?"

"The psycho you told me about last night?"

She nodded. "He was released from prison about a week ago."

"How could that happen?"

"He was only serving time for assault with a deadly weapon, even though they suspect he was involved in at least one brutal murder. The prison psychiatrist cleared him, said he was stable."

"Do you think that's why everyone acted so oddly at the meeting yesterday?"

Kaycee nodded. "Apparently, the board was torn between the pleas of victim's family and the clean psychiatric evaluation. Since there wasn't enough evidence to hold up in court, he was never charged with her murder."

Niki shook her head. "And. . .What else did they say?"

"The work is mine if I want it."

"You don't sound overly excited."

"Trust me, inside I'm doing back flips."

"Then why do you look like you just lost your best friend?"

Kaycee shrugged. "I should be more excited, shouldn't I?"

"That depends on why you agreed to come here. I've told you a million times—if you're moving back to New Mexico because you think I need help, you're making a big mistake. I'm going to be fine."

Kaycee squeezed her hand. "I know. It's just. . ."

"Just nothing. Stay in Tulsa. Don't sell your house. You love that house!"

"But I love you, too. You're all the family I have left."

"So? Are telephones going to be declared illegal? You know, you *can* visit whenever you come here to do work!"

Exasperated, Kaycee stepped back. "Enough! Stop piling on the guilt. I've already put my business up for sale, and the real estate agent has someone who's interested in buying my house. It's too late, the decision has been made."

Niki softly shook her head. "It's *never* too late."

Kaycee nodded, glancing at the falling snow. "I've really got to get going. The weather isn't exactly looking great between here and Tulsa. If I don't get out of Taos soon I'll never make it through the mountain passes before dark."

Niki rolled the wheelchair to the corner by the statue. "You've always loved this angel. I want you to have it." Seeing the skeptical look on her sister's face, she added, "It would give me a good reason to try to start on another one."

Kaycee hesitated, feeling her stomach clench as she glanced at the work of art. "Thanks. When I move I'll take you up on it."

"You know, you aren't fooling anyone. Are you really going to leave without telling me what's wrong?"

"For the hundredth time, *nothing*!" Kaycee snapped, turning away to pull on her heavy jacket. Leaning over, she hugged her sister, blatantly ignoring the look of disbelief in her eyes. "Take care of yourself and call if you need anything. Promise?"

"I promise," Niki sighed.

Kaycee rushed outside, shivering in a wave of frigid air. The wind stung her eyes, another reminder of their family's recent misfortunes—first her parents, then her sister, and now her. Time might heal Niki, but it wouldn't bring her parents back to life. And every passing second brought Kaycee closer to living in a dark world forever.

• • • • •

Willy Thornton constantly checked the rearview mirror as he drove his 4X4 Ford truck exactly one mile an hour under the speed limit. He couldn't take chances at this point, couldn't risk being stopped by the police for any reason.

Unable to wipe the smile off his face, he glanced at the child at his side. She was buckled safely in the passenger seat, one foot curled beneath her small body, her chin resting against the inside of the door just below the window. To his surprise, he realized she had inherited his eyes and strong chin. What could only be described as a wave of paternal pride washed through him.

On her head was the gift he'd brought her—a Dr. Seuss-like velveteen ski hat so tall it crumpled to one side. She softly stroked it in silence, two fingers delicately tugging a loose thread on the top seam.

Willy wondered how long it would take before her mother missed her. Ten minutes? An hour? It made no difference. She'd never track them down—not in a million years. He wished he could see her face when she found out he wasn't tucked safely in prison anymore.

"Doin' okay, Maggie?" he asked.

She nodded.

"You're about four years old now, right?"

"Five."

"Like that hat, don't ya? I saw it when I was skiing in Vail and I knew it was made for my princess." Watching her nod, he sighed. "When you were a little baby I used to read *The Cat in the Hat* to you. Bet you can read it all by yourself now." *Kids will believe anything!* In truth, he had bought the hat an hour ago, and the only time he'd seen Maggie was when she was a baby. Hiding in the bushes behind her house, he stole a few quick glimpses before her mother rushed her inside and locked the doors.

Maggie never answered, so he carried the conversation by asking, "Has it snowed here yet?"

This time her head twisted back and forth beneath the huge, unmoving brim.

"What are you thinking about?"

"Why Mommy didn't tell me you were coming."

"She didn't know, princess. I wanted to surprise both of you."

"But she'll worry. I know she will. She told me I could only ride my bike to Jamie's house if I called her when I got there. And I'm never supposed to get in the car with strangers."

"I'm not a stranger!" Taking a deep breath, he tried to sound calm. "I'm your father. I left a message on your mom's answering machine—"

"But—" she interrupted, then abruptly stopped, fixing her eyes on the passing scenery.

"But nothing. Your mom knows exactly where you are. I told her I have your bike, and that we're going to go play in the mountains for a few days to get to know each other. You can call her later to say hi. Okay?"

This time the child didn't answer. Instead, she shrugged, squeezing her eyes tightly closed.

"We're going to play a game in a little while. Have you ever seen a real gold mine?"

She shook her head, never opening her eyes.

"You will today." The week-old image of Levi's body blocking the tunnel floated through his mind. Probably stunk to high heaven by now. He'd have to explain it somehow. It would have to be part of the game, a kind of challenge.

With a sideways glance, he wished again his only child had been born a boy. Reaching over, he touched her silky hair. "I'm sorry."

She turned to face him, her eyes pleading. "Please take me home."

"When I was a kid, I didn't understand either. I even ran away once. Still got the scars from my daddy's belt to prove it."

Sobbing, she grabbed his arm. "I want to go home!"

"After you've learned a few things, we'll see. Don't you worry, though. I won't take a belt to you. All that did was make me hate my daddy." Wiping a tear from her cheek, he added, "Little girls are supposed to love their daddies. No matter what."

CHAPTER 3

The wind spit fine, glittering sheets of snow across the winding mountain pass. The knuckles of Kaycee's clenched fists matched the white world outside as she anxiously gripped the steering wheel and cursed herself for not leaving earlier, before the winter storm unleashed its full fury.

She didn't dare think about the undulating sea of white tree tops just beyond the pathetically small guardrail that separated the pavement from the steep drop. Instead, her gaze was glued on the ribbon of road unfurling ahead, intently watching for patches of ice. A large yellow and black sign indicated another sharp S turn, just as a big Ford truck seemed to appear out of nowhere. Flying onto the highway from what was probably a snow-covered dirt road, it fishtailed into her lane, then barely maneuvered out of her way an instant before they would have collided. She caught a brief glimpse of the driver's profile before his tires threw a blinding sheet of dirty slush across her windshield.

Kaycee kept her foot poised over the brake even though she was only going twenty-five miles an hour, trying to stay calm as the wipers worked to wash away the muck. When she could finally see clearly again, it was too late.

Oh my God! She froze—one heartbeat too long. Two figures were on the far side of her lane, and she was headed directly at them. By the time she realized it was a man walking a dog, she had already hit the brakes too hard, sending both man and beast leaping over the guardrail to avoid being struck. Out of control, the car skidded all over the road before it finally stopped. Kaycee's heart was pounding a rhythm so frantic she wondered if it would leap out of her chest.

Throwing open the car door, she searched the side of the road. There was no one in sight. *Did I hit them?* She didn't think so, but everything had happened so fast she couldn't be sure.

Wondering what kind of nut would be walking in a snowstorm, she climbed into the brutal weather. With each step, a knot grew in the pit of her stomach. *It couldn't happen again. Not here. Not now!* The same fear that had nagged her since she was seventeen made her hesitate. Once before she had stopped to help someone, and paid dearly.

Taking a deep breath, she walked to the last footprints near the rail, carefully peering over the side of the mountain. A rush of relief washed through her. About fifty yards down the snow-covered slope she spotted him—a man lying very still at the base of a tree. At his side, the dog rested one paw on his chest as he steadily barked. Raising her voice, Kaycee called, "Are you all right?"

The dog urgently barked in reply, almost as if it understood the question.

Kaycee called again. The man still didn't move, and the dog continued its steady bark.

Another alarming surge of adrenaline made Kaycee's fingers tingle as she stepped over the guardrail. As if the dog was certain she was on her way to help, he turned around once then lay down to wait, his head atop the motionless body.

In a matter of seconds she lost her balance trying to rush down the steep bank. Falling flat on her back, she slid helplessly out of control until she managed to grab a four-foot-tall pine sapling to stop her awkward descent. While catching her breath, she pushed the hair out of her eyes, then briefly thought about trying to stand back up. One look downhill made her opt for crawling the few remaining yards.

The dog was protecting a man wearing an oversized parka, faded jeans, and cowboy boots. He was sprawled beneath the huge pine tree that had abruptly stopped his fall. The dog's dark eyes never left hers, as she got close enough to tell he was a large German shepherd, mostly white with sable and tan markings around his ears, eyes, and prominent muzzle. She hesitated when she noticed the hair on the back of his neck was on end. He was trembling, apparently very serious about guarding the downed man.

The dog barked sharply as Kaycee crept forward, his penetrating eyes never leaving hers. She stopped in her tracks as he half-howled, half-cried, a long, moaning bay. "It's okay. I only want to help," she said in her most soothing voice.

The answer was another low growl, followed by an ear-piercing series of barks. "Quiet, Stagga," the man mumbled. Raising a hand to his head, he added, "You're giving me a headache."

Relief washed over Kaycee and she inched closer. "Are you okay?"

Rolling onto his side, he groaned, casting an inquisitive, annoyed glance her way. "I've been better."

With a watchful eye on the dog, she helped the man sit up. Brushing the snow off his parka, she nervously babbled, "I didn't mean to force you off the road. I just didn't see you in time to stop and there was a patch of ice and—"

"It's okay. Really."

Guilt overwhelmed her when she saw the patch of crimson snow where his head had been. "You're bleeding! Let me help." Pulling a wad of fresh Kleenex out of her coat pocket, she dabbed at the trickle of blood from the small cut on his forehead.

For the first time she noticed the man was disarmingly handsome. His eyes were green, but flecked with brown tones that matched the brittle pinecones scattered about him, apparently knocked loose by his recent collision with the tree. As he shifted to sit more upright, the hood of the parka fell back to reveal a thick head of hair in the same dark, rich coffee color that outlined the tips of his dog's ears. Nodding toward the animal, she asked, "Does it bite?"

"It's a he, and he definitely does not bite."

"Could've fooled me. He seemed rather intent."

After pushing himself up, he reached down to help Kaycee stand. "Stagga was only doing what he was trained to do."

"Scare away help?"

He smiled. "No. *Get* help. He's a certified SAR K-9, a search and rescue dog. He was trying to tell you someone needed help. Did you notice how he stayed at my side and barked until he was sure he had your full attention?"

She nodded, still skeptical. "True, but I got the distinct impression he didn't want me to touch you."

"I suppose being a little too protective is okay. He probably thought this was another drill. We've been through a lot in the last week." Bending one knee, he hugged the dog and whispered, "Good boy, Stagga. Good boy." Turning his attention back to his human company, he added, "By the way, my name is Max Masterson. Stagga and I are pleased to meet you."

Holding out her hand, she replied, "Kaycee Miller. The pleasure is all mine. Are you sure you're feeling okay?"

Lightly touching the wound on his forehead, he smiled. "Takes more than a kick in the head to keep me down." Brushing patches of packed snow off the back of her jacket he added, "You look like you took a tumble yourself."

She shook her head, dislodging icy clumps from her shoulder-length sable hair. "True. Would you mind if we continue this conversation while we climb back up? There's no shoulder, so I left my car blocking the road."

"Sure. Let's go, Stagga."

Kaycee was slightly amazed at the immediate response of the dog. He was instantly at his master's side, walking in a perfect heel position on the left as they started to attack the precipitous grade. "If you'll dig your feet in like this, you won't be as likely to slip."

"Thanks." She tried to mimic his confident strides, barely managing to keep up with them. Her thigh and calf muscles were burning as she asked, "You two are pretty good at this, aren't you?"

"We were in the mountains for a course on avalanche rescue, so we've learned a few tricks about plowing through snow and steep grades. Would you by any chance have a cell phone in your car?"

"Do you actually think a lone female would try this road under these conditions without one?"

"Mind if I use it to call a wrecker? My 4Runner decided to conk out on me just around the next curve, and I forgot to pack the battery charger for my own phone." He pulled three flares from inside the heavy coat. "I was walking back to warn oncoming traffic with these."

"Glad to know you weren't just out giving Stagga some exercise." Kaycee spontaneously smiled when she noticed the dog's ears perk at the mention of his name. Watching closely, she said, "Stagga." The dog let out a shallow whine, but kept walking beside his master. "That's an unusual name."

"As a puppy he was stubborn and aggressive, two characteristics that almost kept him out of the SAR training program. The name Stagga just seemed to fit him."

Stagga barked as he gracefully hurdled the rail, his tail wagging a challenge. Max followed, extending his hand to help Kaycee over.

Opening the driver's door, she asked, "Why don't you set your flares, then I'll drive you back to your truck while you call for help?"

"Deal."

Kaycee watched them disappear around the bend, dusted the snow from her boots and jacket, then climbed into the welcome warmth of her charcoal gray Lexus. As Max and Stagga jogged back toward the car, she noticed that Max was not only good-looking, he was tall, over six feet. He and Stagga made quite a dashing pair.

Pulling open the passenger door, Max took one look at the car's spotless leather interior and stopped. "I think it would be better if Stagga and I walk back to my truck." Casting a rueful look at the clumps of snow matted on the hair of Stagga's paws and belly, he added, "We're really a mess."

"Don't be ridiculous, it's freezing out there." She grinned slyly. "Besides, some maniac might run you off this narrow road if you walk."

"Good point." Opening the back door, he brushed as much snow off Stagga as he could, then ordered, "Stagga, in. Hide." The dog happily obeyed, leaping onto the floorboard where he curled into a surprisingly small ball. Max knocked the snow off his boots then folded himself into the front seat.

"Hide?" Kaycee asked.

"One of his tricks. You'd be surprised how often it comes in handy, especially at places that don't allow pets. He'll stay there until I give the next command."

"I'm impressed. My last dog was a Yorkie who was so spoiled she'd give me the evil eye when I expected her to do her business outside in the rain. Heaven forbid she might actually get her paws wet!" His laugh warmed her heart.

"My friends accuse me of being more attached to Stagga than I am to them. So far, I haven't found a kind of weather that he doesn't do well in. I only let him sleep inside on really hot summer days or when we're traveling. SAR dogs have to be tough. You never know what kind of conditions you'll be trapped in, or for how long. Besides, he sheds like crazy."

By the time Kaycee spotted his black 4Runner, Max had already contacted a towing service on her cell phone. "They said they would be here in an hour, two at the most," he said.

A quick glance at the clock on the dashboard was all it took to make Kaycee's shoulder and neck muscles coil into hard, stiff knots. "But the sun will be down by then!"

With a wistful smile, he said, "I'm not afraid of the dark."

For several seconds Kaycee simply stared at him, her fingers unconsciously toying with her necklace. It had been her mother's—a beautiful gold cross. Her mind was racing through a million excuses why she needed to leave, but it never dawned on her to tell him that her night vision was rapidly deteriorating, so much so that she was the one who was *afraid of the dark*. She was surprised at how weak her voice sounded when she finally offered, "Then I guess I'd better wait here with you, just in case they don't make it. . ."

The subtle change in Kaycee had not escaped Max, nor had the hesitant glance at her own reflection in the rearview mirror. *What could possibly have spooked her?* he wondered.

Max had spent a good part of the last eighteen years working with people who desperately needed help—both those in trouble, and their frantic relatives. He had learned to channel their fear, to turn its crushing strength into something more constructive—the energy to challenge fate, even against overwhelming odds.

Opening the car door, he smiled warmly as he stepped outside. "It's okay. Stagga and I don't mind waiting alone. Stagga, heel." The dog bounded happily out the door to his master's side.

"But what if the wrecker can't find you? You could freeze to death. At least keep my cell phone. You can mail it back to me."

"The wrecker *will* make it, and we'll be just fine. Thank you very, very much for the use of your phone, but I wouldn't think of keeping it. What if you have car trouble a few miles down the road?"

"But—"

"Really, I insist. I hope we meet again someday under better circumstances."

The degree of indecision in those gorgeous eyes was disturbing. They reminded him of stone-washed denim—creamy blue spiked with subtle shades of grey—a soft blend of sophistication and simplicity. She was obviously torn. Afraid to leave, yet equally afraid to stay. "Is something wrong?" he asked, studying her every move.

Kaycee's eyes jumped from place to place as she nervously twisted the chain of the gold cross. "Nothing's wrong. I'm just worried about getting through this pass before the weather makes it impossible."

It was so easy to read the lie on that beautiful face, so easy it made him shudder. *Don't ever play poker,* he wanted to tease, but sensed she was in no mood. Instead of pressing her, he backed away with a trusting, friendly smile and a wave. "You really should get going. It was nice to meet you!"

Flipping open the glove compartment, she grabbed a pen and pad of paper. "This is my cell phone number. I'll be spending the night in the next town, Cimarron. Would you mind calling me when you get there? That way I'll know everything turned out okay."

"I promise to call as soon as I can. Really, you shouldn't worry. Stagga and I have made it through much worse times than this. Much, much worse."

"Okay. But if I don't hear from you by eight o'clock, I'm sending out the highway patrol or the national guard, or whatever kind of law enforcement they have in this God-forsaken place."

Max shouted, "You'll be hearing from me soon!"

Long after she drove away, Max could easily picture Kaycee. Her provocative blue eyes perfectly complemented the rich shade of her dark brown hair. The gentle sound of her voice curled effortlessly inside his mind, bringing a smile to his face until he remembered the moment her entire body tensed. She was afraid of something, no, more like *terrified*.

Shifting nervously as he waited, Max stared into the swirling snow and absentmindedly scratched Stagga behind the ears. *What could have instilled such fear in Kaycee Miller?* he wondered.

Leaning over, he hugged Stagga. "According to her car tag, she's from our neck of the woods. I'm going to help her, boy. You in?"

Stagga nuzzled approvingly against him, more than up for another challenge.

·   ·   ·   ·   ·

"I don't like this game! I want to go home!"

"You're not going anywhere until we finish playing. Understand?"

Maggie nodded, knowing that she had to do what he said. Now she knew why Mommy was so afraid of him. She was, too. He had lied to her. He lied about telling her Mommy where she was. He lied about letting her call home.

As she crawled, the rocks hurt her knees and hands, and the cold made her shiver. That awful smell was getting stronger, it made her stomach feel funny. But she kept going, moving slower as the tunnel got smaller.

"Stop for a minute while I catch up."

She sat back on her heels, waiting. The flashlight beam bounced about, illuminating what lay behind the shadows just long enough to make the walls seem alive. "I'm scared! I want to go home!" she cried.

"But we're just getting to the good part." Scooting beside her, he patted her on the back as he pulled something out of his pocket. "You're doing real good, kid. Better than I expected."

"What's that for?" she asked, her voice trembling with a new layer of terror.

"This is where the game gets really fun!"

Maggie shivered, but didn't say a word as he tied the blindfold in place.

CHAPTER 4

Kaycee was relieved to see the small town of Cimarron, New Mexico as she finally emerged from the mountain pass. It was still snowing heavily, and she could tell from the rapidly decreasing light that the sun had already dipped below the western horizon. As was the nearby national forest, everything in the town seemed to be named after Kit Carson, so she pulled into the parking lot of The Kit Carson Luxury Motel.

From the looks of the office, the definition of luxury must have changed in the last twenty-five years. The furniture and carpet were clean, but dated and worn. An older woman in a thick terrycloth robe and lamb's wool slippers emerged from the back room with the sound of a sitcom laugh track at her heels. "Need a room?" she asked.

"Yes. Just for tonight."

"Only got three left. The best of 'em is number 22—next to last door on the end 'round back. It's really a suite that adjoins the room next door to it, but there's a lock on your side. That okay?"

"Sure." Kaycee paid the woman, turned to leave, then stopped. "Do you know what time sunrise is?"

"'Bout six-thirty, I think. You need a wake-up call?"

"Yes, please. Six o'clock would be perfect."

A smile and a quick nod were her reply before she withdrew to finish watching her television show. Kaycee drove the Lexus to the rear of the one-story motel, disappointed to see that the parking lot was dark and the snow had formed a two-foot drift in the last close parking spot.

For a minute after pulling the key from the ignition, she simply stared outside, trying to memorize the short path to her room before she turned off the headlights. When she did, she started to unlock the car door, but froze. A fresh wave of fear caught her completely off guard, one so strong she actually flinched. *Get used to the dark, Kaycee. Soon it might always be dark.*

Her breath caught as she fought to regain control. Scanning the parking area, she was certain there was no one lurking outside, no wild animal waiting to pounce when she stepped out of the car. As cold and nasty as it was, she doubted if anyone would be crazy enough to venture from their warm, toasty rooms. Yet the feeling of dread hung in the pit of her stomach. She felt something she could only call *evil* pulse in the air. It suffocated all logic, stole her ability to move, made her tremble for no apparent reason.

In her entire life Kaycee had never experienced anything so frightening. She had always been strong, so strong that the terms "willful" and "bullheaded" popped up frequently in her school records. In her professional life she'd stubbornly fought to gain respect and recognition for a branch of psychology most of her peers considered to be unconventional, and therefore, unreliable. Yet here she was, trapped in her car by nothing. *Nothing!*

A full five minutes passed before she worked up the nerve to unlock the car door and step outside. *Must be a panic attack. The doctor said this might happen. God, for years I've been helping people work through these and I had no idea how truly horrible they can be!* After a few deep breaths, she managed to negotiate the ice covered sidewalk to the door. Fumbling with her key in the dark, she wished she had chosen a hotel that provided security lights in the parking lot. But it was too late to change now. All she wanted was a good night's sleep, and to get safely back home.

When the door finally opened, she tossed her luggage inside, shakily bolted the door, and fastened the security chain. It was a typical motel room. A double bed draped with an old floral bedspread occupied most of the space. There was a window by the door, a small table and two chairs nestled directly below it. Across from the bed was a dresser with an old television set, beyond that the door to the adjoining room the clerk had told her to expect. She was about to make sure the inner door was securely locked when her cell phone rang.

"Hello?" she answered, her voice still shaky.

"Kaycee? It's Max. Just wanted you to know that Stagga and I are safe and sound. We're on our way to Cimarron. Where are you staying?"

"The Kit Carson Luxury Motel."

"I'm headed that way. Would you consider letting me buy you dinner? There's a nice little restaurant on the edge of town."

"Max, I'd love to, but I'm just too tired. How about joining me for an early breakfast instead?"

"It's a date."

"Why don't you meet me in the lobby tomorrow morning at 7:00?"

"See you then." Cradling the phone, Kaycee smiled. He seemed like such a nice man. Niki would be happy that she had agreed to go out with someone, even if it was in the middle of nowhere with a man she'd probably never see again.

Never see again. . .

Kaycee slumped onto the hard mattress and stared at the ceiling. Hot tears rolled down her cheeks for the first time since she'd been to the doctor. Dragging in a deep breath, she wiped her face. Tomorrow she'd be home. First thing the next morning she'd see Dr. Boomer. In a way, her life rested in his hands. Sitting up, Kaycee sighed. It was too early to cry.

Crying was a privilege she'd vowed to save until she was certain she was really going blind.

•   •   •   •   •

Max hung up the pay phone and took a deep breath. Stagga was at his side, his tail wagging. "Sorry, old fella. No time to play."

Stagga barked enthusiastically, then jumped back into the cab of the tow truck. Max nodded at the driver, and they headed off again.

It wasn't long before they spotted the sign for the Kit Carson Luxury Motel. Max agreed that the service station across the street would be the best place to leave the 4Runner for the night, even though it was already closed.

After the tow truck pulled away, Max unlocked his truck and commanded, "Stagga, hide. I'll be back in a few minutes." Stagga leaped into the back seat, then crawled onto the floor. Curling his body into a tight circle on the narrow floorboard, he held perfectly still, like a fluffy white rug.

Max rushed across the street, noticing the sign dangling in the office doorway—Absolutely No Pets. Quickly glancing back toward the seemingly empty 4Runner, he thought, *Luckily, a certified SAR K-9 is by no means a mere pet.*

．　．　．　．　．

Going to sleep proved to be a challenge that evening for Kaycee, even though she couldn't remember ever being more exhausted. Tossing and turning in the pitch black room, she couldn't escape the uneasy feeling that had plagued her since she arrived. At midnight, she crawled out from under the covers long enough to turn on the bathroom light. Leaving the door ajar brightened the room just enough to make her feel a little more secure in the strange surroundings.

Deep sleep eventually pulled her into its welcome embrace. She rested comfortably at first, surrounded by the dreamless solitude where she so rarely found peace anymore. Then it began. The nightmare that was painfully peeling her self-confidence away layer by layer.

Total darkness consumed her. The wind sang in the distance. Confusion was replaced by terror as she tried to move first her arms, then her legs. No matter how hard she fought, it was no use. She was hopelessly trapped. Then the horrid rumbling began, shattering the eerie quiet with the moans of more rocks, more dirt falling on top. Crushing. Suffocating. Stealing every beam of light. . .

Kaycee's eyes flew open, her breath ragged as she placed her hand on her chest. As always, her heart was pounding wildly beneath the damp nightshirt. But this time something was different. Slowly turning her head, she was sure she must still be asleep, even though her eyes were wide open.

Standing next to her bed was a child.

CHAPTER 5

Kaycee tried to rub away the remnants of sleep, certain she was either trapped in a nightmare or hallucinating from another panic attack. But before she opened her eyes again, the light touch of a hand on her shoulder brought home reality—she wasn't dreaming, couldn't be. Oh, God. Someone really is in here!

A scream started to rise in her throat, but she didn't make a sound. Even in the dimly lit room, she could see the little girl was holding a finger to her lips, begging her not to make a sound.

Kaycee's trembling hand seemed to move in slow motion as she reached out to touch the child. Except for big, wide eyes, the girl's face was dirty, smudged with streaks of grime. Yet as her trembling hand tenderly made contact, it was soft, warm, and very real. Pushing aside the matted, sandy-colored bangs, Kaycee caught a chilling glimpse of the terror that filled the girl's huge brown eyes.

Untangling her legs from the blankets, she bolted upright. Motioning for the child to lean closer, she whispered, "Who are you?"

"Help me."

The child's timid, quivering voice was so weak it made her want to cry. "How did you get in here?"

Big eyes darted toward the door that led to the adjoining suite, then back to Kaycee in another silent plea. Kaycee was surprised to see the door was slightly ajar. Pushing past the girl, the hardwood floor was cold on her feet as she tiptoed across the short distance. Mustering all her courage she gazed into the connecting room.

A dim light glowed on the nightstand in the suite next door, allowing her to see inside. There were two beds. One was empty, but atop the other were two figures. At first, she could only make out dark lumps, but after a few seconds of staring Kaycee could tell there was a man, and possibly a woman. The woman was turned away, buried completely beneath the covers, yet from the size and the sound of her light breathing Kaycee felt sure it was a woman. What Kaycee found odd was that the huge man at her side was fully clothed, sprawled on top of the bedspread. He was so tall his feet hung off the edge of the mattress. In the eerie red glow of the alarm clock she saw the gleam of a gun securely wedged into a leather shoulder holster at his side.

The weapon was enough to convince Kaycee that the child did, indeed, need help. Very slowly, she eased the door closed, then took what seemed like an eternity to slide the old bolt securely into its latch. Crossing back to the little girl, she knelt at her side. "Who are those people?"

The child simply stared at her, then at the floor, as if telling the truth might make Kaycee change her mind. The words, "Help me. Please," were barely understandable.

"I will." Fumbling for the phone she knocked her mother's gold cross off the nightstand, then started to dial 911.

"No!" the child said forcefully, yet quietly, as she pushed a finger on the disconnect button. "Get me away from him! Hurry! He'll take me back to that place! Mommy said he might come some day. She said not to go! She's probably really mad at me!"

Pulling her into her arms, Kaycee soothed, "It's all right. You're safe now, and your mom isn't going to be mad."

"He's a liar! We don't have an answering machine, so he couldn't have told Mommy where I am! I want to go home!"

Kaycee started to dial, and once again the child cut her off. "The police will come and help. You'll be safe with them."

"No! He'll wake up! We have to hurry!"

The image of the gun flashed through Kaycee's mind. The girl was probably right—they would both be safer somewhere else.

The alarm clock glowed 3:23 a.m. Where could she find help at such an ungodly hour of the morning? Would a town like Cimarron even have a police station? She hadn't noticed one, but it had been getting dark. Maybe there was an all-night gas station. . .

The girl rushed toward the door. "Please!"

"Just let me get my clothes." Flipping on a light, she grabbed an old purple Northwestern sweatshirt from her open suitcase and tossed it to the child. "Put this on!"

Her eyes went wide and she shook her head. "I'm too dirty!"

"It's okay."

The girl silently obeyed, but Kaycee could tell her appearance embarrassed her. The sweatshirt swallowed most of her body, but at least it would keep her warm. Kaycee tugged on a pair of jeans and pulled a baggy sweater over her nightgown. Quietly closing the suitcase, she dug the car keys out of her purse and grabbed the child's hand. She was instantly sorry when she felt her recoil in pain. Looking down, she saw her palms were raw and swollen.

"We'll get you fixed up first thing," she whispered as she peeked out the window into the empty, black world. As quietly as she could she twisted the deadbolt, then slid the chain off and let it dangle. She had barely turned the knob when the door flew violently open. It was kicked so hard it knocked both her and the little girl back into the room.

There was no time to scream, no place to run. They were trapped.

· · · · ·

Five rooms away on the opposite side of the hotel, Stagga shot up from the cozy spot on the blanket Max had placed beside the bed. Ears erect, he sat stiffly, cocking his head to listen with every part of his body. Minutes passed. What started as a soft whine soon escalated to a full-fledged barking fit.

"Stagga, hush!" Max rolled out of bed, his head cradled in his hands as his feet touched the cold floor. "What's wrong, boy?" he asked, snapping on the light.

Stagga ran to the door and sat down, obviously wanting to go outside.

Max groaned and muttered, "No way. You know the rules. It's

after three o'clock in the morning. Use the newspaper." Shutting off the light, Max crammed his feet into the warm covers and fell promptly back to sleep.

With a whine, Stagga sat by the door and rigidly waited.

· · · · ·

The man held the gun steady, training it right between Kaycee's eyes. She had never seen a face like his, never felt an aura so powerfully evil. Instincts she didn't even know she had suddenly kicked into gear. She wanted to freeze, to run, to scream, to kill him before he killed her. The momentary confusion left her paralyzed, her mouth slightly open.

Calmly, he kicked the door closed behind him and smiled. "Move a muscle. Scream. Do anything besides lay there quietly and you're dead. Understand?"

Kaycee barely nodded, turning her head only slightly so she could see the child on the floor beside the bed. When the two of them made eye contact, she watched in horror as the girl flinched beneath the hatred that flowed so easily from him. Still frozen, she saw the child crawl like a dog to his side, her eyes never leaving the floor. "I'm sorry . . ."

In a beastly snatch, his huge hand swept her up beneath his arm. "Maybe she should join our little game . . ." he taunted. "She could help you dig!"

"Please! Daddy, no!"

He came toward Kaycee then. She was certain he was going to kill her. Still holding the child, he smashed the gun directly where her head would have been had she not rolled away at the last moment.

Turning the gun toward the child's head, he laughed. "Come here, or I'll blow her brains out."

A whimper escaped the girl's mouth. She shook her head back and forth. "No, Daddy. Please, no."

Kaycee quickly weighed her choices. She stepped closer, her eyes defiantly meeting his as she said, "Leave the girl alone!"

His laugh filled the room. The last thing Kaycee saw was a single tear roll down the child's terrified face.

•   •   •   •   •

Truly irritated, Max shook himself awake for the second time in ten minutes. Stagga had never alerted in the middle of the night before, much less when there was nothing wrong. Fumbling in the darkness, he found the light switch again. "Quiet, Stagga. You're gonna get us thrown out of here at—three-twenty-seven in the morning!"

But Stagga was no longer at his side, he was back on alert, scratching furiously at the door then nudging the curtains with his brindled muzzle to look through the window. Every few seconds he would glance back toward Max with a pleading, frustrated look in his eyes.

Max had learned a long time ago to trust his dog's instincts, but he was tired and frustrated from being roused twice in only minutes. Rolling off the edge of the bed, he sharply ordered, "Stagga, sit!"

Stagga glanced back at his master, sat down, then growled. The growl was apparently directed as much at his owner's lack of immediate action as it was at whoever or whatever was outside. Max grabbed the only lethal looking thing in sight—a metal coat hangar. Sensing Stagga's warning, he felt the hair on his own neck stand on end as he crept cautiously toward the window.

Pulling back the heavy curtain, he finally saw why Stagga had tried to warn him. Across the street, a truck peeled out from behind his 4Runner. In the moonlight, he could see chunks of the back window glittering atop the fresh layer of snow. Had he paid attention to Stagga a couple of minutes earlier, he might have been able to stop the thief. "Damn it!" he muttered. "Next time bite me or something!"

For a moment Max wavered, wondering if he could catch them on foot. The truck wasn't headed for the highway, it was going the opposite direction, behind the motel. He had no idea what was down that country road, no idea where it might lead.

Deciding it was hopeless, he tossed aside the useless coat hanger then crossed the room to dial the police.

· · · · ·

"Hurry up!" Willy ordered through the window of his truck.

Running a hand through her disheveled hair, his girlfriend nervously glanced around the room one last time. The woman was unconscious beside the bed, but at least she was still breathing. There were no traces of dirt and snow left on the floor. The deadbolt adjoining the suites was securely fastened. Even the chain on the outer door was back in place. Spotting the gold cross on the floor, she tucked it into the pocket of her jacket and rushed to the window. After crawling outside she pulled the curtains closed, then slid the heavy pane of glass down until the dual spring-loaded locks snapped back into place.

"I got the stuff we spotted earlier, and I think it's even better than we thought. Get in!" he called.

"I can't! I'll have to meet you later. I've got to change the sheets in our room in case the police decide to check it."

"Okay. Meet me at the mine this afternoon. I'll know by then what we need to do."

She nodded, then watched him speed away. *Grandma's gonna kill me if she finds out I screwed up again!*

· · · · ·

The sound of church bells echoed in the distance. Kaycee was surrounded by darkness, teetering precariously on the edge of a murky void. *Why are they ringing the bells?* she wondered just as they stopped.

A few moments later, they started again. This time the noise seemed closer. Annoying double rings, spaced seconds apart, so loud they hurt. Slowly she came to realize that it wasn't bells, it was a telephone.

Kaycee tried to open her eyes when she rolled over, but doing so made her head throb. Taking deep breaths, she fought to control the waves of nausea that ripped through her. She knew from the cold, slick surface that she was on a floor. But where?

Slowly, cautiously, she opened her eyes, praying she would see *something. Anything.* Even though the light was welcome, it made her cringe. First she saw only blurred shapes, then her vision finally returned. Directly in front of her was a bed. Reaching out, she touched the dangling bedspread to be sure. Farther up was a night stand. From atop it came the unbearable noise of the telephone. Pushing herself, Kaycee reached out and grabbed the receiver.

· · · · ·

"It's six a.m., Ms. Miller," the desk clerk declared and started to hang up.

"I need. . .help," the woman in Room 22 whispered.

"Excuse me?"

"Send help!" she groaned with more force.

"What kind of help?"

"A doctor. . ."

"Hello? Are you still there?"

But there was no answer. As she cradled the phone, the wide-eyed desk clerk watched her granddaughter, Kim, rush into the lobby. Stomping her snowy feet on the mat, she froze under the woman's pressing stare. "What's the matter, Grandma? You look like you just saw a ghost."

"Something's wrong with the woman in room 22. She wants a doctor."

"So call Doc Randle. I'm sure he'd come."

"She sounded really bad. Kim, would you go wait with her while I get the doctor?"

Kim nervously ran a hand through her short, frosted hair. "You'd make a better nurse than I would. How about *I* cover the front desk and call the doctor while *you* go check on 22?"

Nodding, the older woman grabbed a spare room key and a jacket, then slipped into her snow boots. Shaking her head, she muttered, "Last night a car gets robbed just across the street, now this. Maybe it really is time to sell the old place."

·　　·　　·　　·　　·

Kaycee heard the knock on the door and a woman calling, "Are you all right?" Sitting up, she saw sunlight stream in as the door was unlocked and cracked open until the security chain stopped it.

"There's a doctor on the way, Ms. Miller. If you'll unhook the chain, I'll come in and stay with you until he gets here."

Groping her way to the door, Kaycee reached up and slid off the thin chain. "You'd better call the police, too. Something terrible is going on in the room next door."

The woman merely nodded politely as she helped Kaycee onto the bed. "Just calm down, honey. What seems to be the matter?"

Touching the tender lump where her forehead met her hairline, she replied, "My head. He hit me."

Startled, the gentle older woman asked, "Who hit you?"

Kaycee's eyes darted toward the door to the adjoining room. Although her voice was low, it carried an unwavering urgency. "The man in there! He has a gun!"

"Take some deep breaths, dear. Everything is going to be all right now. My name is Sarah. I'm going to fix you a cold compress for your head. I'll be right back." Grabbing the unused plastic bag from the ice bucket, she stepped outside and filled it with fresh snow. After gently placing it on Kaycee's head, she asked, "Are you sure you need the police? Looks to me like you fell and hit your head on the night stand."

"No! There was a little girl, and a man with a gun!"

Sarah walked to the inner door and unbolted it. Throwing it open, she shook her head. "There's no one in there. See?"

Exasperated, Kaycee snapped, "They were there *last night!*"

Sarah forced Kaycee's shoulders back against the headboard. "Okay! If you'll lie back down I'll call the sheriff. But you really should be still. That's a nasty bump you have on your head."

With closed eyes she nodded and listened as Sarah placed the call.

Kaycee could tell from the placating tone of her voice that the old woman hadn't believed a single word she had said.

· · · · ·

After Max fed Stagga, he left him in the room and went to meet Kaycee in the lobby. Pacing back and forth, he was surprised to see a young woman come out of the back room. She was nothing like the clerk who had checked him in last night. This girl was probably in her late teens or early twenties. Her short dark hair was streaked with a variety of colors from golden blond to almost white in places. "Need help?" she asked, popping a wad of gum between her molars as she shrugged off her jacket and hung it on an old brass coat rack. When she did, something fell out of the pocket.

"Not really," Max stated. The girl shot him an interesting look—tired, bored, worried, maybe annoyed—he couldn't tell. "I'm supposed to meet a friend here," he added, leaning down to retrieve the necklace that had fallen to the floor. Intrigued by the gold cross, he turned it over, openly studying it. "This is a beautiful piece of jewelry."

"Thanks," she muttered, holding out her hand until he reluctantly dropped it onto her palm.

"Looks like an antique. How long have you had it?"

Her mouth stopped in mid-chew. For a few moments she considered her answer, then snapped, "Since I was a kid. Grandma called it my Madonna phase." Tugging the clingy material of her long-sleeved t-shirt at the neckline, she dropped the cross, chain and all, inside so it landed in the cradle of her bra. With a snide smile, she patted the thin layer of fabric covering it.

Max kept his eyes on her. "Funny, I have a friend who has one just like it. In fact, she stayed here last night."

"Small world." Turning away, she muttered, "I gotta go make more coffee."

He suddenly wished Stagga was at his side. Meeting people always made him yearn for the simple honesty of dogs. If Stagga didn't like someone, it was obvious. Besides, if that necklace was Kaycee's, he might have caught her scent, acted in that funny, confused way he had that usually signaled trouble.

After pacing in the lobby for ten minutes, Max impatiently stood at the counter. The girl was nowhere in sight, so he leaned far enough over to see the screen of the computer. Using a pencil to reach the keys, he quickly made his way through the menu. Kaycee Miller was registered in Room 22.

Rushing back to his room, Max opened the door and called for Stagga. Careful not to be spotted with him, they took the long route around the building, crossing through the deep snow in a brush covered area on the north end to get to the rooms on the back side of the building.

Room 22 was the second from the end. Parked directly in front of it was a charcoal gray Lexus blocked in by a sheriff's car.

CHAPTER **6**

Kaycee pushed herself up until she was sitting against the head-board, holding the half-melted bag of snow to her head. "I swear. That's what happened." The sheriff looked awfully young, probably a few years shy of thirty. His strong cheekbones and jet black hair were clear signs of his American Indian heritage, and she suspected he made sure his lean frame had just enough muscle to make criminals think twice before trying anything in his presence.

"Call me Fred. I'll submit your report, but I'm not sure what else I can do at this point," he said, then turned to answer a sharp knock on the door. Instant recognition crossed his face when he pulled it open. "If you're here about your truck being broken into—"

Max pushed past the sheriff. "Kaycee! Are you all right?"

She smiled, then winced. "Yesterday you said it takes more than a kick in the head to keep you down. Guess I had to find out for myself."

Sheriff Fred shifted impatiently. "I take it you two know each other. . ."

"She was nice enough to help me when my 4Runner broke down." As Fred jotted on his notepad, Max explained, "Unfortunate-ly, the sheriff and I met a few hours ago because someone stole every-thing out of the back end of my truck. It was parked at the service sta-tion across the street."

Kaycee softly shook her head. "Guess we picked a bad night to stay in Cimarron."

"Mr. Masterson, would you mind stepping outside with me for a moment?"

Max shot Kaycee a questioning look. She shrugged and smiled, indicating she didn't mind being left alone.

Once they were outside, the sheriff pulled the door closed. "How well do you know that woman?" he asked, his words floating in puffs of fog that quickly vaporized in the crisp morning air.

"We only met yesterday," Max said, stooping to scratch Stagga.

"How did she seem then?"

"Fine." Reacting to the sheriff's odd tone of voice, he added, "Listen, Kaycee seemed like any nice, normal person. What's going on here?"

"She *claims* a little girl came into her room from the adjoining suite begging for help. Says the girl's father bashed her on the head and kidnapped the kid."

"Then I'd believe her."

"But she even admits the door between the suites was bolted *from her side* when she came to. And the chain was on the front door when the motel's owner, Sarah, arrived to help. No one could've gotten in or out of that room. Besides, Sarah says the adjoining room hasn't been rented for almost a month. Says the hot water heater broke and they haven't replaced it yet.

"Plus—" he lowered his voice— "Doc Randle says she's had a lot of traumatic things happen in the last few months, things she didn't want to talk about. In fact, when I brought it up she got really agitated and told me that the past had nothing to do with it. Doc thinks all this may be some sort of delayed reaction to stress. Kind of a cry for help."

Max nodded, standing back up to meet him eye to eye. "So what's your take on all this, Fred?"

"I think she hit her head on the nightstand. It was a pretty hard blow, hard enough to give her a mild concussion. She says she's a psychologist who specializes in analyzing handwriting, especially *criminals'* handwriting. Claims parole boards use her to help decide if a prisoner should be released or not."

"So?"

"So, the whole thing sounds pretty far-fetched to me."

Max resisted the urge to point out that there were a lot of things he'd probably find far-fetched that were actually quite true. "When does she claim this happened?"

"Around three-twenty this morning."

"And don't you think it's odd that my 4Runner was robbed about that time?"

Fred glanced at his watch. "Stranger things have happened. Besides, it was a full moon."

"Which means?"

He smiled. "Ask anyone in law enforcement. Full moons always bring out the nutcases."

·   ·   ·   ·   ·

Since he was holding a heavily laden tray of food, Max gently tapped at Kaycee's door with his boot instead of knocking. He was welcomed with a smile so natural and tender that it made the winter day seem suddenly warm.

"Good morning, again. Thanks for bringing breakfast. You really didn't have to," she said, holding the door open. She had changed into a fresh denim shirt and jeans. With her hair pulled into a high pony-tail, she looked young and innocent, a little less shaky than before, yet still on edge. Noticing the sizeable purple knot at her hair line, he gently touched his forehead, saying, "You win."

"I'd have preferred not to be in the race at all."

Setting the tray on the table at the foot of the bed, Max declared, "You're looking absolutely stunning this morning. I've brought scrambled eggs, toast, pancakes, oatmeal with walnuts and brown sugar, milk and orange juice. Hopefully, there's something that will appeal to you."

"It all sounds wonderful. I really am hungry. I can't thank you enough. . ."

"You should have taken me up on dinner last night. Who knows? We might have both been better off."

Kaycee laughed. "I doubt it. My streak of bad luck is practically set in stone. Sorry if some of it rubbed off on you."

"I take it you've had a rough time lately."

Toasting him with a glass of orange juice, she said, "You could say that."

"Then it's time the streak ended. Stagga and I will be happy to loan you some of our good karma."

"Considering you're stranded here, I don't think that's a wise idea. Your good karma may have taken the last train south."

"Stranded is a relative term. We'll get by." Max noticed the way Kaycee was watching the dog and added, "Stagga usually lays on the floor by my feet during meals. That okay with you?"

"Of course."

They each started to take a seat at the small table when she suddenly stopped. Glancing at the window, then back at the table, she slid into the chair and shook her head.

"Something wrong?"

She barely shrugged. "The table and chairs were in front of the window last night. I put my suitcase on the table. I wonder why he moved it."

Max noticed her phrasing. It wasn't *I think this*, or *they moved that*, it was assertive, specific—*he* moved it. Without a second thought, he crossed the room to examine the floor just beneath the window. Since there was no carpet covering the hardwood floor, it was impossible to tell if the small table had been recently moved. His gaze lingered for a moment on the window sill before he took a seat at her side and asked, "Mind if we talk about what happened?"

"As long as you promise to be honest with me."

"Why wouldn't I?"

"Because everyone besides you thinks I'm a certified lunatic."

Max laughed. "Well, are you?"

"In my own professional opinion, I can guarantee you that I'm definitely not a candidate for the nuthouse. At least, not yet."

"Who knows? It might be a nice place."

"I'm as sane as you are," she remarked, lightly kicking him under the table. Stagga instantly alerted.

"Down, Stagga," Max ordered.

"Sorry, I forgot he's a little overprotective. Did the sheriff tell you anything?"

"You're right about him. He thinks the blow to your head made you hallucinate."

"Then why were the lights on when I woke up? Who moved my things? What happened to my necklace and my Northwestern sweatshirt? Why did I have clothes on over my nightgown? Does he really think I woke up, hit my head, then ran around doing weird things before I lost consciousness?"

"Slow down! What was that about your necklace?"

"It's gone."

"Where was it?"

"I always put it on the nightstand when I go to bed. Always. I'm very careful with it, because it's so. . .special. I've looked everywhere and it isn't here."

"Did you tell the sheriff it was missing?"

"I didn't notice it was gone until I changed clothes."

Max hesitated, stalling by eating a piece of toast as he wondered if he should tell her about the girl in the office. "Would you recognize your necklace if you saw it on someone else?" he finally asked.

Kaycee's heaping spoon of oatmeal stopped halfway to her mouth. Her anxious eyes searched his. "You saw it, didn't you?"

"I think so."

"Where?"

"A young woman working in the office had one like it in her coat this morning. But don't get your hopes up, gold crosses are a pretty common type of jewelry. When we check out, I'll see if I can get her to show it to you. Maybe Stagga can help."

Kaycee was shaking her head. "If she stole it, I doubt if she's going to let *anyone* see it again. It's very special to me. My mother's mother gave it to her. It's a family heirloom. I've only had it for a few months. . ."

Max nodded, instantly sensing the depth of her recent loss. "I'm sorry. Was it an illness?"

"A sixteen-year-old drunk driver. He killed both my parents and his two best friends. It was a terrible tragedy for everyone involved, especially the boy, since he was the only one who survived."

"That's horrible."

"I know it sounds strange, but I'm not mad at him. Everyone does something stupid once in their lives, and his mistake cost so many people so much. I worry about him, about what he has to live with now."

"I'm sure you do. At least you're handling it well. Doing rescues, I've run into far too many people who spend all their energy condemning people for the tragedy. It eats away at them."

"I'm lucky. I have my sister, Niki, and we both inherited our father's ability to handle a crisis with humor. I'm sure some people think we're insensitive, but wallowing in fear and self-pity just isn't our style."

"I wish I could've met your parents. They sound like great people."

Kaycee shook her head. "Let's see, we've known each other less than twenty-four hours. By now Mom would've had us married with triplets on the way. She was getting pretty impatient to have grandkids."

Max laughed, taking her hand in his. "I want you to know that I believe you actually saw a little girl, Kaycee."

She paused, casting him a skeptical glance. "Why?"

"I promised to be honest, so don't take this wrong."

Kaycee leaned back, as if distance might soften his words.

Max took a deep breath, his eyes locked on hers. "At first, I thought the sheriff was right. After all, I don't really know you, and it is a pretty far-fetched story. Both doors being locked *from the inside* seems to contradict everything you said, and even when I met you on the highway, you appeared to be under a great deal of stress."

She nodded, painfully aware of how things looked and embarrassed that a total stranger could read her so easily.

"At first, I thought maybe I wanted to believe you because you helped me on the road yesterday. I'd even decided that the necklace was probably just a coincidence, that I was looking for something that just wasn't there so I could keep seeing you." Max relaxed as her expression softened.

"So what changed your mind?"

"Stagga."

"Excuse me?" Kaycee asked.

"Stagga alerted last night at the same time you claim everything happened. He went crazy twice. The first time, I'm embarrassed to say, I chalked up to the call of nature. By the time I believed him the second time, my truck had been robbed. A good handler always trusts his dog, and I should have trusted Stagga from the moment he alerted. In a way, I blame myself for all this."

"You shouldn't." Kaycee leaned down to stroke Stagga's soft, white neck. "Thanks, boy. Can I give him some bacon as a reward?"

"Later, if you don't mind. Like a seeing eye dog, he pretty much goes everywhere I go, so I ask people not to slip him table food. Begging is not acceptable behavior. Remember, he has to stay tough."

"Like you?"

Max smiled slyly. "Actually, begging works quite well sometimes. You agreed to have breakfast with me, didn't you?"

She returned his smile with a dazzling one of her own. "I meant that you have to stay tough."

"In some ways. Doing rescue work gets in your blood. It's a lot of work, you have to stay in top physical condition and exercise your dog every day. But when you find someone in time, the payoff is worth every bit."

"Payoff, as in reward?"

Max laughed. In response to her quizzical stare, he explained, "Rescuers volunteer all their time, and frequently pay their own expenses. Our reward is the look in a child's eyes when they see their parents again, or knowing we saved someone trapped under tons of concrete because a dog told us where to dig."

"Sounds expensive. You must be independently wealthy."

"Not by a long shot. I pretty much break even raising thorough-bred horses, and I earn a few bucks doing contract computer work."

"Out of your house?"

He shrugged. "Or wherever I happen to be. Most of what I do can be done on my laptop, but I do have an office at home. My grand-parents left me their ranch a few years back. There's no mortgage, so I don't have much overhead. I spend most of my free time and money doing rescues."

"Where's your ranch?"

"Just outside Shamrock."

"Shamrock, Oklahoma?" she asked, shocked.

He nodded.

"It's not that big white house with pillars on the hill south of town, is it?"

Max smiled. "Actually, it is. Geez, if you sneeze you'd miss Shamrock. I'm not sure it's even on the map anymore. How do you know about my house?"

"You can see it from the Turner Turnpike! I was all over that coun-try when I was doing a background check on an inmate for the parole board. I even came to your house, but no one was home."

"It's a small world, isn't it?"

Kaycee frowned. "If you run a ranch, how will you manage with-out your 4Runner?"

He shrugged. "Good question. The tow truck driver said he'd heard quite a few 4Runners are blowing head gaskets. The whole engine will have to be redone. Apparently, I may be without my truck for quite some time."

"How are you planning to get back to Shamrock?"

"The sheriff told me he could give me a lift to Liberal, Kansas later today when he gets off duty. I have some buddies doing a double search there, and I can catch a ride back home with one of them. Then, I guess I'll be driving a rental for a while."

"I've got a better offer for you. I'm going back to Tulsa today. You'd be doing me a favor if you'd drive my car as far as Liberal. The doctor wasn't very happy about my being behind the wheel so soon, and there's no way I'm going to spend another night here."

"Are you sure it wouldn't be too far out of your way?"

"Not at all. As a matter of fact, I've never been to Liberal. Maybe I'll see something fascinating there."

Max threw back his head and laughed. "Don't count on it! Even the SAR *dogs* get bored in Liberal. It's flat, barren country."

"Who are your friends searching for?"

"An elderly man who wandered away from a nursing home a couple of hours ago, and a little girl who's been gone two days. She was riding to a friend's house and disappeared—bike and all. This one isn't looking good. It was hot, windy, and dry the day she vanished, pretty much the worst conditions dogs have to deal with. Heat makes the scent rise, then the wind scatters it. The tracking dogs lost the scent just down the block from the house, which implies she got into a car. Then the cold front came through, complete with a line of showers. By now, so much time has passed they're switching to air scenting dogs."

Kaycee shivered, easily imagining the pain the missing child's parents must be feeling. A sudden rush of adrenaline made her gasp. "You don't suppose the little girl I saw—"

"—Is the one we're looking for?" Max shrugged, skeptically shaking his head. "Anything's possible, but I wouldn't bet on it."

"I'm sure you're right."

He beamed a dazzling smile as he took her hand. "If anyone can find her, we can. Some of the best searchers in the country are there. Most of the time, we succeed."

"The other times must be really hard."

"They're hell. No one ever wants to give up, but there comes a point when our presence does more harm than good."

Kaycee sighed, trying not to be overwhelmed by her raw emotions. She blushed, certain her frayed nerves were as obvious to Max as Stagga's wagging tail. Shifting to safer ground, she said, "If they want your help, then Stagga must be able to air scent."

Max nodded. "Trail and tracking dogs search using the scent left behind by a specific person, like the Alzheimer's patient. If the trail gets too old, or is disturbed by the weather, they can't follow it. Air scenting dogs look for any person in a particular area. They do well covering large pieces of undeveloped land. When people call in tips to the police, they contact one of our teams and we go check the area."

"What kind of searches does Stagga do?"

"He's certified in air, track, trail, avalanche, and disaster."

"Disaster?"

"People trapped under debris. Tornados, earthquakes, bombs."

Directing her question to the dog, Kaycee playfully scratched his head. "Does he work you night and day?"

Max smiled. "Sometimes. That's why he has to stay tough."

Still talking to the dog, she added, "And he doesn't let you get a word in edgewise, does he?"

Stagga sat up, his tail mopping the wood floor behind him.

Max answered, "I've trained him to do all sorts of amazing things, but I think I'll let *you* handle teaching him to talk."

Kaycee smiled and stood. "Fine. I will."

Max just shook his head.

"Can you be ready to leave in an hour?" she asked.

"SAR teams are always ready. Besides, everything except the few things I had with me—the clothes on my back, my overnight kit, and my laptop—were stolen from the truck. The only thing I have to do is arrange for someone from a nearby Toyota dealership to come get the 4Runner." One swift hand signal and Stagga was perched on his hind legs in perfect begging stance. Max tossed him a strip of bacon, which he caught in mid-air. "Good boy. Let's go."

The dog raced to the door. Although he appeared to be sitting, every muscle was tense as he waited for Max to open the door and throw his favorite toy—a tennis ball.

"See you in a few minutes," Kaycee said.

Max watched Stagga bound through the snow with the prized tennis ball in his mouth. As they walked back to his room, he couldn't help but notice what a beautiful day it had turned out to be.

• • • • •

Willy had just finished changing the tags on his truck when Kim finally pulled up. His gloved fist was clenched as he shouted, "Where the hell have you been? I've been waiting for over two hours!"

"Grandma had to lie down. All the commotion last night and this morning gave her a headache. Which reminds me, why in the world would you steal something out of that truck across the street? Talk about stupid!"

"We both saw all that loot. It's high-tech stuff. It'll be worth a ton."

"But you promised! You know I can't afford to get in trouble again, and you just got out on parole! Are you—" Kim's voice trailed off as she scanned the area, a sinking feeling growing in the pit of her stomach. "Where's the kid?"

Willy glanced toward the hidden entrance to the mine.

Kim's eyes flew open. Every muscle tensed as she asked, "You left her in there? Alone?"

"She's got food and water. It's only for a day or two while I take care of some business."

Kim stared at the man she thought she knew, thought she loved. When they met in drug rehab four years ago, he was a perfect gentleman. Even when he was in prison, he had written her almost every week. His letters told of the dreams he had for a better life, and each was always signed in closing, "Mine forever, Willy."

Suddenly, Kim felt the suffocating weight of those simple words. "You're not really going to leave her in there, are you?" she asked, her voice weak with shock and disgust.

He nodded, his eyes challenging hers. "It's her own fault. Last night the kid proved she couldn't be trusted. You got a problem with that?"

"N...No." Even though Willy had never hurt her, never even come close, Kim knew that violence was a part of him—a part she had no desire to see, much less provoke. Rather than force his hand, she backed away, her eyes fixing on the freshly cut tree limbs that he had partially buried to camouflage the entrance to the mine.

"Good," he said. "What happened when the sheriff came?"

"Not much. He didn't buy her story. Thought she was hallucinating 'cause of the blow to her head."

Willy smiled.

"But the guy who owns that stuff you stole believed her. He kept looking at me funny." Kim shoved her hands in her pockets, suppressing a shudder when her fingertips touched the gold cross nestled deep inside.

"How do you know he believed her?" Willy asked.

"I took the cleaning cart and made up the room next door while they had breakfast. If you lean against the wall, you can hear everything they say."

"That's my girl! Think they have anything that could lead them to us?"

Her palms were sweating now, the memory of their conversation about the missing necklace making her throat dry. If she told him, she was certain he'd freak. Instead, Kim simply shook her head and shrugged. When she was sure she could sound confident again, she added, "The guy has some kind of trained dog. It went crazy when you stole the stuff from his car. You'd better be careful."

"When are they leaving?"

"Grandma said they checked out early this morning." Kim didn't bother to mention that they had specifically asked if they could talk to her, and that her grandmother had lied to protect her.

Willy nodded, thinking for a few moments before saying, "I've got to run into Taos. You'd better lay low today, just in case. Meet me at the usual spot at sundown."

Kim glanced angrily at her watch. "What am I supposed to do here the rest of the time?"

He climbed into his 4X4 Ford. "I don't care what you do. Just stay *out* of the mine."

Spinning tires showered a veil of small rocks in his truck's wake. Kim slumped to the ground, pulling the necklace out of her pocket. Watching the sunlight glisten off the gold, she trembled as she slipped it around her neck.

She was in more trouble than she'd ever been in before. If she stayed with Willy, sooner or later he would treat her like he did his own daughter, if not worse. Yet if she ran, who would help her grandma? Besides, where could she go this time? All her relatives thought she was trash. Everyone except Grandma.

Wiping away a cloud of blinding tears, she glanced at the hidden entry. *He'll kill me if he finds out about the necklace. The maniac left his poor kid in that hellhole! God, how cruel! How could I have been so stupid?*

It took half an hour for her to decide. She had time to get the child, take her to a friend's house between Angel Fire and Taos, and still meet Willy at dusk. When he came back to the mine the next day and found the girl gone, he'd think she had run away on her own— that she was wandering lost in the forest. He wouldn't suspect Kim had helped her escape. After all, he was always telling her how much he loved her, needed her support.

A surge of hope fixed Kim's resolve, gave her the strength to stand. Rushing to her grandma's car, she popped open the glove box, but groaned in frustration when she saw it only held registration papers. A glimpse of her reflection in the rearview mirror made her gasp. Her eyes were shallow, surrounded by dark circles. Touching her cheeks, she looked at the person she had become. Slipping off the earrings her grandmother had given her last Christmas, Kim dropped them in the ashtray for safekeeping and mentally promised to somehow make all this up to her.

Stopping just outside the mine's hidden entrance, Kim turned to face the forest. Listening intently, she watched for any sign of life before pushing aside one of the freshly cut tree limbs to step in. Just inside the entry was a box marked GENERATOR, and a strange looking clear rope. Bending down, she touched it, holding the end near the beams of sunlight so she could examine it more closely. It was soft, flexible, and unlike anything she'd ever seen before. *What's Willy going to do with this stuff?* she wondered as she searched through the knapsack and pulled out a high- power flashlight. Switching it on, she sighed at the sight of the bright path it cut through the darkness.

Shivering, staggering, she moved away from the safety of the entry into the lonely, malignant darkness. The beam of the flashlight shook in her unsteady grip as she thought of what would happen if someone tripped the wire of one of the booby traps. Then it dawned on her—had he set more traps along the way without warning her? An involuntary tremble made the flashlight beam shake as it cut through the pitch black tunnel that lay ahead.

Trying her best to be brave, Kim said, "Maggie, I'm coming."

CHAPTER **7**

"How's the headache?" Max asked as he maneuvered the car off the Guymon exit to Oklahoma Highway 54.

Kaycee instinctively felt her forehead. "Better. How about yours?"

He touched his temple. "The lump is practically gone. We make quite a pair, don't we?"

"We certainly do."

Kaycee was in the front passenger seat, her body turned toward him as he drove. For the last hour as they casually chatted, her pencil had rarely left the drawing pad precariously propped on one raised knee. With a sigh, she carefully turned to a clean page, then hesitated. Although he was certain she had intended to draw something else, she abruptly flipped back to the first sketch.

"What's that?" Max asked.

"Oh. . .Nothing."

A few seconds later, he leaned over, catching a glimpse of a child's face. "Is that her?"

Kaycee nodded, apparently embarrassed.

"It's very well done."

She shrugged. "My sister has the real talent in the family. Her work is so realistic you're sure it has a life of its own. I do okay with angles and lines, but my art doesn't have the energy to make it distinctive. I guess that's what intrigued me about analyzing handwriting. It's unproven ground, still open for a unique perspective."

"Would you analyze my writing sometime?"

"Sure, but you have to understand that an analysis is like a photo. It only reflects that instant in time."

"What if it shows I'm some sort of kinky freak?"

She laughed. "I'm pretty sure it will! That's the kind of luck I have."

"*Used* to have. That's all behind you now."

"Want to make a bet?"

Extending his hand, Max claimed, "Sure. I'll bet you twenty bucks that in the next two weeks nothing horrible is going to happen to you."

Kaycee shook her head, remembering the doctor's appointment she had in the morning. She pulled back her hand just before it reached his. "This isn't fair. I can't take advantage of such a trusting soul."

"You won't get a chance." With a gleam in his eye, he added, "At least not financially. But there are other ways. . ."

Kaycee elbowed him and smiled.

"Really. Nothing bad is going to happen."

Practically beaming, she took his hand. "Okay, I'm not stupid enough to turn down easy money. But don't say I didn't warn you."

A few miles later, the silence was broken as Max asked, "Mind if I take a good look at your sketch?"

With a shrug, Kaycee tilted the pad toward him. "I knew that if I didn't get that face down on paper, it would haunt me. Her eyes—" she laid the pad down and stared at Max—" the way her tears left streaks in the dirt on her cheeks. It was the saddest thing I've ever seen."

"And you've seen more than your share of sad things lately, haven't you?"

She stiffened a little. "I suppose so. That's why you shouldn't have taken that bet."

"Listen, I don't mean to pry. Sometimes talking about things helps. The sheriff mentioned that you'd been through a lot lately."

"The doctor must have told him about my parents and my sister." *But nothing else! Thank God she hadn't told that country doctor everything. Obviously, he couldn't be trusted.*

"I know about your parents, but what happened to your sister?"

"She was paralyzed by a stroke eleven months ago. That's why I'm moving to New Mexico. I'm planning to get a job there so I can be closer to her."

"Let me guess. She thinks you should stay in Tulsa."

Kaycee's eyes went wide. "How did you know?"

"Just a hunch. I thought maybe that stubborn streak you have might be a family characteristic."

"Ouch! You certainly don't pull any punches."

"I didn't mean it as an insult. In fact, I find strong-willed people the most interesting to have around."

"Interesting?"

"Sure. They're always good for lively discussion."

Her anger diffused, Kaycee nodded and studied him. His profile was strong, his chest thick with solid muscle. On his right wrist was a simple, yet elegant, thin silver bracelet. She was surprised she hadn't noticed it before. Reaching out, she pushed back his shirt sleeve to have a better look. "It's been a long time since I saw a man wear something like this."

It was his turn to tense. "I never take it off."

"Would you mind telling me why?"

He suddenly seemed a million miles away. Finally, he answered, "Not today. Maybe later."

"That assumes there will be a *later.*"

Glancing her way, he grinned. "I hope so. In fact, as soon as I get back home, I'd like to have you over for dinner. I'm not one to brag, but I grill a good shish-ka-bob. Right, Stagga?"

Stagga cocked his head and whined, then went back to sleep.

Kaycee started to speak, then stopped. Suddenly the passing scenery held much more interest than their conversation.

Max felt the same fear flow from her as he had the first time they met. "Let me guess. You can't do dinner."

"That's right," she said flatly. "But I'll agree to lunch if you'll throw in a tour of your ranch."

He laughed. "Then lunch it is! If you're trying to be mysterious, it's working. Are you getting hungry?"

"A little."

"There's a restaurant about a mile off the next exit." Pointing at her sketch, he added, "We can stop there and try to find her."

"How in the world can we do that?"

"They may have stolen all my new rescue equipment, but my laptop was in my room. Trust me, I'm pretty familiar with using the Internet to help find people. One of the first things I do when I go to a rescue is load a picture of the missing person into the national database. The universe works in mysterious ways. You never know who will see a picture and call in."

Kaycee reached past Max's seat to scratch behind Stagga's ears. "I'm afraid I mainly use the Internet for e-mail. How many pictures of missing kids are there?"

"Hundreds, maybe thousands. I've never cared to count. I think it would be wise for you to check the most recent ones before you drop me off in Liberal."

"I think that's an excellent idea. Mind if I ask a nosy question?"

"Fire away."

"Why isn't a handsome man like yourself married?"

With a sly grin, he took her hand. "Would you believe I was waiting for you?"

Shaking her head, she snapped, "No. As a matter of fact I wouldn't."

"How about because I find real canines to be much easier to get along with than—"

At his slight hesitation, Kaycee finished his sentence. "—than some of the real bitches in the world! Now *that*, I'll buy!"

"What about you?"

"I think I may fall into that real bitch category."

"Somehow, I doubt that."

Proving her point, Kaycee threw back her head and howled. From the backseat Stagga's puzzled gaze slowly shifted from Kaycee to Max, then back to her. As if he understood the joke, he pointed his muzzle toward the sky and loudly joined in.

• • • • •

The horrific smell almost convinced Kim to turn around. Never in her life had she experienced anything so vile. The narrower the tunnel became, the worse it seemed to hang in thick, choking layers. Although she had no idea what it was, she was certain it was from something that no child should have to see. She hated Willy for doing this—hated him for leaving his kid in a dark, scary place that would scar her for life.

When she could no longer walk because of fallen rocks, Kim dropped to her hands and knees and called, "Maggie. Can you hear me?"

As the echo rolled back, bits of earth sprinkled down. In the distance, she could hear a child's voice, but she couldn't understand the words. *How could he leave her in here!* Picking up her pace, she crawled toward the sound as fast as she could.

The stench was overwhelming, but it was nothing compared to the sudden sight of the corpse. She was only two feet from it when the light caught his face—or what used to be his face. Dropping her flashlight, Kim gasped for air, certain the mine was collapsing around her. Keeping her eyes tightly closed, she fought tears and nausea until she realized she could hear Maggie's voice clearly now.

Maggie was close, and she was singing softly.

Squeezing past the body with her face turned away, Kim made it ten more feet before the passage was too narrow for her to fit through. Suddenly, she knew why Willy had brought Maggie to this horrid place.

Backing up, she started pulling mounds of dirt toward herself with cupped hands. Even though she hated it, she pushed the dirt against the decaying body. By the time she finished opening the path thirty minutes later, most of the corpse was buried. Too late, it dawned on her that Willy would wonder how the dirt had been moved.

But Kim knew there wasn't time to dwell on such things. Crawling through the narrow opening, she was just thankful to finally be in the cave where she could stand. "Maggie. It's Kim. Remember me? I met you the other night."

Maggie didn't answer. She just kept softly singing *Jesus Loves Me*.

Kim brushed the dirt off her legs and arms. Thankfully, the odor was being sucked toward the entrance of the mine, and she relished long breaths of clean air. She had been to this part of the mine once before. It was actually a natural cave that the shaft intersected. About the size of an average bedroom, it had a high ceiling where a beam of light peaked in. Unlike the rest of the tunnel, the cave hadn't been affected by whatever caused the partial collapse.

When the flashlight illuminated Maggie against the far corner, Kim gasped and rushed toward her. The child was blindfolded. Her feet were tied together, but her hands were free. She wore a huge purple sweatshirt, and in her lap was a knapsack, which Kim assumed held whatever food and water Willy had decided she might need.

Setting down the flashlight, she untied the blindfold and whispered, "It's all right now, Maggie. Everything's going to be okay. I'll get you out of here. I promise."

For the first time, Maggie quit singing. She blinked in the dim light and rubbed her eyes, but Kim felt as though she were looking right through her. "Maggie? Are you okay?"

No answer.

"I'm going to untie your feet, then we'll get out of here. Okay?"

Still not a sound.

Working on the knot, Kim tried in vain to untie it. She needed a knife, something sharp, but she only had a flashlight. "Tell you what. Since I can't get this rope off right now, how about you crawl right behind me at first, then I'll carry you when the tunnel gets wider?"

Maggie shook her head.

Kim glanced at her watch and her stomach tightened. Trying to sound patient, she asked, "Why not?"

"Daddy said I'd get hurt if I didn't play by the rules."

"What rules? What are you talking about?"

"The game. We're playing a game. I'm not supposed to move until he calls out the secret word."

Kim's heart sank. It was obvious Maggie was terrified of Willy—with good cause. Lying, she said, "But I'm playing, too. And he told me that we have to stop the game because it's time to go home."

Maggie's eyes raised as high as the gold cross on Kim's chest. Her face showed little trust as she asked, "Really?"

"Really." Pulling the cross over her head, Kim gently slipped it around Maggie's neck. "I liked the song you were singing. Why don't we sing it on the way out?"

•   •   •   •   •

Kaycee was impressed with Max's ability to travel the world with only a laptop computer, especially from a rundown diner in the middle of nowhere. "Can you teach me how to do some of this?" she asked.

"Will you have dinner with me?" he said.

"That's blackmail."

"No, it's inquisitiveness."

"I think your personality matches your dog's," she said.

"Thank you. I'll take that as a compliment."

"I was referring to the stubborn part."

"I know." The pictures he'd been searching for appeared and he turned the screen toward her. "These are the postings for the last month. Recognize any of them?"

Kaycee carefully examined each face, studying mainly the eyes. Discouraged, she slumped against the cold leather booth as she replied, "No."

Wrapping his hand around hers, he said, "Don't give up. This isn't over."

"But there isn't a thing I can do!"

"It will come," he said.

"What's that supposed to mean?"

"Some leads take time and come in strange ways. You just have to be vigilant and blindly follow."

"Really? Why?"

"Handling dogs has taught me perseverance and trust. Real, genuine, *trust.* What people see isn't always all that's there. If it were, we wouldn't need dogs to help us. There's a gut instinct that tells you when you're getting close." He squeezed her hand and pointed at the sketch. "Mine's telling me that this little girl picked the right person to go to for help."

•　•　•　•　•

"You can take it off now, Maggie," Kim said.

Maggie stopped crawling long enough to tug the blindfold until it fell around her neck. "Why does it always smell so bad in here?" she asked.

Kim lied, "A bear died back there. It's pretty disgusting, isn't it?"

She wrinkled her nose and nodded. "I'm glad this game is over."

"Me, too."

"I want to go home."

"I know." Kim didn't want to think that far, didn't want to admit to herself that either way she was in big trouble. If she took Maggie home, they'd probably arrest her, and God only knew what Willy would do to her when he found out.

They had finally reached the part of the mine where they could both stand. Kim swept the little girl into her arms and ran as fast as she could toward the entrance. A few welcome rays of light broke through the camouflage of pine boughs, illuminating the path to freedom. In her hurry, she almost forgot to step over the booby traps. Freezing at the last moment, she jerked Maggie to a stop. "If you ever come back here, be careful! Touching one of these wires can hurt you really bad."

Maggie looked down at the wires, and nodded abruptly. Kim's heart sank as she realized that at five years old, Maggie was becoming accustomed to worrying about things like booby-traps and the smell of decaying bodies.

Since Maggie's feet were still tied, Kim stepped over the wires before setting her down long enough to move aside one of the branches. Picking her back up, she rushed into the afternoon sun. It was a beautiful day, the sky so blue it seemed like it might shatter. Scanning the forest, Kim was relieved to see they were alone as she headed for her grandmother's car.

Talking more to herself than to Maggie, Kim said, "That took a lot longer than I expected. We'll have to hurry. I'll have to find some clean clothes for both of us. You can stay with my friend for a couple of days until I figure out what to do." Opening the passenger side door, she carefully placed Maggie inside and buckled her seat belt. Glancing up, she was relieved to see the keys were still in the ignition. Rushing around to the driver's side, she stopped in her tracks.

Willy was sitting beneath a nearby tree, carefully polishing his gun.

CHAPTER **8**

A makeshift headquarters for volunteers had been set up at a local motel about a mile from the child's home in Liberal, Kansas. As Max drove Kaycee's Lexus into the parking lot, Stagga began to fidget and whine as though he instinctively knew it was time for some action.

Kaycee was surprised to see a helicopter in the far corner of the parking lot. Nodding toward it, she asked, "Another volunteer?"

Max grinned. "Crazy Cal. He was a chopper pilot in 'Nam. Now he has his own company. Does maintenance on helicopters and small-engine planes. If there's a search in the Midwest and he hears about it, he'll be there."

"Does he bring in the other volunteers?"

"Sometimes. Right now, the main thing he does is transport teams to wherever they're needed. There are a lot of times when a road isn't handy."

Stagga's tail was wagging and he jumped to put his paws on Max's chest. Kaycee laughed. "I guess he isn't afraid to fly!"

"He loves it. Of course, we train the dogs to ride in helicopters, planes, you name it. You never know what kind of terrain you'll be up against. Stagga has always liked being lowered in his harness. He's got an adventurous spirit."

"You're adventurous, too. Does that mean you like being harnessed?"

With a glint in his eye, he replied, "I can think of better places to be tied up than hanging from a helicopter, if that's what you mean."

Kaycee blushed, then stopped. They had reached the entrance to the motel's lobby, where two other dog handlers were having coffee.

As they stepped inside, she knew she was being scrutinized by a sea of faces—some human, some not. One was a man about Max's age, the other a woman. At their feet were two of the most well-behaved dogs she'd ever seen, a large brown boxer and a black lab. It amazed her that they stayed calmly at their master's sides in spite of Stagga's presence.

Max quickly introduced everyone. "Kaycee, meet Joan and Randy, and their dogs, D.C. and Smokey."

"Nice to meet all of you." Admiring the lab's shiny black coat, Kaycee said, "Smokey's name is pretty obvious, but what does D.C. stand for?"

Joan laughed. "Actually it's for Double Chocolate. I'm afraid I'm a hopeless chocoholic. Would you join us for coffee? We're celebrating! We found Mr. Wade. He's going to be fine."

Max beamed. "That's great!" Turning his attention to Kaycee, he added, "Come on, have some coffee. I promise they don't bite."

Slightly embarrassed, Kaycee smiled and sat down. "Just for a minute. I'm afraid I need to get moving if I'm going to be home before dark, and I still have a long day of driving ahead."

Max leaned back and stretched as Joan poured them cups from the self-serve coffee bar. "Looks pretty slow around here. Any hits at all?" he asked.

Randy shook his head. "The girl just vanished. There haven't been *any* sightings since late yesterday. The hot line has only rung twice, and they were false leads. Plus, the mother says the father has a long history of violence. Apparently, he's done time in prison and he's threatened to take the girl before. The police are treating it as abduction by a parent, especially since they discovered he just got out on parole."

"Then why are we still here?"

"The mother asked us to stay one more day, just in case something turns up."

"What's the girl's name?"

"Margaret Mary Thornton. They call her Maggie."

"Age?"

"Just turned five."

"Has her profile been loaded into the database yet?"

"No, we were hoping you'd take care of that."

"Sure. We'll have to find a scanner somewhere. Mine was stolen, along with my survival gear and Stagga's custom harness. What really upsets me is losing the new light line and generator donated by the Warren family. I only got to use it once."

Everyone in the room seemed to suddenly come to life. "How'd it work?" Joan asked.

Seeing the puzzled look in Kaycee's eyes, Max explained, "Light line is a soft, lightweight rope of clear, flexible plastic that glows. It has white light sections separated by green and red lights. Red leads away from safety, green shows the way back. It's powerful enough to light the way through thick smoke. I used it to help a ten-year old boy who fell into an abandoned oil shaft. We couldn't risk using anything that might ignite the fumes, so the light line worked perfectly. The kid thought it was the greatest invention in the world."

"I'm so jealous!" Randy laughed.

"Let's just hope my insurance will cover it."

Joan asked, "What do you do for a living, Kaycee?"

"I'm a psychologist specializing in handwriting analysis." Kaycee had a hard time not grinning. She could tell from the knowing glances they exchanged that a thousand witty remarks popped into their minds. But Max's friends were warm, kind people, far too polite to crack tacky jokes just minutes after meeting someone. Unable to help herself, she added, "And, no, Max isn't seeing me on a professional basis. At least not yet."

They all laughed, even Max, as Randy added, "You know, he's a pretty lonely guy. Probably wouldn't be his first time to turn to a professional. . ."

"Funny. Keep it up and I'll tell Joan about that time in Wyoming."

Randy hopped up. "Anyone need another cup of coffee?" As he waited for a fresh pot to brew, he grabbed a file and carried it to Max and Kaycee's table. "By the way, here's the information on the girl we're looking for."

Kaycee gasped as her eyes fell on the 8 x 10 glossy photo. Meeting Max's gaze, she didn't say a word.

He quietly asked, "You're sure?"

She nodded.

Standing, Max explained, "Call the FBI. This search is over."

∙   ∙   ∙   ∙   ∙

"Since I promised to quit trying to convince you to wait here, will you let me walk you to your car?" Max asked.

Inhaling a deep breath of fresh air, Kaycee sighed. "I *have* to be home *today*. We both know the FBI can question me in Tulsa as well as here. Right?"

"If you say so."

"I say so. Thanks for driving this morning. I really appreciate your help."

"You're the one who did me a favor, remember? And don't forget you promised to come to the ranch for lunch when I get back." Grabbing his laptop and small bag, he reached inside his pocket and took out a tennis ball. "May I?" he asked.

"May you *what?*"

"This." Max took the ball and playfully rubbed it over her head and down her back.

"That tickles! What in the world are you doing?"

Dropping the ball back into a plastic bag, he said, "It's my insurance."

She stared at him as though he were a lunatic, waiting for an explanation.

Max grinned. "If you don't come to lunch, I'll have Stagga hunt you down. I've got your scent now. No matter where you try to hide, he'll find you."

"Did anyone ever tell you that collecting human scent is a little eccentric?"

"Come to think of it, it would make things a lot easier if you'd just give me your phone number."

Reaching into her purse, she pulled out a business card. "This has my address, home and office phone, fax, e-mail, and cell phone numbers. If you want more than that, you'll have to bribe the FBI. They already asked me for everything except my blood type on the phone."

He handed her one of his business cards. "Seriously, Kaycee. Call me if you need anything, or just want to talk." Gently touching her cheek, he asked, "Are you positive you don't want to stay here until after they question you? Just to be sure that bump on your head is okay?"

Casting him a sideways glance, she warned, "You promised! But thanks for the concern. I really have to get going." She slid into the car, adding, "Grilled shish-ka-bob, right?"

"The best you've ever had!" Leaning toward her, he brushed a wayward strand of her hair aside and added, "Promise you won't wait too long."

"For lunch? Trust me, I'll be on your doorstep before you have time to buy groceries."

"Actually, I was referring to the other sketch. I know it's hard, but you can't let his image fade. You really need to do it soon."

"Unfortunately, the mental picture I have of that man isn't going anywhere. In fact, it'll probably be with me for years. You know, if I didn't know better, I'd think you could read minds."

"Maybe I can." Max watched a look flash across her face—one that declared there was no way he could see beyond the shadows that darkened her every waking thought.

Kaycee shook her head, biting her lower lip for a second before she spoke. "I started to sketch him before, but I didn't want to face that monster again."

"It's always easier to push unpleasant memories aside. Facing them is much more difficult."

Especially alone. As Kaycee drove away, she shivered as she thought of what the FBI agent had told her on the phone. The man they suspected was a cold-blooded killer. Be very careful.

•   •   •   •   •

Several minutes later Max was still staring into space when Randy came outside. "How's it going?" he asked.

Max shrugged. "Could be better. Have you ever thought about someone you hardly know to the point where you feel like you're becoming obsessed?"

"Remember—I'm a geologist, not a shrink like your lady friend. Mind being a tad more specific?"

"Even before what happened in the motel last night, I had the feeling Kaycee was running away from something. She says everything is fine, but I can't get her out of my head. It's like she's right in front of me, screaming for help and I have no idea how to help. Like insisting she meet the FBI in Tulsa. What difference could a few hours make?"

"Maybe there's an ex-husband or lover lurking around she doesn't care to discuss. Could even be a stalker."

"She doesn't act like she's afraid someone might be following her. It's deeper than that. Like she's dangling on the edge of a cliff, but too proud to ask for a hand."

"Old pal, I hate to tell you, but it looks pretty bad."

"What's that supposed to mean?"

"That you've fallen for her. Joan's been telling me for years that when you finally found someone it would happen fast and hard. Maybe Kaycee's the one."

Max eyed his buddy, his reply a half-hearted shrug. The words rang too true, touched a part of him that had been cut off for years—a part that he wasn't sure he cared to confront again.

For more than ten years he'd devoted most of his time and energy to SAR work, an all-consuming hobby that was as addictive as heroin. The handful of rescues he hadn't been able to respond to had driven him crazy. He couldn't picture a life without the rush he got from dropping everything to dash to help someone. Yet, as hard as he tried, he couldn't deny the truth. The few hours he'd spent with Kaycee

Miller had changed him. He just wasn't sure how much, or why.

$\bullet \quad \bullet \quad \bullet \quad \bullet \quad \bullet$

"Willy! What are you doing here?" Kim tried to control the panic that had seized her when she laid eyes on him.

Dragging his burly body up, he holstered his gun and calmly answered, "I finished my errands early. Thought I'd spend the afternoon with you." Staring at her filthy clothes, he added, "Looks like you weren't bored while I was gone."

Kim was shaking, almost babbling as she said, "Maggie was scared in there all by herself. Remember what I told you about my daddy? He used to beat me, then lock me in the closet, Willy. I was so afraid of him. That's why I live with Grandma. I couldn't stand the thought of Maggie being alone in the dark." Realizing she was implying he was a bad father, she quickly added, "But you don't have to worry about her at all. She's fine. I'll take care of her. Maggie's a good kid, really sweet. It won't be any trouble. None at all."

Willy opened his arms, his expression pensive as he said, "Come here."

Kim shivered, suddenly cold. Moving into those massive arms was the hardest thing she'd ever done. Every muscle tensed as she waited for him to crush her windpipe or break her ribs. She could hardly believe it when he simply hugged her and backed away.

"I came back early because I felt bad about leaving the kid in there. I'm glad you got her out," he said.

"Y...You are?"

He seemed ashamed as he stared at the ground. "You're right. She's a good kid. She doesn't deserve to be treated that way."

Kim threw her arms around his neck and kissed him.

"Tell you what," he said. "You drive this car and I'll follow you in the Ford. First, we'll go to my trailer and get you two cleaned up, then we'll celebrate at that pizza place you like in Red River tonight. You can watch Maggie for a couple of days while I take care of some unfinished business."

Kim was so relieved she could hardly hold still as she climbed behind the wheel. "Would you untie Maggie's feet before we go?"

"Sure." Willy opened the door and swept the child in his arms. In response to her terrified look, he said, "Don't worry, Maggie. We're just going for a little ride. I want you to go in my big truck, so we can talk." He deposited her in the front seat of his pickup and used his pocket knife to cut her free.

Moments later, they pulled out just behind Kim's car onto the highway. Miles passed without a word as they followed her. Finally, Willy said, "Better put on that seat belt, sweetie."

Maggie tugged it across her lap and snapped it in place. Not once had her eyes looked anywhere besides her own feet.

When they reached the peak of the mountain pass, he muttered, "Hold on, Maggie." Although he didn't notice, Maggie's hand clamped around a gold cross dangling on her chest. She closed her eyes, and began humming softly.

At precisely the right time, he floored the gas pedal to speed down the narrow, winding road. The big Ford truck effortlessly pulled beside the smaller car Kim was driving. She smiled nervously, a question in her eye as she began to ease off on the gas to let them pass.

But Willy had no intention of passing. Instead, he snapped the steering wheel, easily pushing her car off the road. It flipped as it hit the guard rail, took flight over the tree tops, then disappeared.

Turning to his daughter, Willy smiled and said, "Remember this, girl. When people don't play by my rules, they die."

CHAPTER 9

Kim saw it in his eyes. He was laughing at her. Laughing because he knew she was so stupid, so gullible that she'd bought every word he said. White hot anger ignited somewhere deep inside, a fury so strong it crushed all fear.

Her foot slammed on the brakes, a split-second too late. The front fender of the Ford had already knocked the car into the flimsy guard rail. *Out of control,* she thought. *My life, this car. Everything is out of control!*

A scream died before it reached her throat, cut off by the kick in the stomach from the roller coaster descent. For a few moments, she seemed to be driving on a road of lush green treetops, a road that plunged like a waterfall through a blissful void.

But the nose of the car dipped, chewing small, high branches, then spitting them aside. The world slowed down. A huge limb seemed to bend, then snap back right at her face. She should have raised her arms, tried to hide from the impact of certain death. But she didn't.

Instead, she watched in awe as the limb struck the tinted windshield. It splintered beautifully into a million sparkling pieces before it was blown out in chunks. The roar of twisting metal and cracking timber rushed inside, along with the scent of freshly cut pine.

Thoughts of revenge laced with regret as the sunny day turned black as night. *God forgive me!*

•　•　•　•　•

Crazy Cal stretched in the corner. Since he was the only person without a dog sitting patiently at one heel, he stood out. "From what you've told us, that girl you saw with the necklace must know some-thing."

"I'm sure she does," Max agreed.

Nodding toward his waiting helicopter, Cal smiled. "She's gassed up and ready to go. We could drop by Cimarron, then be back in the heart of Oklahoma in no time at all." He glanced at his watch. "You might even make it back to Tulsa before Kaycee does."

"I'd like to talk to that sheriff one more time."

"Then let's get the hell out of here."

The flight went quickly. As Cal sat the chopper down in the mid-dle of the quiet town, Max was fascinated by the crowd they always drew. Less than three minutes after they arrived, every person in Cimarron must have known that a helicopter had landed. People sud-denly found reasons to go outside. A few pretended to sweep fresh snow off the sidewalks, leaving behind a shimmering layer of thin ice. Most of them just stood in groups of three or four, pointing and openly staring at the unusual activity.

Max was trained to work at crime scenes. Now he wished he'd been more adamant about believing Kaycee that morning. There was no way to tell how much evidence had been destroyed during the day. He, Cal and Stagga were waiting outside when the sheriff arrived.

"Didn't expect to see you again so soon," Fred said, extending his hand.

"Sorry to have to call you when you're off duty," Max replied. "This is Cal Stevens." The men shook hands as Max handed him a photo. "Maggie Thornton is the little girl who came to Kaycee's room last night. She was reported missing day before yesterday."

"How can you be so sure?" Fred asked.

"Kaycee sketched a picture of her before she ever saw this photo. They're practically identical. There's no doubt it's the same girl who disappeared two days ago from Liberal."

Fred was shaking his head. Reaching into his car, he said, "The FBI just faxed this information on their prime suspect—the girl's father, Wilfred LaVerne Thornton. He's six-five, last known weight was around three hundred pounds. Goes by the name Willy." The men exchanged an amused glance, before he continued. "Why don't we start by talking to Sarah? She may be able to help."

"Does she own this motel?" Cal asked, unzipping his leather flight jacket.

Fred nodded.

Max patted Stagga. "Mind if I take my dog along?"

"Sure."

It was obvious Sarah had been watching from the lobby. As they approached, she held the door open. "Did you find the things stolen from the truck?" she asked.

Fred replied, "Not yet. Mind if we ask you a few questions?"

Wringing her hands, she stared at the floor and shook her head.

"Have you ever seen either one of these people?"

Max watched carefully as Sarah studied the picture of Maggie, then shook her head. When Fred handed her the photo of the man, she paused for a moment, then snapped, "I'm afraid I can't help you."

"Who was the young woman watching the lobby this morning? Can we talk to her?"

Sarah stiffened. "That's my granddaughter Kim. I'm sure she'd be happy to talk to you, but she isn't here right now."

"Does she usually wear any type of necklace?"

The woman seemed confused. "No."

"A gold cross?"

Shaking her head, she replied, "She has a little silver pinky ring. One of her ears is pierced in three places, the other in one. I know she likes to wear earrings, but I've never seen her wear a necklace." The phone rang, and she excused herself.

In a low voice, Max leaned toward Fred and asked, "Mind if we see if she's telling the truth about whether her granddaughter is here?"

"How are you planning to do that?" the sheriff asked.

"Watch." Crossing the room, Max removed the jacket that Kim had worn that morning from the coat rack. Opening it, he said, "Stagga, ready."

Stagga's ears shot up, and he sat perfectly erect, waiting in eager anticipation. Placing the inside of the jacket under the dog's muzzle, Max let him get the scent, then commanded, "Stagga, find."

Whining in his excitement, Stagga began his search. As Sarah watched wide-eyed, the white German shepherd made his way through the back room, around her legs, then stopped at the lobby door. She hung up the phone, asking, "What's his problem?"

Just as Max opened the door, the Sheriff turned to Sarah. "Would you mind coming with us? We may need the key to a room."

Stagga made his way through the parking lot, around to the back side of the motel. In a matter of minutes, he alerted at the door of Room 21. Max kept his voice low as he told Cal, "This is the room that Kaycee claims Maggie was being held in. It supposedly hasn't been rented for a while."

Fred asked, "Mind if I unlock the door, Sarah?"

Her hands were trembling as she found the right key on the ring and handed it to him. Using a handkerchief, he unlocked the door and pushed it open with his boot.

Stagga rushed inside, diligently tracking the scent over the bed, into the bathroom, until he finally alerted at the inside door adjoining Room 21 to Room 22.

"Anyone in there?" Fred shouted, knocking loudly as he noticed the interior locks weren't bolted from either side. When there was no reply, he cautiously opened the door.

Still tracking, Stagga sniffed the area, stopped briefly to double check the floor by the night stand. Finally, he alerted at the window.

Max nodded and smiled. "I think he just explained why Kaycee's doors were locked from the inside. They left this way." Using the cuffs of his shirt to keep from disturbing any latent prints, the Sheriff pulled in on the two spring-loaded locks at the bottom of the window, then pushed the heavy glass up. Stagga bolted through the open window, then slowed to a circle in the parking lot.

He'd lost the scent—probably because Kim had gotten into a vehicle of some kind. Max called, "Stagga, come! Good boy!"

Reaching into his pocket, he heaved a rubber chew toy shaped like a bone into the distant trees. Stagga happily chased it. As soon as he returned, Max asked, "Shall we confirm if Maggie was in that room last night?"

The Sheriff shrugged. "Probably wouldn't be a bad idea."

Cal ran to the helicopter and brought out Maggie's favorite blanket. At Max's command, Stagga easily bolted back to the door of room 21, alerted at the bed, then followed the girl's scent to room 22. "Looks like she paid Kaycee a late night visit after all," Max said, trying not to gloat.

The Sheriff put his hand on Sarah's shoulder. She seemed to have aged ten years in the last ten minutes. "Thank you for your help. I'm sure the FBI will have a few more questions. When you see your granddaughter, please give me a call, okay?"

Sarah nodded. "Is she in more trouble?" she asked weakly.

"Has she been in trouble before?"

"She was arrested on drug charges four years ago. But she's been clean ever since! What's going to happen to her now?"

Sheriff Fred shook his head. "I honestly don't know. It might be best if you didn't tell her we've been here. Just call me when she comes home."

In shock, Sarah nodded and walked away.

"Now what?" Cal asked.

Fred smiled sincerely at Max. "Looks like I owe your lady friend a big apology."

· · · · ·

Willy never noticed the hush that fell in the forest as he emerged from the mine that afternoon. Brushing the dirt off his legs and arms, he crawled into the cab of the pickup and sighed. Having all day to think made him realize what a mistake he'd made the night before. He couldn't believe he'd listened to that conniving, lying woman! Then again, what did he expect? They were all manipulative and deceitful, every stinking one of them.

It was Kim's fault he'd have to drive all night, her fault he would have to track down that woman Maggie found in the motel and snap her scrawny neck. His mind summoned the last memory of Kim—the way her face changed just before the end. First confusion, then outrage.

Willy's hand wrapped around the grip of his gun. He should have trusted his gut, ended it last night at the motel. But no, he'd listened to Kim whine about getting blood everywhere! Listened to her cry about not killing that woman while Maggie was watching! Now she was out there, and she'd seen him clear as day, and Maggie, too.

Opening the glove box, he found a Snickers bar and ripped it open. Washing it down with a lukewarm Coors, he rummaged through the box until he found the little leather luggage tag he'd tucked in his pocket last night, just in case. Pulling it out, he peered through the clear plastic to read:

> *Kaycee Miller*
> *3417 East Sherlyn Lane, Tulsa, OK*
> *Please call 918-555-2050 if found*
> *In case of Emergency contact:*
> *Niki Miller 505-555-1998*

Willy laughed. "Kaycee Miller, here I come!"

· · · · ·

Two years ago, Kaycee bought the house in a spacious suburb of south Tulsa, certain she'd live there forever. It was the home she'd always dreamed of owning—a contemporary two-story with a spacious yard that held the promise of an enormous garden.

Leaves were scattered on the street as she wove through the neighborhood and into her driveway. One look at her house made her heart sink. The 'For Sale' sign planted in the front yard was a disheartening reminder of what her future held. Admitting that the dream was over, she shook her head—in a million years she would never have imagined that it would end this way.

Deep down, Kaycee knew it was time to stop running from the truth. In a few short hours she'd know for certain. Sitting on her doorstep was a flat of pansies, no doubt the ones she'd ordered from the enterprising teens who lived across the street. They were gorgeous—deep velvety purple with splashes of yellow in the center. Touching one, she stared, memorizing every single detail. Then she closed her eyes to visualize the flower, but it wouldn't come. She was simply too tired to try to prepare for the future.

Right now, all she wanted was a nice long soak, and a good night's sleep. As quickly as she could, she carried her bags upstairs and unpacked most of her things. After running a hot bath, she slipped into the sea of bubbles, and dialed her sister's phone number on the portable phone.

"I'm home!" Kaycee announced.

"I was worried sick! What took you so long?"

"I had to detour through Liberal to drop off some friends." Kaycee could almost hear Niki mulling over the unexpected tidbits of information. "I met them on the highway on the way home. . ." She briefly ran through the story of what happened at the motel, and about the missing girl from Liberal. When she was finished, she asked, "So, what do you think?"

"I'm a little overwhelmed. In the last day you've had more adventures than I've had in a year."

Kaycee laughed. "I meant about Max. He seems too good to be true. And we both know my track record with men is less than spectacular."

"Then be careful. But, Kaycee—"

"Oh no. Here comes the lecture."

"No lecture. I just want you to remember that life is too short to question every single thing that comes your way. Looking back, there are things I wish I had done when I had the chance, and now it's too late."

"Niki, it isn't too late for anything."

"Maybe, maybe not."

Kaycee closed her eyes. For several moments there was silence on the line. "You were right about me selling this house. I really don't want to, but I don't have any choice."

Niki sighed. "Really, Kaycee, I'm doing great on my own."

Even though she'd practiced this speech a million times in her mind, the words still didn't come. Just as she was about to tell her the truth, the doorbell rang. "Sorry, Nik, someone's at the door. I have to go. I'll call again soon."

Grabbing a robe, Kaycee peered down through the second story windows. The dwindling light of dusk revealed a handsome balding man at her door. His navy suit matched the dark blue sedan parked at the curb, and his wide stance gave him an authoritarian air. "Coming!" she called, rushing downstairs.

When she opened the door, she greeted him with a pleasant smile. He nodded, flipping open his FBI identification. "I'm Special Agent Terrance Jones. I understand you're a witness in the Thornton kidnapping case."

Kaycee nodded, showing him inside. "Would you mind if I slip on some jeans? I wasn't expecting you so soon."

"Every minute in a case like this could make a difference."

"Oh." She felt guilty for even suggesting that she change clothes. "Why don't we sit at the kitchen table? I'll put some water on for tea, or make coffee, if you prefer."

"Tea would be fine. I didn't mean to imply you couldn't go change. It's just that the sooner we get confirmation that it was Margaret Thornton's father you saw in Cimarron last night, the sooner we can put out his description."

He handed her five pictures. They were all grainy black and white, obviously produced by a fax machine. "Can you tell me if any of these are the man who attacked you?"

She spread the pictures on the marble counter top. Scanning them, her eyes met his. Even in two-dimensional black and white, they were intimidating. Clutching the terrycloth robe at her chest, she pointed to the photo, not willing to even touch it. "That's him."

"Are you positive?"

Kaycee tensed, taking offense at the man's arrogant attitude. Moving across the room, she picked up the pad of paper and flipped it open. On the page beneath the drawing of a little girl with tears streaking her dirty face, was a sketch of a man. "I drew this at a rest stop on the way home. Now if you'll excuse me, I'd like to go change."

"Mind if I use your phone to call this in?"

"Not at all."

The agent watched her scurry away, then placed the photo next to the drawing. They were definitely the same man, only one difference was clear. In the sketch, Wilfred LaVerne Thornton's eyes were so evil, they made him shudder.

A s night thrust the house into darkness, Kaycee moved from room to room flipping on lights. Agent Jones tagged along, observing the ritual with open curiosity. Now that she had confirmed Thornton's identity, all Kaycee cared about was getting Jones out of her house so she could rest.

Stretching to ease her knotted neck and shoulder muscles, she noticed that it was only a few minutes past six o'clock. It felt more like midnight. The ring of the doorbell revived her spirits by breaking the rigid silence that hung between them. Excusing herself, she practically ran to the door. Spotting Max on the porch, she whipped it open and smiled. "How in the world did you get here so fast?" she asked, then added before Max could answer, "Where's Stagga?"

"Stagga's at the ranch. Cal flew me from Cimarron to my front door. Trust me, it's the only way to travel."

"I'll say. Come in. Max Masterson, this is Special Agent Jones. He's been going over what happened last night—" she shook her aching head, "—I mean this morning."

Max shot an irritated look at Jones. Leading Kaycee to an over-stuffed chair in front of the fireplace, he said, "You really should be resting." Directing his attention back to the agent, he added, "Ms. Miller may have a mild concussion, plus she's been on the road all day. I'd be glad to answer your questions if there's anything I can help you with."

Jones smiled pleasantly at Kaycee. "Would you mind if I ask Mr. Masterson a few questions in private?"

"As a matter of fact, I would. I'd prefer you talk to us together so we can wrap this up as quickly as possible."

"Fine," Jones muttered, glaring at Max. "Do you have the information we needed on the items stolen from your truck?"

Max dug a slip of paper out of his shirt pocket and handed it to him. "This is everything I could remember."

"Did your trip back to Cimarron prove beneficial?"

Max quickly summarized Stagga's successful tracking at the motel that afternoon, adding, "I have a gut feeling our kidnapper is still in New Mexico."

"We're sending in a team to check." Tucking his notepad into his pocket, he stiffly smiled. "Both of you have been very helpful. Hopefully, we'll find Maggie Thornton before it's too late."

Kaycee and Max exchanged a somber look.

"Will you be spending the night here, Mr. Masterson?" Jones asked.

Before Max could answer, Kaycee snapped, "His name is Max and he's just a friend. I don't need a babysitter, if that's what you had in mind."

Jones scowled through a placating shrug. "Sorry."

Kaycee held her temper, saying as politely as she could what she'd been thinking for the last thirty minutes. "Did I offend you somehow? You act as though you'd rather be anywhere in the world than here."

Taken aback, Jones suddenly found the pattern on the ceramic tiles of the entryway very interesting. When he looked back up, there was a genuine sincerity in his eyes. "I apologize. Cases involving parental child abuse really get to me. But I shouldn't have let it effect my professional demeanor. I'm really sorry."

It was Kaycee's turn to blush. "I think we could all use a good night's rest."

"Your safety is my responsibility, and I take my job very seriously. I didn't mean to imply anything about the two of you before, but I really don't think you should be alone. At least not until we get some idea of where Thornton could be."

Kaycee sighed. "He doesn't know my name, and I'm almost six

hundred miles from Cimarron."

"You said yourself that the last thing you remember was being hit on the head. Who knows how long he hung around? He could've gone through your purse, your luggage—"

Max protectively wrapped an arm around Kaycee, as if it might shield her from the rush of bitter memories.

Kaycee shook her head. "If he's the cold-hearted killer we all think he is, why didn't he finish me off when he had the chance? It doesn't make sense."

"Maybe something interrupted him," Jones said.

"Or maybe he's not a big enough jerk to murder someone in front of his own kid," Max added.

Kaycee sighed. "Listen, I'm absolutely drained. We can talk about all this tomorrow afternoon, but for now, my head is going to roll off my shoulders if I don't get some rest. I'm sure I'll be safe tonight. Even if he knew where I lived, Thornton couldn't possibly get from Cimarron to Tulsa this fast."

Jones raised one eyebrow as he stepped out the door. "I believe Max just did exactly that. Call if you need me."

•   •   •   •   •

Downshifting, the semi tractor trailer finally managed to crawl to the top of the mountain pass just as the last of the sun's warm breath was swallowed by a bank of ominous clouds. Roger Adams cranked up his new Garth Brooks CD, singing along with his favorite ballad as he felt the truck crest the peak and begin to coast downhill. At thirty, Roger was slightly younger than most of his trucking buddies, which probably explained why he was the only one who truly loved driving through the mountains even in the dark. It was always a challenge, something that made him feel totally energized.

His reward would be at the other side of the mountain, when he'd pull over long enough to capture the experience in his journal, then maybe catch an hour or two of sleep before heading on. Trucking paid the bills so he could someday chase his real dream—writing full time.

As he crossed the nation he recorded every thought, every emotion aroused by the wonders the land and its people held, determined to weave it into a best-selling novel someday.

Shifting and braking to keep the truck from gaining too much momentum, he watched the road ahead, concentrating on the path of the headlights as they bobbed along the curving, narrow shoulder. At first, he thought his mind was playing tricks on him when he saw it. "What the hell?" he muttered, braking so hard the wheel vibrated beneath his unyielding grip.

Although he squinted to focus better, the peculiar image had disappeared as rapidly as it had materialized. Unable to stop the rig quickly, Roger downshifted again, straining to catch another glimpse of whatever it was. Braking, he intently watched the oversized mirror fastened along the passenger side door, but the slushy wake revealed only the dark red shadows of the glowing brake lights.

The sudden, grotesque image that had flashed for only a second in his headlights wouldn't fade no matter how hard he blinked. He was sure he'd seen something. Something pale, ghastly, downright *weird*. A person? A ghost? Suppressing a shiver, he knew that whatever it was, it was back there, and he couldn't just ignore it.

Praying the heavy-duty parking brakes would hold on the steep incline, he coaxed the reluctant semi to a full stop and pulled on his thick overcoat. With a flashlight in one hand and a baseball bat in the other, he started the short hike back up the long grade of the hill to check the place where the guardrail was crushed. That much he was sure he'd seen.

By the time he hiked up to the edge of the curve, his leg muscles were burning. Breathing hard, first he searched the snow-covered pavement with his flashlight, then the spot where he'd seen *it*, scanning the downhill slope last. The flashlight beam prowled the black night until it fell upon what looked like a row of stalagmites jutting toward the sky from the forest floor. It was a path, a trail of destruction marked by craggy white stubs of pine branches torn asunder by whatever had plummeted down the side of the mountain.

Aiming the light just in front of his feet, Roger crouched to touch the snow along the narrow shoulder. Something had been there. The snow was packed, recently disturbed. His stomach clenched as he tightened his grip on the baseball bat. "Anybody need help?" he shouted, listening with growing fear as the haunting echo rumbled deep into the silent mountains.

Roger's mind began playing tricks. The wind swayed the pines in haunting swells as limbs cracked and groaned. Falling snow clumped on his eyelashes as nature's energy spawned horrific visions fueled by too many late-night horror movies. Half-sliding, half-running down the hill, he rushed back to his rig to call for help.

Climbing into the warm cab, Roger's breath was ragged as he tried to quiet his pounding heart. He was thoroughly spooked, and his hands were shaking. Closing his eyes, he swiped at the melting snow, then focused on calming thoughts. At last he leaned back and sighed, smiling at the depth of his imagination. "This'll make one hell of a story," he murmured, turning the music up as he softly shook his head.

While he collected himself, a thin line of melting snow was trick-ling down from the sleeping cabin behind his seat, mingling into the pool beneath his own boots. If Roger had looked down, the red tinge of the liquid would've wiped the smile right off his face.

· · · · ·

Kaycee leaned against her front door, closing her eyes. "I guess I'm just tired. I shouldn't have snapped at Agent Jones like that."

Max shrugged. "I don't envy anyone in law enforcement. It would be tough to see so much of the bad side."

"And to know that most of us take them for granted. We just assume when we need help, someone will be there."

"Because usually someone is. After all, you stopped to help me."

"Some people wouldn't consider running you off the road to be of much help."

"True, but everything still came out okay. I can see why you and

Agent Jones didn't exactly hit it off at first." Reacting to her questioning look, he added, "You both want to run the show."

"I'm sorry. I hope I didn't embarrass you. It's just been an incredibly long day, and I have an early appointment in the morning."

"Then I should be going, too. You need your rest."

"Actually, it'll take me a while to unwind. I'd really like to talk to you for a few minutes about what happened in Cimarron. How about a cup of hot tea? Decaf, of course."

"Sounds delicious."

Max described every detail of Stagga's search as Kaycee microwaved some water, then dunked tea bags in delicate china cups. When they were settled on the sofa in the den, Max said, "Your home is beautiful. Did you supervise the construction yourself?"

"Yes. It was a lot of work, but I loved every minute of it."

"Yet you're selling it."

With a faint smile, her eyes met his. "Sometimes we have to do things that aren't easy."

"And sometimes we don't," he said with an incorrigible grin.

For a moment, Kaycee simply looked at him. "More tea?"

"No, thanks. Did you install a security system?"

She visibly tensed. "Why?"

"I think Agent Jones was right. Willy Thornton might come looking for you."

"Willy?"

"The FBI says that's the name he goes by."

"Willy. Sounds like a cute little boy, but the man who broke into my motel room was more like a bull elephant on steroids."

"My point exactly. He's a big, mean guy. And if he watches any television at all, he's going to realize someone nailed him. The story about Maggie's kidnapping will probably be on every news show across the nation first thing tomorrow."

Kaycee softly shook her head. "Sometimes I wonder if I'm the only one who can hear my voice." Slowly, deliberately, she leaned toward him and said, "Remember, he doesn't know who I am!"

"Okay, let's assume he doesn't. I'd still feel better if you weren't alone."

"Max, that's sweet. We don't really know each other very well, so let's just say that I learned to roll with life's punches a long time ago. I don't take unnecessary chances. I'm careful, but not to the point that I'm obsessed about it. And, yes, this house has an alarm system."

"Good. Did something bad happen to you at night?"

Kaycee was puzzled by his odd question, by the curious look on his face. Remembering that night, that horrible man, gave her goose bumps. "As a matter of fact, I was attacked at night on a highway when I was just seventeen. How did you know?"

"I'm so sorry. I tend to notice things that most people don't. Guess it's my rescue training. . ."

"Like what?"

"Let's see. . .You were afraid when you stopped to help me the first time. You desperately wanted to be in Cimarron before dark. And you won't have dinner with me at the ranch, but lunch is okay." He paused, motioning with one hand. "Plus you keep your entire house lit up like a Christmas tree after dark."

Cornered, Kaycee looked up, as if an answer that would satisfy him might miraculously fall in her lap. It amazed her how easily he could read her, how right he was in some ways, yet wrong in others. "You're awfully observant, aren't you?" she asked.

Raising one brow, Max smiled. "Answering a question with a question—a classic avoidance technique. I'm not surprised you've mastered the conversational sidestep."

His breezy attitude and sly grin were contagious, stealing the edge from her indignation. "Definitely. Since you've analyzed me, it's only fair that I get a shot at you. Why do you prefer the company of dogs over people?"

"Who says I do?"

"Me."

"Aren't you ever wrong?"

She grinned. "Sometimes. But I'm a pretty good judge of character."

He smiled. "You must think I'm okay, or you wouldn't be sitting here alone with me. Tell you what, if I promise not to pry into your past, can we just forget this conversation ever took place?"

"I suppose. Go ahead."

"Go ahead and what?" he laughed.

"Promise! Swear you won't ask me again!"

"All right, I promise not to ask you about. . .What exactly was it that we were discussing, anyway?"

Kaycee grabbed a pillow and whacked him playfully on the head. As she was laughing and gently flailing him, he pulled her into his arms. Their lips touched, softly at first, then with unexpected passion.

Pulling back, he searched her eyes. "I honestly didn't mean to pry. It's just that I'm worried about you."

It felt wonderful to languish in his embrace. Resting her head on his shoulder, she replied, "I appreciate your concern, but I really can take care of myself. I've done it for a long time now."

"So long that you've forgotten how to lean on someone else every once in a while?"

Closing her eyes, she sighed. "Maybe."

"Just remember, I'm pretty good at coming to the rescue. All you have to do is call."

. . . . .

Roger slouched, tilting his head back as he anxiously waited. The burst of nervous energy that had accompanied seeing whatever it was on the side of the road had left him exhausted. Checking his indiglo watch, he was sure the State Police would be there any minute. With closed eyes, he wondered what they would find. What if a whole family had plunged off the road? What if someone was still alive, slowly freezing to death? Guilt wrapped around him even though he knew there was nothing he could do alone.

His thoughts were shattered by a sound inside the cab. For the second time in only fifteen minutes, his heart was hammering. Reaching forward, he punched off the CD player, leaving only the sound of the wind slapping the truck. Surely it wasn't his imagination. *God, I must be really losing it!*

Turning slowly around, he peered over his tall seat, pulling back the curtain that separated him from the area he considered home. It was dark. Empty. Flipping on the interior light switch, he glanced at the narrow rumpled bed, the box of books on the floor. Twisting to reach his journal, he noticed his hand was shaking. Recording his feelings would have to wait. For now, he was just too unnerved.

Shivering, he closed the curtain and muttered, "I wish they'd hurry."

· · · · ·

It was just after 4:00 a.m. when Thornton slowly drove past the address listed on Kaycee Miller's luggage tag. Even though every other house in the neighborhood was dark inside and out, the place he was searching for gleamed like the beacon from a lighthouse. If he were a superstitious man, he'd have sworn the lights were a sign that she was waiting for him, inviting him into her home. But Thornton tried not to read between the lines, because it usually just slowed him down. To him, most of life was easy to understand. *The man on top wins, everyone else loses.*

A chandelier dangled from the ceiling of the second story, lighting the tall entryway so well that he was certain a quick peek through a first floor window would allow him to plan every move he would need to make. She must have stayed up all night, or she was a very early riser. Either way, he was too tired to risk being seen. He needed sleep, and time. Time to decide how and when to kill Kaycee Miller.

Enjoy yourself. I'll be back soon. Maggie can't wait forever, he thought as he slowly drove into the night.

CHAPTER 11

T he ring of the telephone near his head roused Max so quickly that he bolted upright. Disoriented, he ran his fingers through his disheveled hair and leaned against the headboard of his bed. Even after years of being rudely awakened, he still wasn't used to it. Grabbing the phone, he grumbled, "Hello."

"That you, Mr. Masterson?"

"Yeah. Who's this?"

"Sheriff Fred out in Cimarron. Thought you'd like to know we found something that was stolen from your 4Runner."

"That's great! Is it my light line?"

"Not exactly. More like a fancy flashlight. Your name's engraved on the side. It was in the motel owner's car when it went over the edge of a mountain pass."

"Was anyone hurt?"

"Max, I don't mind telling you that this is the strangest case I've worked in a long time. The truck driver who spotted the place where the car went off the road claims to have seen something in the woods."

"Something? Don't you mean someone?"

"That's what's so strange. He's a level-headed guy. Says he never drinks. Yet, he claims he stopped because he thought he saw a ghost or something. The man was so scared he was shaking. Can you believe it?"

"I'd believe anything right now."

"I can tell you this—it wasn't a ghost. There was blood on the steering wheel, and on what was left of the windshield. That car ended up a long way off the road, teetering on a pretty treacherous incline. We had a helicopter spotlight the area a few minutes ago, but didn't turn anyone up. The sun will be up here soon. We'll start a ground search then."

"Do you think it was the girl who stole Kaycee's necklace?"

"Most likely. Her grandma said she borrowed the car early yesterday morning and she hasn't seen her since."

"Stagga and I will be there to help search."

"That's really not necessary."

Max sighed. "Yes, it is."

· · · · ·

"You really shouldn't have!" Kaycee exclaimed as she buttoned the top of her tailored black silk suit. Motioning for Max and Stagga to come inside, she quickly closed and locked the door behind them.

"I wanted to. Last time we shared breakfast was such a treat I thought we'd try it again," Max softly whistled. "You look gorgeous."

"What I think you mean is—" she switched to a Western drawl— "that I clean up real *purty.*" Laughing, she added, "Come to think of it, you haven't exactly been around me in the best of circumstances."

"True."

"Do you always drop in with breakfast?"

"More like occasionally. I have some news to tell you."

"I really only have a few minutes before my appointment. Why don't we eat on the deck? It might be a little nippy, but my yard backs a beautiful creek, so Stagga can make himself at home in the grass. But it's not fenced. Will he wander off?"

"Not without permission. Eating outside sounds perfect."

After loading a tray with a pot of coffee, two cups, and two plates, Kaycee led the way to her backyard. Max spread the feast on the glass table—fresh bagels, strawberry cream cheese, and a small baker's box of caramel-pecan cinnamon rolls.

"Knowing you could lead to a serious weight problem," Kaycee observed.

Eyeing her slender figure, he asked, "What do you usually have for breakfast?"

Shaking her head, she replied, "It's too early for lectures, so I refuse to answer on the grounds that it might incriminate me."

"Must be something really bad. Let me guess. Cold pizza?"

Scrunching her nose, she grimaced. "Not since college."

"Caviar? Leftover pie? Lucky Charms?"

"Okay! You win. A cup of instant cappuccino and a handful of granola. Low fat, of course."

"Of course."

Responding to the disgusted look on his face, she added, "I know it sounds terrible, but it travels well. I'm usually on my way to the office by now."

"Which brings up why I'm here. They found something stolen from my 4Runner. I'm leaving for Cimarron in a few minutes. Cal is going to fly us out as soon as we get to his hangar. They're searching for the girl we think stole your necklace."

"Searching?"

"Her grandmother's car went off a mountain road, but the driver was missing." He shook his head as he worked on a particularly chewy bite of bagel. "They'll have found whoever it was by the time we get there. If not, Stagga can give it his best shot."

"Promise you'll both be careful?"

"We always are. I should be home sometime tomorrow. Since it'll be Saturday, why don't I pick you up when I get back in town? I'll give you a tour of the ranch on horseback or by four-wheeler. Your choice. I'm afraid I won't have time to break out the charcoal, but I'd love to treat you to dinner at O'Malley's Landing."

Kaycee glanced at her watch, wondering if she would be in any shape to be around anyone after her doctor's appointment. "Isn't O'Malley's pretty far out of town?"

"Yeah, but it's well worth the trip. Their food is to die for." Reacting to the resistance that strained her face, Max quickly added, "By the way, did I mention that I won't take no for an answer?"

"Then I guess it's a date," Kaycee weakly promised.

. . . . .

Even though Roger Adams had been driving for hours, he couldn't shake the creepy feeling in the pit of his stomach from discovering the abandoned site of the car wreck. The glow of sunrise in his rearview mirror reminded him that more than twelve hours had passed since he'd stopped to eat and sleep. Veering off onto the exit ramp of the next rest stop, he parked the rig and closed his eyes.

For a few minutes, he simply leaned his head back. The same personal demons that always came out when he was tired crawled into his mind—the insecurities, the anger over the divorce, the need to find a place to settle back down. A yawn helped push them aside as he crawled onto his bed.

He noticed a lump on the floorboard directly behind the driver's seat. Throwing the covers back, he gasped.

It was a girl. No, a young woman. She was curled into a ball, either sound asleep or dead. Dried blood stained her clothes, apparently from the deep abrasions on her forehead and arms. Moving closer in the dim light, he could barely see the rise and fall of her shoulders as she drew a shallow breath.

"Thank God," Roger sighed as her eyes slowly opened. Startled, the woman flinched, apparently causing a flash of pain so intense she screeched and grabbed her head. Extending his hands, he declared, "It's okay. I'm not going to hurt you."

Crushing fear pushed her as far away from him as the small space allowed while she responded in a terrified whisper. "I can't go back there! Don't make me go back!"

"What are you talking about? How did you get in here?"

"He'll kill me next time!"

Suddenly, the evening's events made sense. "Oh, my God. You're what I saw."

She nodded.

"When I went back to investigate, you crawled in here and hid." His eyes widened, then narrowed. "The police are looking for you."

"No!" Bolting upright, she held her head and started to cry.

"Okay! Okay! Calm down. I'll get you to a doctor."

"No! I need to go to Taos. I have a friend there who will help me. Please!"

Roger shook his head. "We're a hundred miles from there. Besides, I could get in big trouble. I'm on a deadline, and this whole situation seems pretty suspicious."

Tears streamed down her face. "Please."

Roger sighed. She was so young. Logic told him to drop her off at the nearest hospital and run. But he was a true romantic at heart. Glancing at the fragile young woman one more time, he knew there was no way he could add more pain to her already heavy load.

Crawling back into the driver's seat, Roger found the next turn-around on the highway and headed back into the rising sun.

• • • • •

Kaycee understood why her palms were sweaty, she'd even planned for it by tucking one of her mother's antique white hankies in the breast pocket of her suit. But she hadn't expected another full-fledged panic attack. Not in broad daylight. Not at a stoplight just two miles from her home.

Yet as she glanced in the rearview mirror, she realized that she was absolutely terrified. With unsteady hands, she managed to drive the rest of the way to the medical building and park. Ever since the first ophthalmologist diagnosed her condition, she'd been mentally preparing herself for this day. She just wished it hadn't arrived quite so soon.

Sitting alone in the car, Kaycee softly recited the thought she had found most comforting in the long hours between dusk and dawn: "We're here to do the best we can with what we're given. I can deal with anything. I will be *independent,* no matter what fate throws my way."

Opening the door, she stepped into the sunshine, held her head high, and marched inside.

•   •   •   •   •

The Greater Tulsa Area telephone book listed two phone numbers for Kaycee Miller: a residence and a business. When Willy parked his truck near the entry to her neighborhood that morning, he had planned to follow her to work. Instead, he had carefully trailed her to the Warren Clinic, a towering medical building on the south side of town.

Parking several rows away, he watched with voyeuristic pleasure as she sat in her car, apparently talking to herself. In his mind's eye, he pinpointed the exact place where a bullet could strike her ample breasts, laughing, "Gotcha!" He imagined she was preparing for a speech, some important business presentation that paid for the fancy house, the expensive car. The longer he watched, the more intrigued he became. By the time the vision in black disappeared inside the building, he was breathing hard.

Willy found this unexpected twist fascinating. Kaycee Miller wasn't the type he usually lusted after, yet the arousal he felt clearly said otherwise. As the sun crept higher in the sky, Willy's plans changed. This beautiful, powerful woman was his to do with as he pleased.

Visions of simply killing Kaycee Miller were long gone. She needed to be taught a lesson. He would play with her, teach her a few things that he was sure she'd find enlightening. They'd play a different kind of game than the one he was playing with his daughter, but one that promised to be infinitely more fun.

•   •   •   •   •

Max shielded his eyes from the blowing snow, trying his best to watch Stagga's descent onto the open slope.

Cal was doing a good job of keeping the dog away from the trees as he was lowered from the helicopter. As Stagga floated lower and lower, Max recognized the usual blend of excitement fighting the instinctive panic in his eyes.

"He seems to like this!" Sheriff Fred called over the commotion of the helicopter.

"More than I did! It's really cold under the wind from the rotors," Max called as he swept Stagga into his arms. Lowering him to the ground, he disconnected the cable and signaled to Cal that they were clear.

The helicopter's nose tilted slightly down before it swept across the morning sky. In moments it was out of sight, leaving Fred to break the welcome silence as he said, "Have to admit, I'm impressed."

"Crazy Cal's the best."

Kneeling beside Stagga, he ran his hand over the dog's warm, bright orange vest. "I meant by your dog. He didn't struggle at all."

"We practice staying calm from the time they go in training. SAR K-9's have to be very sociable animals under the most extreme circumstances. Some victims can be hostile from fear, lack of food, even mental disorders."

"So they're nothing like attack dogs?"

"Far from it. Within reason, they'll yield to a human every time. They're trained to go back to their partner if there's a problem." Nodding uphill, Max asked, "How far are we from the road?"

"About seventy yards." The men had crossed into the heavy woods where the demolished car rested. Fred continued, "The FBI people told me to remind you that this area is part of a crime scene in an ongoing investigation. They've already had a crew out here to get lab samples, but we'd like you to see if there's anything else inside the vehicle that belongs to you."

The body of the car rested pretty much upright, although the entire back end was elevated by a five-foot-high stump. The contrasting fresh blanket of snow gave the entire scene an eerie feel.

The windshield, windows, dashboard, and virtually everything plastic was either gone or shattered. Someone had already dusted for fingerprints, and Max noticed scrapes across a spot that looked like blood. Peering inside, he checked for the generator and coil of light line. When he saw the trunk and empty back seat, he muttered, "Damn!"

Answering the sheriff's inquisitive stare, Max shook his head.

"This sure would've been easier if it hadn't snowed all night."

"We've worked in worse," Max replied.

Holding up an evidence bag with a sweater inside, Fred asked, "Can Stagga do his stuff with this?"

"He can try. Stagga, ready." The familiar whine and eager anticipation filled the air as Max held the bag so Stagga could sniff its contents. "Stagga, find."

Bounding through the snow, Stagga headed back up the hill. A heavy guide rope had been tied from the guard rail to a tree near the wreckage to make the trip less treacherous on foot. The Sheriff followed that path as Stagga and Max found a parallel route in the woods. Halfway up, Max shouted, "Looks like there's a trail over here, and some spots of blood under the fresh snow!"

"Mark it and we'll send the photographer back down."

Stagga continued to follow the trail up the steep incline. Twice, Max had to struggle to keep up with him. By the time they emerged at the side of the road, they were both breathing heavily. But Stagga didn't stop. Instead, he twisted back into the woods, weaving through the trees parallel to the road. A quarter mile down the hill, he headed back up to the pavement to pause and circle.

Fred was walking toward them down the highway. "Is this where the trail ends?"

"Seems to be," Max said, obviously disappointed.

"This is exactly where the guy's semi was parked last night after he spotted the wreck."

"You mean the one who claims he saw a ghost?"

Fred nodded.

Max rewarded Stagga with a hug as he remarked, "Good job, boy. Now we know we're searching for a ghost that not only bleeds, but likes to hitch rides."

Kaycee could hear everything the doctor said, yet she had long ago stopped grasping the meaning of his words. Recessive genes, results of the electroretinogram, diagrams of how the photoreceptor cells would degenerate, none of it mattered. The one thing that did matter—not being able to see—was now definitely a part of her future. The only question was when?

Still reeling, she interrupted him. "How long do I have?" The sound of her own voice surprised her. It was level, cold, resigned.

Rolling his chair closer, the kindly older gentleman took her hand. "Ms. Miller, you mustn't think like that. Yes, discovering you have retinitis pigmentosa is a life-altering blow, but it isn't the *end* of your life. You'll be amazed at how well you can adapt, just by changing how you interact with the world. The next few years will be a bridge, a time to build a strong foundation for the rest of your life."

A tear slid down her cheek. "A life in a dark cocoon?" She drew a ragged breath. "I'm sorry. I thought I was ready for this, but no matter how much I try to tell myself that I can get through this, I feel like I'm being buried alive."

"I promise you, the life you find will be far more meaningful than anything you can imagine at this moment. Quite frankly, I'd be very concerned if you *weren't* scared to death right now."

"Then you've got nothing to worry about!"

He laughed. "And it's that sense of humor that will get you through this." Standing, he motioned for her to remain seated. "If you don't mind, I'd like you to wait here for a few more minutes. One of my nurses will be right in to discuss a few things with you."

"Thank you, doctor."

He slipped out the door, leaving Kaycee alone with her thoughts. Grabbing a tissue, she dried her eyes and fought the urge to break down and sob. When the door finally opened, an attractive woman walked slowly into the room. Slender with blonde chin-length hair, she nodded politely as she introduced herself. "Ms. Miller, my name is Ellen Henderson. I'll be your case coordinator."

"Please call me Kaycee."

"And I'm Ellen." Ellen extended a hand in Kaycee's general direction, then waited for Kaycee to take it.

"You're..."

"Blind? Not completely. My RP is at a more advanced stage than yours. I can still see light, but all the images are indistinct. I want you to know that I'm here to help. Feel free to call me any time of the day or night. I know firsthand how frightening this can be."

Kaycee studied her face, startled by the perfectly applied makeup, the confident tilt of her chin. "How long have you known?"

Ellen sat down. "About thirteen years. But it's different for everyone. Sometimes RP progresses quite rapidly, other people live most of their lives only dealing with mild inconveniences. Unfortunately, the medical crystal ball doesn't work well with this particular disease."

For the first time in weeks, Kaycee no longer felt like she was alone in a world spinning out of control. Ellen's warm smile filled the room, even though it was a room she couldn't fully see. "What was your first clue something was wrong?" Kaycee asked.

"I was a nurse at St. John's Hospital and my supervisor filed a report on me. She accused me of being an alcoholic because she kept noticing that I wasn't walking straight."

"That's terrible!"

"Yeah, but I had the last laugh. You should have seen the look on her face when I told her I was going blind!" Ellen leaned forward. "How about you? What was your first clue?"

"Double takes. I'm constantly doing double takes."

"Look at it this way. The eyes just feed information to the sight center of your brain. Before, the images were always sharp and clear.

You could easily figure out what you were seeing. But now, those images are starting to become fuzzy. Your mind's working overtime trying to form mental images, but with far less detail than before."

Kaycee nodded. "My night vision is the worst. Being in the dark scares me half to death."

Ellen extended her hand, waiting to speak until Kaycee took it in hers. "I'm not going to lie to you. This will be the biggest challenge of your life. If anyone tells you otherwise, just reel back and smack 'em!"

"I'd probably miss!" Kaycee joked.

"Didn't you know? That's why they give us canes!" They both laughed. When Ellen regained her composure, she continued, "But seriously, it really, truly isn't going to be as bad as you think it is. Right now, all you can see is becoming dependent, your loss of freedom. But there are so many wonderful inventions available that can give most of that freedom right back to you. In fact, I think we should get started today. Can you spend part of your afternoon with me?"

Kaycee nodded, blushing when she realized Ellen was still waiting for a response. "Of course. What will we do?"

"We'll start with the basics. I can show you some tricks to help heighten your awareness. It's time you started teaching your other senses to be a little more useful. You'll be amazed how much touch, hearing, and smell can compensate."

Kaycee hesitated. "It's overwhelming."

"That's why we'll take it slowly. The only *good* thing about RP is that you have time to adjust to the idea that you'll have to live a little differently."

"What was the hardest thing for you to give up?"

Ellen thought for a moment. "I think the toughest is not being able to drive."

Kaycee nodded, another fear confirmed.

"I know what you're thinking, and you're wrong. I'm here, aren't I? I'm still nursing full time. I've met the most wonderful friends *because* I must commute. You'll find the best comes out in people if you give them a chance. Problem is, most people are too busy to notice. In an odd way, losing your sight will give you the chance to really *see*."

·   ·   ·   ·   ·

The phone in Kaycee's office was ringing as she jiggled the lock, trying to coax it open. Finally, the bolt slid free and she rushed inside, past the empty reception area and into her private suite. Dropping her briefcase and purse on her desk, she grabbed the phone and breathlessly answered, "Kaycee Miller."

"Kaycee, I was afraid I'd missed you. This is Bob Palmer, with CSI. We met the other day when you presented your skills to the parole board."

"Good afternoon, Mr. Palmer."

"Guess we'd better set things straight. My name is Bob. I'll get right down to why I called. I was quite impressed with your abilities. So much so that I wondered if you'd be interested in joining our organization."

"You mean work for the state prison system?"

He laughed. "Not at all! I'm referring to working for my company, Confidential Services & Investigations. We're based in Taos, but you could take your time deciding whether you want to relocate. Plus, you could still do contract work for parole boards on the side."

"Which brings up an obvious question. Why not just handle your firm's needs on a contract basis?"

"I thought about it, but I think you could be a very valuable resource. A lot of what we do is based on gut feelings, intuition, whatever you care to call it. In order for you to truly understand the scope of a case, I think you'd have to be in on the ground floor. Will you at least consider it? Come back to New Mexico long enough to interview for the position?"

Kaycee hesitated. Now, more than ever, she was torn. She knew she should tell him the truth about her limited future, yet it could be years before her ability to work would be seriously impaired. The soft bell that signaled someone had come into the office gave her a few seconds to compose herself. "Could you hold on? I gave my secretary the day off, and someone just came in."

After putting him on hold, she crossed into the reception area. It was empty. Noticing she'd forgotten to turn on the recessed lights, she flipped the switch then peered through the glass on each side of the door into the hallway. There wasn't a soul in sight. An uneasiness settled in her bones. Quietly moving toward the back of the office, she checked the small break area that doubled as a home for the copy machine, then stopped in front of the only other room.

For a few seconds, Kaycee stared at the bathroom door. Gathering her courage, she picked up an umbrella and briskly opened the door. Turning on the lights, she looked twice, relieved to find it empty.

Slumping into her desk chair, she sighed, disgusted by her own fear. Grabbing the phone, she said, "I'm sorry you had to wait, Bob. You wouldn't believe how crazy my life has been since I last saw you."

"It's been pretty rough here, too. You know that man you warned us about? I heard that he's a suspect in a kidnapping. Obviously, you were dead right about him."

Kaycee's mind flashed to the handwriting samples she'd examined, every detail suddenly as real to her as if she were holding them in her hand. Although his face alone was enough to scare the hell out of her, for some reason connecting *him* with the overwhelming evil she'd sensed in his writing made her shudder. More to herself than to Bob, she mumbled, "Oh, my God! The initials on the back were W.T.— Wilfred Thornton."

"How'd you know his name?"

"He's the reason my life has been so crazy." She quickly ran through what had happened in Cimarron.

"Kaycee, you really must be careful. I'm not at liberty to go into the details, but I can tell you that our firm had a person watching Thornton."

"And?"

"And we haven't heard from him in days."

"Oh. . ."

"Promise me you'll call if he makes any attempt to—" it was obvious he was carefully choosing his words, "—contact you. To put it mildly, CSI has a vested interest in this case."

"As I've told the FBI, he doesn't know who I am. But I promise, you'll probably hear me scream all the way from New Mexico if I so much as lay eyes on him." She took a deep breath, then added, "Could I please have a few days to think over your job offer?"

"Take as long as you need. In the meantime, would it be too much of an imposition for us to overnight handwriting samples if the need arises? As I said, I was quite impressed with your abilities."

"Not at all."

"Take care, Kaycee."

"I will."

Kaycee glanced at her watch. It would be dark in an hour, just enough time to check her messages, answer e-mail and drive home before sunset. After jotting down the calls taken by the answering service, she started to turn on her computer, then stopped. Unnerved and tired, she decided the rest could wait until next week. Switching off the lights, she gathered her things and double checked the locks on the way out. When she emerged into the crisp air outside, she felt a little better, but still rushed to her Lexus.

Sliding inside, she shivered, glancing into the back seat to be certain she was alone. The same feeling she had in the parking lot Wednesday night in Cimarron hit her. Swallowing hard, she started the engine and drove home, wondering which was worse, being afraid of a life of darkness, or of Wilfred Thornton.

When she was finally in her own kitchen, she took a deep breath and vowed to call Ellen first thing in the morning. Being terrified for no reason was driving her crazy, and she wondered if it was a symptom of RP, or merely a result of her own sudden inability to handle stress.

Cooking was always relaxing, so she rummaged through the refrigerator, pulling out what she would need. Even though she knew every ingredient by heart, she dug out her grandfather's hand-written recipe for chili cheese omelets. In moments, a spicy aroma filled the kitchen and she expertly folded the concoction onto a plate. Turning to place it on the counter, out of the corner of her eye she glimpsed movement outside the window.

The plate crashed to the floor as her hand flew to her mouth, but the petrified gasp quickly changed to a sigh of relief. The neighbor's black cat was perched on the windowsill, its probing iridescent eyes mocking her foolish human behavior.

After cleaning up the mess, Kaycee whipped up a second omelet and sat down to eat. Picking at the food on her plate, she realized that no matter how hard she tried to pretend this was just another day, there was no denying her dark mood, or the causes of it. A few moments later, it dawned on her. Losing her eyesight might be out of her control, but there was no need to spend the night afraid of her own shadow.

Her hand trembled slightly as she dialed the home phone number listed on the card. "Agent Jones? This is Kaycee Miller."

"Are you all right? Have you remembered something?" he asked.

"No. I just think you may be right. Could you have someone come by for the night?"

"Did you see someone? Something?"

Hearing children in the background, she fought a wave of guilt. "No. . .It's just a feeling I have. I know it sounds silly, but I'd rest more comfortably if I knew I wasn't all alone. Just for tonight. I'll be with Max all day tomorrow and hopefully by Sunday you'll have caught the guy. I'm sorry to be such a bother."

"It's not a problem. I'll have the local police stop by and check your house while I arrange for an agent to spend the night."

"I really appreciate your help."

"Lock your doors, set the alarm, and don't let anyone in."

"I won't."

Remembering Ellen's suggestion, Kaycee closed her eyes and visualized every detail of the kitchen. She was too tired to try to learn to get around in the dark tonight, and far too scared. Working her way upstairs, she turned on every light along the way.

Sitting in her grandmother's antique rocking chair, she finally broke down. Tears tumbled down her cheeks. She cried for her parents, her sister, and finally, for herself.

· · · · ·

Thornton didn't bother to follow Kaycee. He was so sure she was going straight home that he waited fifteen minutes before leaving the parking lot. Taking the now familiar route toward her house, he parked his truck in front of a grocery store less than a half mile from her neighborhood.

As the brisk November day folded into night, a handful of joggers made their way through the quiet neighborhood. Wearing a baseball cap and a brand new pair of dark green sweats, Thornton lumbered along at the side of the road, thankful for the diminishing sunlight.

Turning into Kaycee's neighborhood, he nodded pleasantly at a woman walking a runt of a dachshund. It barked and strained against its leash so furiously as he passed that the woman swept the obnoxious dog into her arms and hurried back inside. Thornton imagined the yappy little beast trying to bite him and laughed. He'd punt it into next week given half a chance.

Even though the houses were only a few years old, the builders had left large oak trees scattered through the yards to give the neighborhood a rustic quality. Thornton was about to turn down Kaycee's street when he spotted a Tulsa Police car parked at the curb of her house.

Another change of plans. Retracing his steps in the darkness, he knew he only had one more day before he had to get back.

Tomorrow he would take care of Kaycee Miller. She would make the long, boring trip to New Mexico much more interesting. In fact, he was really beginning to look forward to it.

CHAPTER **13**

Kaycee reached for the clouds, then bent slowly at the waist to stretch her aching legs. "I wish every day were Saturday."

"Don't we all?" Max laughed.

"It's been a long time since I've ridden a horse. I guess I'm a little out of shape."

"Riding certainly uses different muscles than most sports. I try not to miss more than a week, or I pay for it the next day."

"Who takes care of the horses when you're away?"

"A wonderful woman named Robin Hessel. She has a stable of her own to run, but she still drives down from Stillwater when I go on rescues."

Kaycee noticed how his eyes had softened as he thought of her. "Have you known her long?" she asked.

"Long enough."

"Are you—" suddenly embarrassed, she turned her attention back to the ranch house, "—oh, never mind."

"Seeing her? Well, we've been friends since college. She and I have a unique relationship."

"Really?"

Max grinned coyly. "I grow hay. Her horses eat hay. It's a match made in heaven. Seriously, Robin is happily married, and if you're wondering if I'm involved with anyone, the answer is no." He tossed a stick for Stagga to fetch.

"Good. I'd hate to have dinner tonight with a man who's cheating on someone."

"Then you're in luck." Gazing down the slope of scrub oaks and blackjacks, he asked, "What do you think of the place so far?"

"I love it."

"And I saved the best for last." Grabbing her hand, Max urged her toward the house. Up close, it looked even more impressive than it had from the highway. As they walked past the two-story white pillars that stood like sentries on the porch, Kaycee ran her fingers along the smooth, cool surface, wondering what kind of stories the wood would tell if it could.

Max proudly opened the massive front doors and motioned her inside. She could feel his anticipation as they walked into the heart of the old ranch house. Her genuine surprise and amazement didn't disappoint him.

"Oh, my," she whispered. "Your grandfather built this?"

"Most of it. I've made a few changes recently, but the basic structure was his design."

"I assumed it was two stories, but it isn't, is it?"

"This central room is one story with an eighteen foot ceiling. There are two bedrooms with full baths on each end that have lofts with sliding doors that open to let in the night breeze. Modern houses this size have at least a dozen rooms, but this one has five."

Kaycee stood in the doorway, sensing more than seeing the home before her. Her heart beat faster, and she slowly came to appreciate that it was because the house felt so familiar, as though it was spreading its arms to embrace a long lost friend. She soon realized it was the sheer simplicity that dazzled her—open space filled with natural light.

The ranch house was actually one enormous room with a double doorway on each wall. An oversized fan suspended on a long chain hung between enormous skylights carved out of the slatted oak ceiling. Its slow-turning blades cast lazy shadows across the polished wood floors. Beneath the groupings of furniture were beautifully woven rugs. One third of the room was an enormous kitchen area, with its own open-hearth fireplace. A line of aging copper pots dangled from a rack over the free-standing marble-topped island. Crossing to admire it, Kaycee asked, "Did you remodel the kitchen?"

"Last year," he proudly replied. "How'd I do?"

She walked over to touch the luxurious surface. "You did great. Did you have help?"

"I had to stick to the basic floor plan, but I built these cabinets, and installed new appliances. A friend handled the marble and glass etching for me."

"This is the granite counter top I picked for my kitchen, and the same ceramic tiles on the floor."

"I noticed." Max moved beside her, so close he could feel her warmth. "Then again, you're the one who notices everything, aren't you?"

"I'm better when I'm not distracted." She turned into his arms, tracing one finger slowly along the outline of his cheek.

"Are you distracted right now?" he softly asked.

"I'll say."

•   •   •   •   •

Thornton had resigned himself to wait all day Saturday if necessary, but he was rapidly losing his patience. Spending the afternoon strolling from house to house in Kaycee's neighborhood, he assessed his escape route while stuffing fake lawn service flyers into people's front doors. When he finally stood on Kaycee's porch a little after five p.m., he stole a glimpse through the window before casually pretending to head toward the next house.

At the last moment, Thornton veered off the sidewalk to hide behind a row of shrubs. After waiting there for several minutes, scanning the area to be sure no one had noticed his sudden disappearance, he ambled around the side of the house into the spacious backyard. Thornton was relieved to see the grass slope down to a wooded creek bed—no row of nosy neighbors, fewer chances of witnesses.

Clinging so close to the house that the bricks snagged and tugged at his flannel shirt, he slowly inched up to peek into the kitchen window. All was quiet. No lights were on. A sticker in the corner of the window boasted that the place was protected by Advanced Security.

He was sure that if she had a dog, it would have announced his presence by now. It would be dark soon, and he needed to find a place to wait as quickly as possible.

Moving along the back side of the house, Thornton was certain her bedroom was the one upstairs with a balcony. At his height, it was easy to jump up and grab one of the boards of the railing, but swinging his massive weight upward required a tremendous amount of effort. By the time he had struggled over the rail, he was practically panting. Slumping onto the white wood deck, he stayed low, crawling slowly along.

French doors opened onto the balcony. Trying his luck, he slowly grasped the shiny gold knob and twisted. As expected, it was locked. Testing the strength of the thin wooden frame, he was confident it would easily snap if he simply threw his weight into it, then jerked the doors back out. But not yet, not until later when she was there to see him coming. Remembering the look on Kim's face just before he forced her off the road, he smiled. Terror at the prospect of impending death fascinated him. After all, what good would it do? Death was simply the end of living. Nothing else. One of the simplest of life's lessons.

Pressing cupped hands against the glass, Thornton looked inside. This was definitely her room. A low-cut navy and emerald cocktail dress was arranged on the elegant bedspread. Beside the dress was a blue lace bra and a matching pair of panties.

Moving into the growing shadows, he was certain this would be a night to remember. With the lights on in the bedroom, it would be like a private screening of an X-rated movie, but she'd never know he was there—at least, not in time. When he broke through those flimsy doors, the reward would be worth every bit of trouble she'd caused, and then some.

Thornton smiled at the thought of watching her change into that sexy outfit, then envisioned it in shreds. Lights suddenly came to life inside the house, forcing him to creep into the corner, eagerly anticipating the beginning of Kaycee Miller's end.

•   •   •   •   •

"Make yourself at home. I'll be ready in a flash," Kaycee called to Max before sprinting upstairs.

Closing the door of her bedroom, she leaned against it and smiled. The day had been magnificent. She couldn't remember having more fun, or feeling so at ease with any man. It made her wonder what was wrong with him—why some other lucky woman hadn't snatched Max Masterson off the market years ago. But for now, she didn't care. He was the perfect cure for what worried her—which was the only thing she was allowing herself to think about. "If you take each day as it comes, you can handle it," Ellen had promised.

Flipping on the recessed lights, Kaycee crossed the room to perch on the edge of the rocking chair just long enough to tug off her riding boots. For a moment she stopped, staring at the shadows outside the French doors. Walking to them, she gazed through the panes of glass. In the darkness, she couldn't see the stars, but she knew they were there, sparkling beautifully. The realization that she'd probably never see them again hit her like a blow to the stomach. The contentment of just moments ago instantly faded. With an involuntary shiver, she rushed into the bathroom, hoping a steamy shower would help her find enough courage to make it through the night.

But it didn't. After quickly rinsing off, she wrapped a soft towel around her body and hurried to get ready. Sliding into the chair in front of the vanity, Kaycee looked at the magnified image of her eyes in the makeup mirror. Applying a thin layer of eye shadow and liner to bring out their almond shape wasn't as easy as it had been just a few months ago. Throwing down the brush, she froze, suddenly angry and afraid.

How much longer will I be able to do this? Quickly taking a deep breath, she remembered Max was waiting downstairs, then thought of all the things that could have happened with such an amazing man.

What will he do when he finds out the truth? she wondered.

•   •   •   •   •

Thornton shivered, pressed against the cold wall so the light pouring through the French doors wouldn't reveal his presence too early. Just moments ago she had come so close, he was sure she was going to open those doors—sure she would walk right into his hands! But then she'd turned around. Patience, he thought. Everything worth a damn in life takes patience.

Leaning slightly at the waist, Thornton could see more than half of Kaycee's bedroom. Seated at some fancy makeup table, her head was tilted back as though she were trying not to cry. *Come on, hurry up! I don't want to sit here all night, but I will if I have to!*

As if she had heard him, Kaycee seemed to collect herself. In a matter of minutes she applied her makeup, brushed her hair into a sexy French knot, and crossed to the bed. Grabbing the pile of lingerie, she walked back into the bathroom.

When she emerged, the sight of creamy breasts pushed high by a scanty navy bra temporarily made him forget why he was there. His eyes shifted down, only to drag slowly up the sheer nylons until they vanished beneath a short, navy slip. When she turned away, his breath caught as she bent to put on her heels. Still half-naked, she rushed to open the bedroom door. Raising her voice, she called, "Everything okay down there?"

A man shouted back, "Just great."

"I'll be ready in a few minutes!"

"Take your time. Our reservations aren't until seven-thirty."

"How long will it take to get to O'Malley's Landing?" she asked.

"Twenty, twenty-five minutes max. There's no hurry."

"Sure there is!"

"Why?"

"Ask me later!" she laughed and closed the door.

Thornton leaned against the wall, breathing hard. *Damn it! She isn't alone!*

•　•　•　•　•

"Wow!" Max sighed, slowly taking in Kaycee's transformation

from cowgirl to femme fatale. Her short navy and emerald dress high-lighted everything beautiful about her, from the length of her slender legs to the sparkle in her intelligent eyes.

"I'll take that as a compliment."

"As it was intended." He held the delicate matching shawl open for her, finding the view from behind equally breathtaking. Leaning close, he whispered, "You look gorgeous."

"Thank you. Are we ready?"

Max nodded. "Want me to turn off a few of these lights?"

She quickly shook her head. "I prefer to leave them on."

"Let me guess. You're trying to single-handedly make the electric company's stock split?"

As they stepped onto the porch, she wrapped her arm tightly around his. "Would you believe I prefer to have it look like I'm here even when I'm gone?"

"I suppose. If you want people to think an entire army is home, you've definitely achieved your goal." Putting his arm around her, Max looked into her eyes. To his surprise, she softly kissed him.

"Are you always this affectionate at night?" he asked.

"Sometimes. That was just in case I forget later. I want you to know what a very special day this has been for me. For a while, I actually forgot all my troubles. Thank you."

"You're welcome." After kissing her again, he opened the door to the Isuzu. "I agree with you. I haven't enjoyed myself this much in years. What could possibly happen later to spoil such a splendid night?"

Kaycee sighed. "Considering the year I've had, I wouldn't be shocked if a sinkhole swallowed us both right now. I got so unnerved I actually called Agent Jones last night. One of his people slept on my sofa. Between the men coming and going at all hours of the night, and the police routinely showing up on my doorstep, my neighbors probably think I've opened a house of ill repute."

"The best little whorehouse in Tulsa?" he joked.

"Of course! Nothing but the best!"

"I'll be sure to tell all my friends, Madam Miller. Madam Miller
—," he repeated, "—you know, that actually has a nice ring to it."

"Well, I suppose if there's a slump in business—"

"Are you sure you didn't mean hump?"

She slugged him.

"Ouch! Where's my overprotective dog when I need him?"

"Good point. Maybe I could borrow Stagga until all this blows
over. I'm getting tired of hearing noises and getting the creeps."

"Or you could just stay with me. My door is always open. You'd
have an entire wing to yourself, and I promise to act like a gentleman."

"How gallant."

"Unless, of course, you'd prefer me not to act like a gentleman.
Either way, it's up to you."

Shaking her head, she replied, "Decisions, decisions! It's funny—
one side of me thinks I'm crazy for being such a chicken while the
other is screaming, *Run away, run away!* Why does life have to be so
hard?"

"Probably because you're the type of person who needs to be in
control. It's throwing you to know that jerk is out there."

Sliding into the Trooper, Kaycee's gaze seemed far away.

When Max was at her side, he purposely changed the subject. "So,
you promised to tell me why we were in a hurry to get to dinner…"

"Would you believe that I'm absolutely ravenous?"

"No."

"Okay. How about because I'm really looking forward to spending the evening with you?"

Starting the engine, he replied, "Then let's get on with it."

As they backed out of the driveway, the headlights washed over
the perfectly manicured shrubs. Neither Max nor Kaycee noticed the
slight movement of the bushes, or the man who brazenly stomped out
just seconds after they drove away.

Heading east on Route 66, Kaycee and Max chatted as the lights of suburban Tulsa faded in the distance. By the time they turned off the highway onto the country road, both were beginning to shake off the edgy pressure they felt to impress the other on their official first date. Gravel crunched beneath the tires as they entered the dimly lit piece of unpaved land that served as a parking lot for O'Malley's Landing. The open, light atmosphere combined with excellent food as the evening slowly revealed its secrets.

Leaning back in her chair, Kaycee beamed. "This place is marvelous. Do you come here often?"

Max grinned. "Only when I'm trying to dazzle a woman."

"So you're a regular customer?" she quipped.

"Actually, this is my second time. My aunt was quite captivated on her last birthday."

"Your aunt?"

He nodded. "My parents both died when I was a kid. I was raised by my grandparents. Aunt Viv is the only relative I have left."

"Does she live nearby?"

"Reasonably close. She's got about 320 acres south of Tulsa, with a kennel and obedience training facility."

"So cavorting with canines runs in the family?"

"I suppose. Indirectly, she's the reason I got into search and rescue, although her specialty is training dogs to help the handicapped."

Kaycee stiffened slightly, her voice almost brittle as she asked, "Like seeing eye dogs?"

He nodded. "Actually, she doesn't train dogs to help the blind." Sensing her tension, Max hurriedly added, "There are a variety of different programs other than those for the blind. My aunt pre-trains some dogs for police departments—you know, drug and bomb sniffers. But mainly she targets para- or quadriplegic people, and she has a program for people who suffer from seizures. But what Aunt Viv does that's so special is train each dog to fit the unique needs of the individual. She takes the time to discover what each person hungers to do again, and does her best to give it back to them."

"Sounds like quite a lady."

"She is. I've been trying to get her to expand for ages—her waiting list is over two years. But she insists that doing it right takes time, and of course, being a Masterson, she's too stubborn to delegate very much." Trailing a finger gently along the back of her hand, he asked, "Are you okay? You've gotten awfully quiet."

"I'm fine. Just a bit too much good food and wine. Did you get Stagga from your aunt?"

Max grinned. "Of course. He was rejected early in the process."

"Rejected? You mean some dogs flunk out of training?"

"Some aren't cut out for it. Being a service dog is pretty demanding. They have to have the right temperament and a willingness to work. And once they're trained, they have to bond with the person they'll be assisting. They're special animals."

"Like Stagga."

He beamed, but shook his head. "Stagga was a little too aggressive. Besides, he stands 28" at the shoulder."

"Which means?"

"He was too tall. Standard service dogs stand 23" to 25". If a harness is used, it has to be adjusted to the height of the owner."

"When do they decide which ones to train?"

"Service dogs are socialized by living with volunteer families until they're old enough to go through the training program. Our family raised one every year when I was growing up."

Kaycee's eyes softened and she shook her head. "You had to give away a puppy you loved every year?"

"That's how it works. It was my job to take them through basic obedience classes, make sure they got lots of exercise and love, then turn them over to Aunt Viv's school. The first time was really hard, but she made sure I watched that pup go through the whole program. When I saw how much that dog touched the life of his new owner, I sat down and cried. From then on, I always knew what a dog's future held—more love than any normal person could possibly give. I felt lucky to be a part of it."

Fighting tears, Kaycee quickly sipped her drink, thankful the cold water coated the rising wave of self pity long enough for her to suppress it again. This was a man like no other she'd ever known. Caring, open, unafraid to expose his heart. At a time when she should have been looking forward to building a relationship with him, all she could feel was the nagging sense of loss that kept crawling into her thoughts. Without looking up, she said, "I'm sure you did a great job nurturing those puppies."

"I must have. Not one of the dogs we raised ever failed."

She managed a smile, unable to resist the sparkle in his eye or the pride in his voice. "I admit, I'm amazed. You must have the patience of a saint."

"For some things . . ."

Straightening her shoulders, Kaycee shook her head to push away the remnants of her insecurity. Finding a shred of her old self-confidence, she asked, "Okay, I know I asked once, but this time I'd like a truthful answer. What's wrong with you?"

"Excuse me? Are you calling me a liar?"

"You're handsome. You live in a stunning house. You love animals, you're genuinely polite, and you might just qualify for sainthood. There should be women lined up at your door. I know you told me that you're too busy, but I'm not sure I buy that."

Looking guilty, he shrugged. His voice was sincere as he answered, "I was hoping you wouldn't figure it out so soon. . ."

"Figure out what? That you're afraid of commitment? Have a foot fetish? Wear ladies' lingerie?"

Still serious, he simply nodded. Intense blue eyes held hers defiantly as silence fell between them.

Kaycee didn't know whether to laugh or groan in frustration. Finally, she chose the latter and begged, "Max! What are you talking about?"

"The same thing you are."

"Which would be?"

He grinned. "Why we're here—together. I'll tell you the reason I'm still single if you'll tell me yours. Why would your neighbors find male visitors coming and going from your house so out of the ordinary?"

Kaycee considered his challenge. "Okay. I'm still single because after what happened—" she caught her breath, "—you know, when I was seventeen. Well, after that, I decided to build a business. I didn't consciously intend to ignore my social life, it just sort of happened. There were always clients, late meetings, trips all over God's green earth. Up until this time last year, I lived and breathed my work."

"What changed since last fall?"

"A more appropriate question would be what *didn't* change. I lost my parents—"

"And your sister had a stroke. And—" he left the word hanging, daring her to continue. When she didn't, he said, "And what else? I know there's something. I can feel it."

Her eyes lingered on everything in the room except him. With a sigh, she said, "Max, I can honestly say I'm not ready to deal with all that's happened lately. Not yet. Please trust me on this. It would change everything. How you feel about me, how I react to you. Right now, even though it's cold outside, you're my spring. Flowers blooming, a fresh new start. . ."

"Yet you're already worried about what you'll do when the flowers start to wither, aren't you?"

She nodded.

"Some flowers live for years. There are trees that have made it for centuries."

"I know. But most don't."

"Then think of me as a California redwood."

She grinned as he reached his arms out to impersonate a tree. "I'm really enjoying being with you, and I promise, when I'm ready to talk, you'll be the first to know. Deal?"

Catching her hand in his, he searched her eyes. With a sigh, he reluctantly agreed, "Deal."

Quickly changing the subject, Kaycee countered, "Okay, now it's your turn to confess why you're a solitary man."

"It really is simple. As I said before—rescues."

She waited for him to continue, but he simply watched her, gently stroking his thumb along the back of her hand. His touch made it hard for her to stay focused, hard to wonder why she found herself wishing they had met years ago, before everything had changed. Finally, she asked, "Is that the best you can do? Rescues? I could've figured that out by myself."

"I thought you wanted the truth."

"I do."

"I dated a lot when I was younger, but doing rescues isn't exactly the most attractive thing to women who care about settling down and starting a family. There are only so many hours in each day. I was engaged once to a great woman. She needed stability, a definite plan. I guess I wasn't ready."

"To give up rescues?"

He shook his head. "It runs deeper than that. She didn't ask for anything unreasonable. I just wasn't ready to give. It wouldn't have been fair to either of us."

"Then you did the right thing."

Their eyes met. "That's the hard part. We never really know, do we?"

"I believe things turn out for the best. Sometimes it takes a long time to find the right perspective."

"You know, I've always felt sorry for the left perspective. No one ever gives it a lick of credit."

Kaycee laughed, bringing fresh tears to her eyes. The shine of the bracelet peeking out from under his cuff caught her attention and she pushed back his sleeve. "Are you willing to tell me about this yet?"

He seemed to mull over the idea before saying, "It's a reminder."

"Of?"

"Not to do certain things. And right now, it's reminding me not to spoil a perfect evening by dredging up too much of the past. Why don't we go back to your house for coffee?"

"If you'll stop by Java Dave's and let me pick up some decaf you've got a deal."

As soon as they stepped into the dim parking lot, Kaycee stopped. Max turned back, looking at her with a questioning smile.

"Listen," she whispered.

He did. The night was filled with the music of the wild. Leaves rustled in the gentle wind, and overhead purple martins floated effortlessly through the air. "It's amazing."

"Would you mind holding my hand while we go to the car? This isn't the easiest surface to walk on in high heels."

"I can do better than that." In a flash, Max swept Kaycee into his arms. Despite her giggling protests, he easily carried her across the lot to the Trooper. Opening the passenger door, he bowed. "Your carriage awaits, my lady."

"Thank you, my lord."

Moments later, Max was seated beside her. After a long, captivated look into her eyes, their lips touched in a lingering, gentle kiss.

"I had a wonderful time," she whispered.

"Had?" Max circled her in his arms. "But the night is young," he whispered, his lips grazing her neck.

"True." She tilted her head to kiss him again. It had been so long since she'd enjoyed anything so much, it made her lightheaded. A noise outside made them stop. Straightening their clothes like high school kids caught parking, they blushed.

Max was about to start the engine when Kaycee said, "My shawl! I laid it in the chair beside mine. It must have fallen to the floor."

"I'll be right back." Kissing her one last time, he said, "Promise you won't forget where we were."

"I promise!" she called after him. Leaning her head against the headrest, she closed her eyes to think of him, of what might happen in the next few hours. The future seemed too far away to matter. Right now, being with Max was all she cared to see. Her thoughts were interrupted when her door suddenly flew open. Turning, she said, "That was fast—"

But it wasn't Max. It was *him!*

Thornton's massive hands closed around her neck. Like a helpless rag doll, she was ripped out of the Trooper so brutally she thought the door frame would come with her. Although dazed, she still fought— wildly kicking and scratching so hard she lost a shoe as he slammed her back against the vehicle to make his point. His vile breath was hot on her ear as he said, "Fight again or make a sound and I'll kill you right now. Understand?"

It was black outside, black and still. Like in a nightmare, the world seemed to fade in and out, teasing her with harsh bits of reality mixed with demonic images as she stiffly nodded.

In the dim light, she could see only dark smears, shapes that had little meaning as he dragged her deeper and deeper into the woods. Even her sense of sound seemed sluggish—the snapping of twigs just underfoot echoed as though it were miles away. Her other shoe was long gone now, and the feel of cold, slimy dirt on her stocking feet instantly snapped her out of her daze. *No! Not again. I won't let it happen again!*

Sucking in precious air, she tried to scream, but his vise-like grip made it impossible to take more than half a breath. Using all her energy, she started fighting in spite of his threats. Squirming and writhing, she felt the butt of a gun in his shoulder holster press into her back. Twisting even harder, she managed to land several solid blows that made him gasp. Suddenly he stopped, pulling her so tightly against him that her feet were off the ground.

Kaycee was dangling from the arm he had wrapped just beneath her chin as he whispered, "Keep it up and I'll crush your scrawny windpipe right now!"

She relaxed slightly. A moment later he loosened his grip and started moving again. After a few deep breaths renewed her energy, she lashed backward to jab his eye and claw his face. His skin tore under her nails, making her almost lose her dinner. The warmth of his blood against her frigid hands made her shiver as she twisted to kick him in the groin. As his breath rushed painfully out, his grip loosened for an instant. Kaycee didn't miss her opportunity.

Free! Every nerve in her body tried to compensate for her lack of sight as she fled, thrashing through woods, unable to judge anything in the darkness. Behind her, the silence was broken by a string of expletives as Willy's massive body crashed wildly through the undergrowth to close the gap between them.

"Max, help! Help me, please!" she hoarsely screamed as she ran blindly into the night.

CHAPTER **15**

As soon as he emerged from the restaurant, Max knew something was wrong. The song of the night had vanished, replaced by a stillness that chilled his blood. Even from a distance, he could see the interior light was on in the Trooper, and the passenger door was ajar. Kaycee was nowhere in sight.

Rushing across the parking lot, his heart sank. Spotting the lone shoe on the ground was like a hard slap, followed by an even harder blow when he noticed a smear of blood on the back window. He was certain what had happened, and with that certainty came an all too familiar fear—fear that he was too late. Again.

Searching the area, Max tried to determine where he had been hiding, which way he might have run. If he was parked nearby, they were probably long gone. But if he took her into the woods, he might be able to stop him in time. If he only had Stagga!

Grabbing a flashlight and his cell phone, he scanned the perimeter of the lot as he explained the situation to the emergency operator. Several broken limbs caught his eye, and his pulse quickened. Someone had recently left in a hurry. As fast as possible, he carefully, silently followed the fresh trail.

Listening with his entire body, Max placed each step, moving forward at a frustratingly slow pace. Halfway down a steep incline, he found Kaycee's other shoe. A fresh wave of hope quickened his pulse. Knowing a team of search dogs might need the scent later, Max moved on without disturbing it.

When the forest was pierced by a distant guttural scream, Max broke into a full run, and prayed.

•   •   •   •   •

Kaycee couldn't see. As hard as she tried, as much as she longed to escape, there wasn't enough light for her to make out which way to go. Yet she continued to run. Time after time, she ran into trees, bushes, rocks. Pain pushed her on, kept her going when others might have given up.

After what seemed like an eternity, she finally saw something flash—metal gleaming in the moonlight. The simple vision made her want to cry with relief, but there was no time for celebration. He was so close she could hear his ragged breathing, almost feel the ground trembling under his violent strides. Rushing toward the object, she saw it was a truck parked on the side of a dirt road. "Help!" she yelled with newfound determination, certain someone must be nearby.

Slowing down, she tried to get in, but the door was locked. Beating the metal with clamped fists, she prayed an alarm would sound, but nothing happened. Catching a glimpse of the monster lurching toward her, she realized that it was too late.

Her dress ripped as one of his fists closed around the soft material in the middle of her back. His other hand dug viciously into her hair. Crushing her against the cold truck, his chest heaved as he muttered, "You'll pay for this!"

•   •   •   •   •

Max knew he was running out of time. Another scream led him even closer, and after twenty yards he paused to listen. Nothing stirred around him, nothing moved at all. All life seemed to be holding its breath in dreadful anticipation.

Breaking out of the trees, Max emerged on a dirt road. A hundred yards away a truck roared to life, headlights flipped on, illuminating spindly trees in its path. Running as fast as he could, he met only the cloud of dust in the wake of the truck's spinning tires.

"NO!" Max screamed. Falling to his knees, he tried to catch his breath as panic seized him. The dust settled, but his heart continued to pound. A few yards ahead, something was lying on the side of the road. Moonlight caught its brilliance, dancing on the sea of dazzling beads as he rushed to grab the remnants of Kaycee's emerald and navy dress.

By the time he hiked back to the parking lot, it was ablaze with the flashing lights of squad cars. The various law enforcement agents gathered around as he quickly ran through the story. At the end, one asked, "How can you be so sure it was Wilfred Thornton who took her?"

Max simply glared at the county sheriff. In his hand was Kaycee's dress. He suppressed the urge to slap the man with it.

Agent Jones shook his head and led Max away. "We've got roadblocks on the Interstates, two police helicopters in the air, and every law enforcement officer in Oklahoma, Kansas, and Arkansas on alert. We'll catch him."

"But will it be in time?"

"She's a strong woman. We'll find her."

Thinking aloud, Max muttered, "I can't believe he actually came after her. And how did he know where to find us? I made absolutely sure we weren't followed."

"Max, it isn't your fault. He's a ruthless, clever criminal."

"Which is exactly why I'm so worried!"

"We're doing all we can."

Max nodded, hearing the throbbing approach of Cal's helicopter. "That's my ride. You'll be the first to know if we find her."

"Wait a minute! You can't leave!" Jones shouted.

"You going to try to stop me?" Max called over the growing noise. Since there wasn't a clear place to land, a rope came tumbling out of the helicopter's belly. Experienced at heli-repelling and in-flight pick-ups, Max easily began scaling it, until suddenly the swaying rope felt sluggish beneath his grip.

Looking down, he saw Agent Jones, saucer-eyed, yet determined, at his heels.

• • • • •

Kaycee shivered, leaning against the cool glass of the truck. The clock on the dashboard couldn't possibly be right. If it were, just twenty minutes ago she had been safe in Max's arms. Taking a deep breath, she scanned the inside of the truck without moving her head. Unfortunately, there was nothing in sight that she could use as a weapon.

With her wrists taped together, she knew her options were severely limited. Yet going down without a fight was not a possibility this time. Sitting up, Kaycee flatly said, "I'm cold. I need my dress back."

Reaching over, he traced one finger along the silky cup of her bra. When she recoiled from his touch, he laughed, "Get used to it. You won't get away again. And you *will* do what I say." Grinning, he dug his hand up under her slip, groping as he added, "You'll do whatever I want, as many times as I like."

"Give me my clothes!" she demanded, knowing full well that showing any sign of weakness would be the worst thing to do.

Taunting her, he sneered, "You'll think twice about running off dressed like the powerless whore that you are."

"Spoken like a truly demented soul."

"I'm in charge now. In charge and ready."

He's trying to beat you down. Don't listen to him! Don't let him win! Looking out the window, Kaycee shrugged, muttering, "Yeah, right."

"Funny, you looked pretty scared yesterday afternoon in your office. So which is it? Are you tough, or not?"

She instinctively cringed, realizing her fears were justified. "I can be tough when I have to be."

"Then let's make a bet. When I'm finished with you, I'll bet you're begging me for more."

"That would certainly be poetic justice."

"What's that supposed to mean?"

"Well, if you followed me to my office, you probably know where else I went yesterday."

"To that medical building. Warren Clinic."

She closed her eyes, envisioning his handwriting, how close he was to the edge of sanity. Pushing, she sneered, "So, you can read. I'm impressed."

The veins in his forehead were starting to pound as he snapped, "Why were you at that doctor's office?"

The lie rolled easily off her tongue. "I just found out I have AIDS. Still interested?"

Thornton's knuckles were white on the steering wheel. She could almost hear his brain grinding through what he'd seen that morning. Even from afar, he would've witnessed her emotional turmoil, felt the depth of her despair.

"I can't believe I've wasted so much time on you! Serves me right for not blowing your brains out the first time I had the chance." Slipping his gun out of the holster, he pressed the barrel against her temple. "Maybe I'd better just get this over with now."

She didn't breathe. Didn't close her eyes in fear. Instead, Kaycee said, "How brave of you. That thing really makes you feel like a man, doesn't it? Better be careful, though. This is an awfully small space, and, well. . .blood splatters pretty far, you know."

Wide-eyed, he slipped the gun back into its shoulder holster.

Closing her eyes, Kaycee knew she'd bought a few precious seconds with her lies. She couldn't give up, wouldn't give in, but every second brought more horrid memories to the surface. She felt her chest tighten, felt the numbing fear slithering inside her like a snake coiling around her heart.

Shifting her gaze to the silver door handle, she realized how easy it would be to open the door and jump out. Would it kill her? Or would he pick up her mangled body, toss her in the bed of his truck, and still be the one to finish her off? The last thought made her cringe.

I will not die this way! As she silently repeated the words, her courage began to return. She knew Max would have an army out searching for her, and that her only chance was to gain control—*soon*. And right now, words were her only weapon.

"You know, you'd better get it over with. The police know who you are. They know everything about you. You might as well go ahead and kill me."

"Not before I see how sweet that ass of yours really is. I can almost taste it now. The bed of this pickup will make a fine place to tie you up. I can picture it already. Those legs of yours spread wide. There are ways to keep from getting AIDS, you know. . ."

Kaycee's stomach churned. Breathing hard, she raged, "I'll die before I let you touch me!"

"Really?" Driving with one hand, he grabbed at her breast, laughing as she tried to shrink away.

Through gritted teeth she spat, "Why'd you blow it the first time you had a chance? Because Maggie was watching? Do you at least have enough decency not to kill people in front of your terrified little girl?"

In the light from the dashboard, she thought she saw his eyes darken. Violently raging, he snatched her by the hair, jerking her toward him. His pungent breath struck her face as he screamed, "Maggie saved you the first time. But now you're going to die in the same hellhole she's in right now. You'll be her second lesson. Maybe this time she'll learn not to disobey her father."

Where is she? Kaycee wanted to scream, but instead she focused on her hatred of the man at her side, and on the little girl who desperately needed her help. "Who was her first lesson? Was it the woman I saw you with at the motel?"

"None of your business!" he shouted, shoving her into the passenger side window.

Kaycee knew she had to keep badgering him, had to keep him enraged so he would make a mistake. Waiting, her bare foot tapping nervously in the layer of dirt on the filthy floorboard, she knew she was running out of time. If she didn't find a way out of the truck soon, it would all be over.

"Ever heard of vacuuming?" she grumbled, kicking up dust.

"I thought I told you to shut up!"

"Powerless whores don't take orders well."

His right fist flew into her cheek, snapping her head brutally against the window again. Stunned for a moment, Kaycee tasted blood, felt it trickle from the side of her mouth, then smiled. She knew better than to back down because of pain. Pain was better than death. Better than eternal darkness. When she was seventeen she had taken it. Don't fight, don't resist, they had said. So she had mentally crawled into another world and waited while he beat her, stole everything she had, and left her for dead in the woods.

Not this time! Carefully choosing her words, she asked, "Has it occurred to you that I know all about you? That I know you kidnapped Maggie? That when they catch you they'll put you away forever this time?"

"Why do you think I'm here?"

"You're here because you're so stupid you didn't do the job right the first time. Why did you kill your daughter? What did that poor child ever do to you?"

"Maggie's not dead! She's safe in the mine."

The mine! Certain she was getting under his skin, she shifted closer to him, anxious to push him past his limit. "Sure she is. Probably all by herself. You're exactly the kind of jerk who would leave a frightened little girl all alone. She's in New Mexico, isn't she? In a dark, creepy place with bugs and rats. Right? Is that what you're teaching her? How to be scared of everything? Have you been raping her, too? Or is she just going to watch you rape me? Learn from good old dad how women should be treated."

Kaycee suddenly knew what she had to do. Mustering her courage, she quickly leaned over and bit his massive forearm.

Thornton screamed and flailed as her teeth drew blood.

Pushing her aside like a rag doll, she sneered. "Now you've got AIDS, too. Either way, looks like we're both gonna die."

"That's it! I'm going to blow your brains out right now. That's probably the only way to shut you up!" Swerving off the road, Thornton slammed on the brakes.

Kaycee seized what she knew would be her only chance. Just before the truck slid to a stop, she jerked open the door and rolled out.

Thornton crammed the truck into park and stormed around the front end, temporarily blinded by the glare of the headlights. The passenger door was still ajar, and Kaycee took the opportunity to crawl back inside, careful not to let the latch catch. Thankful there were no interior lights to give her away, she waited on the floorboard.

"Where are you?" he screamed from somewhere near the front fender. A semi whooshed past making her pray the driver would stop to help, but in its fading wake she knew she was still on her own. With her heart pounding so hard she could feel it pulsing in her fingertips, she listened intently until she heard the crunch of gravel as he stepped near the door. Just as his faint shadow darkened the window, Kaycee froze, afraid he would turn around and see her cowering there.

But he didn't. Instead, he moved closer to the door, closer to her trap. With the energy she had left, Kaycee kicked open the door. Her feet landed solidly on the frame, pounding the heavy metal forcefully into his back. The impact sent Thornton flying, sprawling him face down in the muddy ditch.

Jerking the door closed, she locked it and slid into the driver's seat. With her bound hands, she threw the truck into drive as she floored the gas pedal. The truck fishtailed back onto the highway, showering everything in its wake with pebbles.

The last thing Kaycee heard was the sharp, unreal chink of bullets piercing the tailgate, accompanied by an unintelligible blast of obscenities.

. . . . .

Max crawled into the helicopter, strapped on a seatbelt and shouted, "Thanks for getting here so fast!"

"That's what friends are for!" Nodding toward the rope, Cal flashed a twisted grin. "Want me to let him know he's not welcome?"

"Actually, for an FBI agent he's a pretty decent guy."

Disappointed, Cal sighed. "Okay, but how about I give him my government training special as soon as he's safely buckled in?"

Max shrugged. "Fine with me as long as it doesn't slow us down." Checking his harness, he added, "I'm in tight."

Agent Jones dragged himself on board, his face as pale as his starched white shirt. Loosening his tie, he glared at Max, who was pointing at one of the rear safety harnesses. After buckling in, Jones shouted, "Nice stunt! Next time warn me when you plan to use some of your frequent flyer miles."

"Stunt!" Cal said. "He wants me to do stunts?" Ignoring the look of horror on their uninvited guest's face, Cal grinned and swooped sharply toward the ground, back up, then followed the road bobbing from side to side with sickening speed and precision.

By the time they reached the Interstate, Jones' white knuckles were holding on for dear life. Cal glanced at Max with a satisfied twinkle in his eye as he asked, "Which way now?"

"West. I've got a feeling he'll head back to New Mexico."

Sharply turning, Cal soared higher and snapped, "Then west it is."

. . . . .

Kaycee wasn't sure when she started shaking. She wasn't even sure how far she had driven or which direction she was traveling. The only thing that she was certain of was that *he* was back there somewhere, and she wanted to be as far away from *him* as possible.

Perched on the edge of the truck's bench seat, she hugged the steering wheel like a little old lady, barely able to make out the white line along the side of the road in the glow of the headlights. When the tires started shuddering, she finally thought to glance at the speedometer. Squinting, she realized the needle was hovering just past one hundred and ten miles an hour! Easing back on the gas, she caught the first glimpse of red, white, and blue flashing lights in the rearview mirror.

Kaycee had no idea why suddenly everything seemed funny. Flying down the highway in a stolen truck, half-naked, bruised and bleeding from a dozen different scrapes, she started to giggle. By the time she pulled onto the shoulder and brought the truck to a complete stop, she was laughing so hard that tears were rolling down her cheeks.

With a big gulp of air, she regained a bit of control, but lost it as soon as the Oklahoma Highway Patrolman leveled his weapon at her from beyond the tailgate and started screaming for her to give up. *Give up what?* she wondered as she slumped over the wheel laughing again. *The rest of my clothes?*

As if God were showing her the way, the cab of the truck was suddenly flooded with light from above, brightly illuminating the surrounding land enough to allow her to actually see. Catching her breath, she realized there were flashing lights everywhere, virtually all around the truck, and that the beam from above was coming from a hovering helicopter. Wide-eyed, she watched the glare of lights from another helicopter as it landed in the field just a few yards away.

Stunned to be the center of such unbelievable commotion, she wiped away her tears and viewed the world outside with detached curiosity.

Kaycee's trance-like state shattered when the driver's door flew open and Max pulled her into his arms. Wrapping her in his jacket, he hoarsely whispered, "Thank God you're all right!" Sweeping her into his arms, he added, "Cal's going to fly you straight to the hospital."

Pulling back so she could see him, she shook her head. A rush of energy accompanied the realization that she'd survived relatively unharmed. "I don't need a hospital. Really."

"Even so, I think it'd be a good idea."

Shaking her head, Kaycee sternly protested, "Max, I'm okay. Don't you see? It's over."

Rushing toward the waiting helicopter, he replied, "Thank God."

"I think I can walk."

Max slowed, his eyes questioning hers. "You mean it, don't you? You're okay?"

"I'm positive. I just want to go home. . ." She shook her head. "No, he might go back there. Could I stay at your ranch tonight? Would that be all right?"

Hugging her fiercely, he replied, "I'll take you to another galaxy if that's where you want to go."

Delicately placing her feet on the ground, he held her steady while gently removing the tape binding her wrists. They were about to board the helicopter when Agent Jones rushed to stop them. "Where are you going?"

Both Max and Kaycee started to answer at once. Kaycee finally won the battle. "I promise to tell you all the details in the morning."

"I know you've been through a lot, Ms. Miller, but you've got to help us locate Wilfred Thornton. Where the hell is he? How did you escape?"

Her hand trembled slightly as she pointed due east. "He's back there somewhere. I knocked him in the ditch and drove away as fast as I could."

"Can you show us the exact place?"

Frowning, she tried to form a picture in her mind. "It all happened so fast. . .I wish I could. It was very dark, and I just didn't get a look at the scenery." Shaking her head she added, "I don't even know how far I drove. . ."

Another agent chimed in, "The Highway Patrol chased you for almost four minutes. We can start where they first spotted you and work back east. Are you certain it was Wilfred Thornton who attacked you?"

"No doubt about it."

"Is he armed?"

Nodding, she said, "He shot at the truck when I pulled away. I'm sorry, but I think I need to sit down. I'm suddenly very tired, a little dizzy, and my feet hurt."

Max and Cal exchanged a serious look as they helped her into the helicopter. Cal asked Max, "Are you thinking what I'm thinking?"

With a smile, Max turned to Agent Jones and led him away. Once they were away from Kaycee, he asked, "How long will it take to get a K-9 unit out here?"

"There's already one on the way. Where are you going to take her?"

"We'll stop to have her checked by a doctor, then go to my ranch. She should be safe there. There's no way he can follow a helicopter, especially on foot."

"That's good, because I doubt if he's going to just give up. We'll stake out her house and her office. I'll send an agent to watch your place, just in case."

"Trust me, that won't be necessary. One of the advantages of living in the middle of nowhere is that it's hard for anyone to sneak up on you. Besides, Stagga barks if a stranger comes within a mile of the place."

"Fine. But whatever you do, don't let her out of your sight without contacting us. We'll need to go over everything he said to her first thing in the morning."

"She'll be safe with me this time. I promise."

·   ·   ·   ·   ·

Max paced outside the guest room with the first aid kit in one hand, the assortment of bandages, gauze and ointment they'd given them at the Emergency Room in the other. Glancing at his watch for the thousandth time in the last twenty minutes, he called, "Are you sure you're all right, Kaycee?"

The door opened to reveal Kaycee standing before him. His heart ached for her. With wet hair and no makeup, she seemed young and very vulnerable. Wearing his heavy velour robe, which was so big it practically swallowed her, she looked like a child playing dress up. But the picture was spoiled when he looked closer. It was hard to find a spot on her face that wasn't bruised, and there were fresh scrapes and cuts on the little he could see of her feet and legs.

"Quit looking at me like that!" she sighed.

"Like what?" he asked innocently.

"It's a *poor little thing* look. I saw it for months when I was a teenager and I absolutely hate it."

"I'm sorry. I didn't mean—"

Interrupting him, she put her hands on his chest and softly said, "No, *I'm* sorry. It isn't your fault. I really do appreciate all you've done for me."

Nodding, he carefully hugged her.

"I think I'll take you up on some of those pain pills now," she said.

"Why don't you sit by the fire and I'll bring them to you?"

"That would be very nice." Taking a place near Stagga, she added, "He's the prettiest dog I've ever seen."

"Don't say that in front of him. The last thing he needs is a big head. He already thinks this ranch is his domain."

Placing the medical supplies on the coffee table, Max crossed the living area and stopped in front of the kitchen island. "What would you like to wash them down with? Water? Hot cocoa? Tea? Straight whiskey?"

"Cocoa would be wonderful."

Max poured milk into a copper pot and turned the burner on low. He slowly stirred the milk until it started to steam. Adding cocoa, powdered sugar, a dash of vanilla, and a handful of mini-marshmallows, he mixed the concoction one last time before handing the hot mug to her.

After a satisfying sip, Kaycee leaned back and sighed as she watched Max stoke the fire. "This is delicious. Thank you."

"It's my aunt's recipe. Are you sure you're okay?"

"I can't believe I'm sitting here."

Taking a place on the sofa beside her, Max said, "To tell you the truth, neither can I. When I saw that truck take off with you inside, I—" He stopped, swallowing hard before continuing, "—I've never felt so helpless in my life. I'm sorry I didn't get there sooner."

Shifting to face him, she touched his cheek. "Max, if you think any of this was your fault, or something you could have prevented, you're wrong. If he hadn't attacked me there, he would've waited till I got home, or followed me to work again."

"Again?"

She shivered. "Apparently he spent all day watching me. He knew exactly where I'd been."

"I'm so sorry."

"There's that look again! I really, truly do not want sympathy. What I need right now is a bright, perceptive friend who's willing to help me through this."

"I'm not sure about the bright perceptive part, but I'd like to consider myself your friend."

Staring at the dancing flames, she smiled as he moved closer.

His voice softened. "But I am perceptive enough to see your eyelids drooping. I think you'd better get some sleep."

"Could Stagga stay in my room tonight?" Kaycee managed another weak smile when the dog perked his ears at the sound of his name. After stretching by the fire, Stagga sauntered across the hardwood floor to rest his muzzle on her knees.

"That's his way of saying he'd love to sleep with you," Max said. Following Kaycee to the door of the guest room, he gently kissed her goodnight. "Promise to call if you need anything at all."

"I will," she replied before closing the door.

Leaning against it, Max muttered, "Lucky dog."

Suddenly, the door flew back open. With a grin, Kaycee simply stared at him, holding out one hand.

Baffled, Max asked, "Did I forget to give you fresh towels?"

"No. You forgot to pay up. I just remembered our little bet. I believe it was twenty bucks if anything horrible happened within two weeks."

Pulling her into his arms, he softly answered, "Surely you don't consider this horrible? After all, you survived."

C H A P T E R **17**

Max bolted upright, his heart pounding furiously. A noise. He was sure he'd heard something in the house, but what? A quick glance at the clock revealed it was 4:00 a.m. Reaching down, his hand found only cool air, not Stagga's warm fur. Then he remembered Kaycee.

Tossing back the quilt, Max jumped out of bed. He rushed from his room with such urgency that he slid across the hardwood floor, stopping just past the open door to the guest room. Grabbing the door frame, he gazed inside. Kaycee wasn't there. For a moment his mind raced. Where could she be?

"Couldn't sleep?" she asked.

Her voice drifted from somewhere nearby, yet when he turned slowly around no one was there. Moving toward the sound, he spotted them curled on the floor by the fire. Stagga was at Kaycee's side, his head resting on her hip. Kaycee's eyes met his in silent question.

"Are you all right?" Max asked.

She smiled. "Sure. I hope we didn't wake you."

Realizing he only had on boxers, he blushed and explained, "When I heard that noise, I was afraid. . .Well, that you might need something."

"Sorry. The fire was almost out so I added a couple more logs. I tried to do it quietly. I really didn't mean to disturb you."

Max wrapped himself in the Indian weave blanket that had been draped over the back of the sofa. "Do you always get up at four in the morning?"

She shrugged. "Only when I can't sleep. At first, the entire night was just a blur, but then I remembered something *he* said. After that,

I couldn't stop thinking about what had happened, it all came flooding back. How he's been watching me, following me, what he said he'd do to me, everything. I couldn't go back to sleep. When I close my eyes I see his face, his voice echoes in my head, and I can't forget his handwriting—it practically haunts me."

Max asked, "His handwriting?"

Kaycee quickly filled Max in on her conversation with Bob Palmer, adding, "You know, it's really creepy that his path keeps crossing mine."

Max gazed at her silhouette. He'd never realized how warm and soft the rug in front of the fireplace was until that moment. Clearing his throat, he said, "Remember, I'm here to help."

She scowled. "You may not want to this time."

"Why don't you let me decide what I want to do? You might just be surprised."

"I decided I have to go back to New Mexico. I'd like you to go with me, but I'll go alone if I have to."

Max studied the determined look in her eyes. Finally, he shrugged. "Just like that. You're going. Decision made."

Kaycee nodded, her gaze never faltering.

"Mind if I ask why?"

"He's keeping Maggie in a mine there. We can help her. I know it."

Startled, Max asked, "He told you where she is?"

Ruffling the dog's fur, Kaycee admitted, "Not exactly, but I'm sure Stagga could find her. Can he work from dirt?"

"Dirt?"

"Remember how dirty I was? The floorboard of that truck was covered with a thick layer of dirt, and I'd bet a million bucks that some of it came from where he has his daughter hidden. If the police would let us have a little, maybe Stagga could get some kind of scent from it."

Max contemplated her idea, then said, "I doubt if that would work. Dirt's not a specific smell, especially dirt in a truck that's probably contaminated by humans, plastics, you name it. By now, the snow in those mountains will be pretty deep. But Willy Thornton's scent would be in that truck. We could get a rub from the seat, or maybe there's a piece of his clothing they'd let us use. Stagga could easily track a fresh human trail. But no matter what, nothing will work if Thornton hasn't gone back to the area."

"He has to go back, his little girl is there. In fact, he seemed irritated that it took him so long to get to me. I think he's in a pretty big hurry."

"Which is why you have no business going anywhere near there."

"But I have to. Don't you see? Maggie came to me for help! And what did I do? I wasted precious seconds checking her story and trying to call the police. Maybe if I'd just wrapped her in my arms and run she'd be free right now."

"Or maybe you'd both be dead."

Kaycee grimaced. "But I think I know where to look for her." Placing her hand on her chest, she added, "Max, I have to go. I have to try."

Taking her hand, Max smiled. "Trust me, I'd be the last person on earth to question your insight. I'd love to take you, but it's too dangerous. I promised the FBI that I wouldn't let you out of my sight."

"Sorry, but I'll still go alone. My sister Niki will help, plus I'm supposed to interview for a position with CSI. They offered to let me use their resources."

"Is Niki the one who had the stroke?"

Kaycee nodded. "I can stay with her. I'd be safe there."

"What makes you think the FBI is going to let you go anywhere? I practically had to swear on my firstborn not to let anything happen to you. Even if they don't nail Thornton for kidnapping his daughter, they can get him for what he did to you."

"I know, but I also know Maggie's life is in my hands. What's the longest someone's been lost before you found them?"

After a moment's hesitation, Max replied, "Eighteen days. But he had access to fresh water, and foraged for food."

"Then there's still hope."

Max stared into the fire, then shifted his gaze to Kaycee. "Agent Jones is going to have a fit over this."

"Agent Jones doesn't have to know everything, does he?"

"Last time I checked, you were just shy of being classified as a protected witness. If you disappear, all hell will break lose."

"But they can't make me stay here. I haven't done anything wrong."

He laughed. "Well, that probably depends on your point of view. If I remember right, a few hours ago you were leading half a dozen lawmen on a high-speed chase in a stolen car, not to mention being indecently attired and damn near uncooperative."

"But—"

"But that isn't fair, right? Trust me, if they want to make sure you don't go anywhere, they can."

"Then I won't tell them about the mine."

"Kaycee, they could blanket the entire area, launch a massive manhunt."

"I can't explain it, but I know that if they send in a bunch of people Maggie won't make it out of there alive. You haven't seen his eyes, Max, or read the depth of his insanity in his handwriting. He's crazy, and not worried at all about the consequences of his actions. He'll either take her away, or if that doesn't work, kill her if he sees them coming."

"They're trained to help people in situations like this."

"So are you."

Leaning back, Max ran his fingers through his hair in frustration. His gaze fell and stayed on the silver bracelet around his wrist. With a sigh, he asked, "Why are you so certain you know where to look?"

"Remember when I almost ran over you and Stagga? I'm pretty sure I saw that same truck come out of the forest onto the highway just moments before the curve where you were walking."

Max was watching the firelight in her eyes, the clenched set of her jaw. "There are lots of Ford trucks in New Mexico."

"Trust me, Max. Lately, I pay very close attention to everything I see, and I saw that truck. In fact, it may even have been him driving, but it all happened so fast. I can see him behind the wheel, but I'm not sure if it's a real image, or one blended from more recent memories."

"Don't you think the police can find her based on what you've told me? I'm sure the towing company will have a record of where my truck broke down. The authorities can backtrack from there."

"Maybe they can. But I *know* we can, and it would be much faster. Every minute we waste is like driving another nail in her coffin."

Silence hung between them, broken only by the popping and sizzling of burning wood. Finally, Max grumbled, "Okay."

"Okay, as in you'll take me?"

"As long as you agree to play by my rules."

"Which are?"

"You tell Agent Jones what Thornton said about hiding Maggie in a mine. That way, if they have access to some sort of classified maps, they might be able to find her. Meanwhile, we'll go to New Mexico and you can show me where you think the truck came out of the woods. I think Cal will help, and I'll call Randy and Joan, too." Eye to eye, his voice hardened as he added, "But then I take you to your sister's place while we search. Understand? Only the SAR teams will be on that mountain."

"But—"

"Take it or leave it. Professional SAR teams. Period."

Obviously disappointed, she asked, "Why? Do you think I'd bother Stagga if I tagged along?"

He smiled, softly shaking his head. "No. You'd bother me."

•   •   •   •   •

Special Agent Jones sipped coffee as he scribbled notes. Even though it was only eight o'clock on Sunday morning, Kaycee had already spent an hour taking him step by step through the events of the night before. When she was finished, he leaned back and shook his head. "You're a lucky woman."

"I suppose you could look at it that way," she said, the tone of her voice contradicting her words.

Max squeezed her hand. "I'm just glad Kaycee was strong enough to take control of the situation instead of becoming another of this thug's victims."

Jones nodded and moved on. "Tell me more about the mine. Did he say where it was?"

"No."

"How far away?"

"No."

"How big a mine? What kind?"

"He only mentioned it once, when I pushed him about abusing his daughter."

"Are you sure?"

Kaycee sat back, suppressing a yawn. "Do you honestly think that if I knew where he was keeping that poor little girl that I wouldn't do everything I could to help her?"

Jones sighed. "I'm sure you would. This is a tough case. I keep imagining my own kids. . ."

She nodded. "I wish he'd said more."

Standing, Jones stretched. "Sometimes people in traumatic situations recall things in bits and pieces. If you happen to remember anything else, you will call, won't you?"

"Of course."

As if contemplating the wisdom of his words, Jones reluctantly added, "Before you hear it on the news, I think you should know that our manhunt last night did turn up something."

"Really! Did you catch him?" Kaycee asked excitedly.

Jones avoided making eye contact as he shook his head. "No. But we found the bodies of an elderly couple. The coroner said they were shot just few feet off the road, then dragged into the woods. The bodies were covered with a thin layer of leaves and branches, but they hadn't been dead for long."

Kaycee paled. "Oh, my God! You think Thornton killed them?"

"Looks that way. There was a slug left in the tailgate of the truck you were in, so we're waiting on ballistics to determine if they were killed with the same gun. Right now, we're assuming Thornton needed transportation. Most likely he flagged down two trusting souls by pretending to hitchhike."

Max asked, "Does that mean you know what he's driving now?"

Jones shook his head. "There was no ID on either of them. Their prints aren't on file in any of the standard databases, so they could be from near here, or they may have been passing through. At this point, until someone reports them as missing, we're at a standstill. We're working on artist's sketches to release to the media and other law enforcement agencies, which should speed up the identification process."

Max nailed Kaycee with a calculated stare. "That means he could be anywhere."

"Unfortunately, that's true. Even though we had roadblocks on the Interstates, there are plenty of back roads he could've slipped by on."

"Have the New Mexico police come up with any more information on the trucker who found the wrecked car?"

"We know he's lived in that semi for the last eighteen months. According to the locals, Roger Adams is a wannabe writer, a really nice guy. After his marriage fell apart, he started traveling all over the country. We've put out an Attempt To Locate Witness on him, but so far, he hasn't been spotted."

"What about the granddaughter of the woman at the motel?"

"Still missing."

"So now what do we do?"

"That depends. The FBI will provide protection for Ms. Miller."

Kaycee tensed, shaking her head. "I'd prefer to stay here with Max."

Jones stood. "I'll run it by my boss, but I don't think he's going to buy it. He's already making plans for you to stay at a safe house. I'll be back this afternoon, but if you think of anything else, please call."

She nodded, following him to the front door. When he was gone, she leaned against it and smiled triumphantly. "I didn't lie to him, you know. I said I would prefer to stay with you, I just didn't mention where we would be staying."

"True."

"Then why do I feel so bad?"

"Because you're a lousy liar, even when you're telling the truth."

"Max, that made no sense whatsoever."

Hugging her, he whispered, "I know. You have that effect on me."

Burying her head in his warmth, she asked, "How soon should we leave?"

"I'll pack the SAR gear while you get ready. I already called Randy and Joan. Joan is in San Diego for a few days, but Randy can be in Cimarron tomorrow. Cal will probably be waiting for us when we get there tonight. He's really pumped."

"Somehow, I don't think this is going to be fun."

"That's because you don't know Cal. He could make climbing Mt. Everest in a blizzard seem like a walk in the park."

"Speaking of which, I have a major clothing problem. Are there any stores open on Sunday morning?"

"Not near here, but I'll loan you a flannel shirt and—"

"And what? In case you haven't noticed, you're about a foot taller than I am."

Opening a closet, he pulled out a full-length men's coat. "For now, you can wear my oil-skin duster, and I've got a pair of shorts that I think will fit you."

"So you want me to go out in public wearing only a shirt, shorts and a coat that drags the floor?"

Tossing her a cowboy hat, he grinned. "Trust me. No one is going to recognize you."

"Let's just hope Willy Thornton doesn't. . ."

CHAPTER 18

Maggie awoke, happy to see the narrow ray of light far above her head had returned. It must be daytime. A few days ago she would've cried, would've thought about her mother, but there were no tears left. Later, when her work was done, she would sit under that beam and watch the way it touched the pretty cross Kim had given to her. But for now, she had to get busy.

Since her hands were tied, she ripped open a fruit roll-up with her teeth, then chewed on it while she held a juice box between her knees so she could spear it with the mini-straw. Finishing her meager breakfast, she placed the wrapper and the box neatly into the little trash pile, seeming much older than five. Eating alone in a dismal hole in the ground was a part of life she had learned to accept.

Rolling to her feet, she whispered to her invisible friend, "Jeremy! Wake up! You've got to finish your breakfast so you can help. It's time to go to work."

Her daddy had promised he'd be back *soon*, a thought that always struck fear in her heart. Even though it seemed like she'd been in that awful place forever, Jeremy had told her they had to finish all their work before her dad came back for her. Maggie trusted Jeremy. He was a good friend. She needed him.

Scooting across the dirt, Maggie searched the tunnel end of the cave until she found a six-inch oblong rock. Pushing it with both feet toward the cloaking gloom of a cleft in the far wall, she inched along. Like building a sand castle, she was making a little fortress of stone and dirt—sprinkling each rock with loose soil until it no longer showed its true form.

Even on a day like this, when the sun managed to squeeze through the sliver of earth overhead, the fortress was cloaked in shadow. Already, it was as tall as her shoulder. When it was done, she would crawl inside. She and Jeremy would play games, and when Daddy came back, they'd be as quiet as little rabbits.

Jeremy promised her dad wouldn't find her in there, and that she'd never, ever have to go anywhere with him again. *Never!*

·   ·   ·   ·   ·

Roger watched Kim emerge from the motel's dinky bathroom, rubbing her wet hair with a towel. The cuts were beginning to heal, but the bruises had darkened, dragging up the most dismal part of her soul. The combination of her facial abrasions and short, spiky hair made her look like a prisoner of war.

For two days he had stayed with her, nursed her, longed for her. More than anything he wished he could confront the man who did this to her. Just the thought of meeting him made his fists clench.

Kim turned, her eyes meeting his. "Are you leaving now?"

Roger nodded, unable to find words when he needed them the most.

Kim crossed the room, stopping so near him the tips of her toes touched his boots. For the first time since they'd met, she gently kissed him. "Will you come back like you promised?"

Wrapping her in his arms, he sighed. "You know I will, as soon as I deliver my load. The room is paid up for a week, and I left two hundred dollars on the nightstand."

"You saved my life, Roger. I don't know how to thank you, but I'll pay back every cent. I promise."

Softly shaking his head, he touched her cheek. "I won't take a dime from you. I just wish I could do more."

Only the muted sound of the television next door saturated the room. Flustered, Kim's eyes darted from the curtains to the cheesy Monet print over the bed as she said, "I'll be here when you get back."

"Please come with me," he begged.

"You know I can't. I have to finish my business here first."

"Business that could get you killed?"

Her eyes blazed as the slender line of her jaw hardened. "Not this time. This time, he'll be sorry he ever met me."

"Kim, I know there's some reason why you don't want me to find out what happened. But whatever you were involved in is over now. Forget the creep. Sometimes it's best to just go on."

"And sometimes when people go on, a lot of innocent people get hurt because of their selfishness. I've been selfish long enough, Roger. I know what I have to do, and I'm going to do it."

· · · · ·

In the parking lot of Enid's WalMart, Kaycee wiggled into her new clothes—jeans, a thick, soft black sweater, and insulated socks. Tapping on the window, she signaled Max that she was ready while she gently tugged the hiking boots onto her swollen feet.

As soon as he crawled into the driver's seat, Kaycee announced, "I'm a whole new woman!"

"Personally, I liked the other woman just fine."

"She was embarrassed to be seen in public."

"Exactly. She's safer that way."

"There is no way anyone could possibly know where we are."

Max shook his head.

Ignoring his stare, she asked, "Did you remember to get Stagga a treat for me?"

Digging through one of the sacks, he pulled out a chew toy. "Here it is, but you'd better make him work for it."

"How?"

"Ask him to—" he spelled, "S-P-E-A-K."

"Stagga, speak!" Kaycee commanded.

The dog's piercing bark echoed in the interior of the Trooper, making them both wince. "Next time, I'll wait until we're outside." Tossing him the toy, she leaned over and gently kissed Max. "If nothing else, this should be an interesting trip."

Max nodded. "True. Do you need anything before we leave?"

"I'm almost set. Would you mind if I go make a couple of calls from that pay phone over there?"

He tugged out a cell phone as he maneuvered the car out of the parking lot onto the highway. "Use this."

"No. I'd rather put them on my calling card."

"Which the FBI can easily trace."

"Like they won't check your cell phone?"

"They can check my cell phone all they like. This is Randy's. I switched phones with him because using mine would leave a trail a house cat could track."

Kaycee grinned. "Do you always think like a criminal?"

"Only when I'm aiding and abetting a fleeing witness."

Dialing her sister's phone number, Kaycee anxiously waited through twelve rings before the machine picked up. Hanging up, she said, "I think I'd better explain this in person. It might come across a little crazy on the phone."

"True. Why does her machine take so long to answer?"

"It takes awhile to get to the phone in a wheel chair. I must admit, she's made unbelievable progress these past few months. She works out every day. In just the last two weeks, her upper body strength has almost doubled."

"I can't wait to meet her. Maybe she'll be home later. Who else do you need to call?"

"A friend." Digging through her purse, she found a business card for her nurse, Ellen Henderson. As she dialed her number, she leaned away, trying to keep the phone as far from Max as she could. Kaycee was relieved when an answering machine picked up. "Hi, Ellen. This is Kaycee Miller. Don't worry, everything is fine. I know I promised to call and set up another lunch this week, but I had to make an unexpected trip out of town. I may be gone for a few days. I'll call as soon as I get back."

Handing Max the phone, Kaycee asked, "What about you? No one will think it's odd when you just vanish for a few days?"

"Not a soul," Max replied.

"Doesn't that bother you?"

"Why should it?"

"What if something happened to you? Or to your ranch?"

Max shrugged. "Then it happens. Worrying about it isn't going to change anything. Robin does a great job taking care of the place while I'm gone. Besides, bad news travels fast."

"How true," Kaycee replied, closing her eyes. In an instant, she quickly opened them again, unwilling to miss even a second of the sights this trip had to offer.

·   ·   ·   ·   ·

Thornton stood and stretched, barely pushing aside the curtains to glance outside. He'd driven all night, then used a copy of Kim's motel master key to slip unnoticed into room 21 at five a.m. Washing his face, he glared at the fresh claw marks that started just below the dark circle under his eye and ended in the new stubble of his three-day-old beard. Surprisingly, it wasn't anger or hatred that rushed through his veins. Instead, he soared with anticipation, his mind buzzing as though electrified.

It was a few minutes past eleven when he smoothed the covers on the bed and slipped outside. Check-out time at the Kit Carson was noon, and he had no intention of hanging around long enough to risk being seen by Kim's grandmother.

The old El Dorado he'd stolen was parked a few blocks away. Dressed in his new jogging outfit, he loped through the snow along-side the clear road, anxious to be on his way. Although he had planned to stop off at the mine and make sure Maggie had plenty of food and water, he couldn't control his need for revenge. Pulling the luggage tag out of his pocket, he ran a finger down his scratched cheek. Smiling as he read it once again, he recognized the area code and the prefix of the phone number.

> *Kaycee Miller*
> *3417 East Sherlyn Lane, Tulsa, OK*
> *Please call 918-555-2050 if found*

In case of Emergency contact:
Niki Miller 505-555-1998

Niki Miller didn't know it yet, but today she would start to pay for her sister's sins.

· · · · ·

Kaycee relaxed into the leather seat, her head turned toward Max. He seemed lost in thought as he drove, giving her the chance to study his profile. She grinned as she noticed little things—the tightly curled hair at the nape of his neck, the strength in his hands, the glint of the sun dancing on the edge of his silver bracelet.

"Having fun?" he laughed, catching her gaze.

"Sorry, I didn't mean to stare. What were you thinking about?"

"Lots of things. Where we'll stay, how to safely attack the mountain. But mostly, what to do with you."

"That's easy." Scooting closer to him, she explained, "From now on you can pretend I'm Velcro. Wherever you go, I go." Before he could argue, she added, "I seem to recall you're a man of your word. Is that right?"

"I suppose."

"Well, I heard you promise Agent Jones that you wouldn't let me out of your sight. So, the only way you can keep your word is to keep an eye on me. Right?"

Max answered by slowly shaking his head while raising one brow. "Twisted logic won't change my mind."

"What will?"

"Nothing."

"Want to make a bet?"

"I believe with my track record on bets I'd better pass."

"See, I knew you were a wise man." Touching the silver, Kaycee felt an intangible strength in the bracelet's interwoven braid. "You said this was to remind you—" her voice trailed off for a moment before she gathered the nerve to add, "of what?"

He cast another sideways glance her way, pausing for a moment before offering, "An important lesson. In fact, I wouldn't be here right now if it weren't for that lesson." Unfastening the bracelet, he dropped it in the palm of her hand.

Kaycee read the inscription inside:

On each gentle breeze an angel is called home.

"There's no name. Was this a gift from someone you found?"

"Indirectly. One was given to each SAR team member who worked the rescue of Mandy Akins. Her parents were really special people."

Kaycee noticed his hands clenching the wheel. She could practically feel anguish pulsing from him. "She didn't make it, did she?"

He shook his head. "For a little while, but we were too late. She was only three years old. She lived about five hours after found I her. That sentence is inscribed on her tombstone."

"I'm sure you did the best you could do."

Max's voice was low as he breathed, "No. I didn't." Keeping his eyes on the road, he confessed, "I *knew* where we should look! A gut feeling, but still, I should have had faith in it. It was only my second time in the field. The team leader wanted the perimeter searched first, which is standard procedure—start outside and move inward. The weather was horrible—a hard, driving rain with gusts of wind that made the trail practically impossible to follow. After a half a day, I broke out of the designated search pattern and headed Stagga toward the place I'd initially felt she would be."

"And you were right?"

He nodded.

"Did her parents know?"

"No. About a month after her death, these bracelets came in the mail. There was a note attached to each one, thanking us for finding their little girl, and telling us that at the moment she died, a soft wind fluttered the curtains in the hospital room. Her mother swore it was the other angels carrying her to heaven. I've worn it night and day ever since."

Kaycee leaned her head on his shoulder, unashamed of the tears rolling down her cheeks. "I'm sorry."

"Me, too. It won't happen again."

She wrapped the bracelet back around his wrist, snapping it back where it belonged. "Always trust your instincts?"

"Always."

. . . . .

Thornton banged on the solid oak door again, glancing over his shoulder down the winding drive to be sure no one was coming. Apparently, Niki Miller wasn't home. Thankful there were no other houses nearby, he stepped off the porch and casually scanned the area. The drive and sidewalks were clear of snow and ice, recently shoveled and salted. He chose to follow the walkway that led to the back of the house, glad he didn't have to worry about leaving footprints in the snow. Stopping at the first window, he cupped his hands around his eyes and leaned close to peer inside. With a gasp, he jumped back.

He'd been eye level with what he was certain was a person. As his heart's loud thumping began to slow, he realized that even though it looked alive, it couldn't have been real. It didn't jump at the sight of him, and he was pretty sure it had wings. *Wings?* Trying again, a nervous laugh escaped his lips. He'd been scared by a statue—of a stupid angel, no less!

No lights were on inside, no stereo or television, no sound at all. Confident the house was empty, he moved along the back wall, testing each window. When he reached the last one, the metal frame squealed as it budged beneath his pressure. Every muscle tensed while he waited to hear an alarm. When all stayed quiet for a full minute, he sighed.

As a precaution, Thornton pulled his gun out of its holster and checked to see if it was ready to fire. Leading with the gun, he folded his body into the narrow opening, grunting as his massive shoulders crammed through the tight space. As soon as he was inside, he shoved the window closed, snapping the lock. To be certain he was alone, he yelled, "Special delivery! Anybody home?"

Silence.

The gun dangled at his side as he moved from room to room. Each step added a layer to his growing confusion. The kitchen counters and sink were very low, the bathroom had been equipped with rails, and there was a makeshift ramp that ran into the garage. *Niki Miller must be her crippled old mother, not her sister,* he thought. *This should really make things interesting!*

After he was certain he was alone, Thornton hid the El Dorado a quarter mile down the highway. By the time he hiked back and slipped in the front door, he realized he was bone tired. Squeezing into the space between the bed and the wall where no one could surprise him, he placed the gun at his side and promptly fell asleep.

R oger had settled in for a long day of driving when he spotted the highway patrol car in the rearview mirrors. An anxious glance confirmed his speed was two miles per hour under the limit, giving him cause to breathe a little easier. For the next five miles, he occasionally looked back, not really concerned. Even when he saw the flashing lights come to life, at first he didn't believe they were targeting him.

A fresh layer of sweat glistened on his brow as he downshifted and pulled off the road. Crawling from the high cab, he tried not to act uneasy as he ambled back to the patrol car. Wearing his most polite smile, he called, "Good morning, officer. Would you mind telling me what I've done wrong?"

"Are you Roger Quincy Adams?" the officer asked.

"Yes, sir. That's me."

"Did you know you're wanted by the FBI for questioning in connection with a kidnapping?"

A kidnapping? Oh, God, they must think I kidnapped Kim! But how could they possibly know I helped her? His stomach turned and before he realized it, he blushed so deep that he felt the blood tingle from his cheeks to the tops of his ears. Trying to hide what was probably the guiltiest look any officer of the law had ever witnessed, he cleared his throat, then tried to sound unfazed. "No. . .Who was kidnapped?"

The trooper glanced at the computerized data screen and replied, "I'm sure they'll go over everything with you. Would you like an escort into town? I'm headed that way."

An escort. . .They're not treating me like a criminal. . .Maybe this is just a stupid coincidence.

The trooper waited for a reply as he studied Roger's confused expression. Finally, he offered, "Listen, this is no big deal. At this point, all they're asking for is your cooperation. Our orders are to locate you. It would be a good idea to go answer their questions. Obviously, if they think you know something about a kidnapping, then you might be able to help in some way."

Roger was beginning to relax. "Okay. I'll follow you."

The trooper smiled and nodded.

As he walked toward his truck, Roger's head was spinning. *Maybe Kim was involved in a kidnapping. Surely I didn't buy into another stack of lies, just like all the ones my ex-wife fed me. Why do I always fall for women who are pure trouble?*

• • • • •

Kim didn't waste a moment after Roger left. It only took a few minutes to hide her bruises with makeup before she changed into the new clothes he had bought for her. A shiver of guilt laced with fear crept down her back as she slipped out of the motel room. What if Willy spotted her? Or the police?

The sun on her face helped melt some of her anxiety. On a beautiful Sunday like this, downtown Taos had an ample supply of skiers and tourists window-shopping the local art galleries. The heavy foot traffic made it easy for her to blend in as she briskly made her way across town.

Unconsciously, her stride slowed as she approached the run-down apartment building. A new version of an old fear made it hard to swallow, and even harder to keep walking. Stopping outside the weary double doors, she tried to take a deep breath and bolster her courage, but the air suddenly seemed too thick to breathe. Two years. She'd been drug free for two whole years.

With a trembling hand, Kim turned the knob on the outer door and stepped inside. The familiar stale stench of the place slapped her, making her reel back against the foyer's filthy wall. On unsteady legs she made her way to the end of the hall, turned right, then stopped in front of the door marked, "Basement—Keep Out."

Kim's hand was shaking violently as she reached above the dusty light fixture, desperately hoping the key was still hidden there. On tiptoe, she closed her eyes, gently touching the dusty surface until she felt the thin metal outline. Sliding it off, she unlocked the door, then put the key back exactly where it had been.

Terror had stolen her courage. She wanted to throw up, cry, scream, run, be anywhere except this dreadful place. With her hand on the doorknob, Kim froze—shuddering as she remembered.

A few minutes crept by, minutes filled with memories of the drugs, the pain, the horror of rehab. Yet even as bad as that part of her past seemed, recent images of hurting her grandmother, of Willy's face as he pushed her off the road, seemed far worse.

With a deep breath, Kim opened the door and slipped inside. Its murky, musty shadows evoked visions of Maggie alone in that hellhole, petrified of her own father—with good cause. She remembered this place was perpetually dark, too. Long ago, the single window had been painted black to protect its illicit secrets. Punching the inside lock, she pulled the door closed, certain she'd just sealed her own tomb.

Wrapping her fingers around the rough handrail of the narrow staircase, she clawed the bannister, feeling as though each step brought her a little closer to unspeakable agony. The dirt on the concrete floor scratched beneath her new athletic shoes, making a sound she was certain could be heard for miles.

On tiptoe, she flailed her arms until she felt the string of the dangling bare light bulb. Tugging on it, she winced as the room suddenly emerged from darkness, still half expecting a monster to lurch out of the shadows. The place hadn't changed one bit.

Everything had always been hidden among the cardboard boxes stacked almost to the ceiling. Tapping what appeared to be an enormous refrigerator box on the end, she felt it move. Although cardboard on the outside, the inner box was actually reinforced with a wood frame, complete with a door hinge that squeaked as she gingerly pushed it halfway open.

Stepping inside, Kim forced open the false back to emerge next to the table of drug paraphernalia. Seeing the packets of white powder made her cringe, made the track scars on her inner arms ache, then burn with desire. Glancing around, she was sure no one would ever know. One hit wouldn't hurt. Just one.

In slow motion her fingers began to close around the needle. Suddenly, from deep within a voice screamed, *No! You've worked too hard! GET OUT!*

Jumping back, Kim gasped as she loudly crashed against the back row of boxes, desperately fighting a raw physical need stronger than anything she'd ever felt in her life. Sweat trickled down her face, flowed in cold, shocking drops from under her arms. *LEAVE! Now!*

Suddenly, she remembered why she came. Groping with trembling, wet hands under the table, she finally felt it—the gun. Dropping to the floor, she jerked away the X of duct tape, taking the small pistol in her hand. After tugging out the tail of her T-shirt, she stuffed it into her jeans, then froze as the key turned in the lock above. Someone was coming.

Kim cowered, then froze. A voice from above boomed, "Who the hell left the damned light on this time?"

·　·　·　·　·

Closing her eyes for a moment, Kaycee could almost feel the hand of fate dragging them down the highway. She didn't care to admit, especially to herself, that the future might truly be as dark as the recent past. No matter how much she wanted to change what had happened in the last year, she knew she couldn't.

In the weeks since Kaycee had first learned she was going blind, she'd conjured a vision of herself that was unacceptable. Dependent, scared, totally alone. Now she understood why it was so important to meet someone like Ellen Henderson who was winning the battle of life in spite of RP. Ellen didn't fit that incapacitated image—she was *still* strong, able, apparently managing a career quite well.

Ellen's words floated back to Kaycee, her image alive. *It's easy to wallow in self-pity. The challenge is overcoming the fear. Change is hard for most people. It can be devastating for those who use it as an excuse to crawl into a shell.*

Kaycee knew she was right. All her life she'd fought uphill battles. Trying to get professional recognition for handwriting analysis, starting a business on her own, even moving to a strange new city. Yet every time she had truly tried, she had succeeded. Why should this challenge be any different?

Inspired, Kaycee focused on the positive things she'd already started to learn. *As sight diminishes, the other senses will compensate. Sense of touch, of smell, and hearing will fill in gaps. Each person is unique, but if they try, they can speed up the process. Hearing, for instance. We're surrounded by blankets of raw sound. You have to peel back the layers, focus on which sounds are close, which are far away. You'll be amazed at all the tiers you've never noticed before, how you can slice through them. When you begin to sift through the clutter, you'll find the precious tones that will help you navigate. Many noises have a vibration, they shiver, resonate in an identifiable way. Soon, you'll be listening with your entire body without even realizing it.*

Concentrating on the assortment of sounds inside the Trooper, she slowly began to dissect them. There was the drone of the engine, and *yes!* she felt the quiver of the tires beneath her feet. Like an accent, the tone from the tires was unique, one that, even though her eyes were closed, she felt subtly change when Max shifted into a different lane.

Then there was the wind. In her entire life she'd never realized how the song of the wind altered each time the car slightly varied directions. Amazed, with her eyes still closed Kaycee suddenly pictured the fine lace curtains that had hung on her bedroom window when she was a child. She'd spent hours watching them dancing on evening breezes, studying the dainty images cast by the moonlight filtering through their folds. *From now on, I'll hear those curtains, touch the intricate stitches, feel them flutter against my skin. They'll be just as beautiful, even if I can't see them.*

Kaycee grinned. For the first time she had confronted an image of a sightless future, and it wasn't terrifying! She suddenly wondered if she could hear Max at her side, or Stagga in the back seat. Leaning slightly toward Max, she waited until she felt the pattern of his breathing gently caress her ears and the brush of his breath on her skin.

Since her total concentration was directed at hearing, Max's whispered words startled her as if he'd shouted. "Are you awake?"

Her eyes flew open as she recovered with a nod.

Pointing toward an expanse of open grassland on the side of the road, he said, "I thought you might want to see a herd of antelope."

Following his outstretched hand, she struggled to see them, but the sun was blocked by a handful of scattered clouds. There simply wasn't enough light for her to see clearly so far away. After pretending to watch for a few moments, she lied, "They're absolutely beautiful."

"Were you asleep for the last few minutes?"

"No, why?"

He seemed to look *through* her for a second before shrugging. "Just curious. The look on your face was. . .well, interesting."

"I was trying a new—" she hesitated, "relaxation technique."

"Well, it must work. You look more content than I've ever seen you. We'll be in Cimarron in about an hour, then we can decide where to spend the night."

"We'd better choose a different place to stay this time. Just the thought of the Kit Carson Luxury Motel gives me a headache." She paused, adding, "I was just thinking about Agent Jones. Poor guy is probably having a cow about now. I'm sure the note we left that promised you were safe didn't sit well with his supervisor."

She grimaced. "I hate doing this to him. He really is a nice man."

Max started to hand her the cell phone. "Then maybe you should invite him to come along. Might be safer for all of us."

"No way!" Realizing he was teasing her, she punched his arm. Stagga's low growl rumbled from the backseat. Turning to face the dog, she said, "Listen, boy, we need to stick together. Quit taking everything so seriously."

Max raised one brow. "He will, the moment you do."

· · · · ·

Roger leaned back in the chair, far more confident than he had been all day. Glancing at the poster in his hand, he could honestly say he knew nothing about the kidnapping of that little girl. And, thankfully, he'd never laid eyes on the oversized cretin they said was named Wilfred "Willy" Thornton. He was almost ready to go when another agent stepped into the small interrogation room.

The photo slid to a stop right in front of his chest as the weary agent asked, "What about her? She look familiar?"

Roger bit the side of his tongue, trying to decide what to say. Even though the hair was dark and long, there was no doubt it was a mug shot of Kim, probably a couple of years old. He mumbled, "A little. Who is she?"

"She disappeared about the same time you found her grandmother's wrecked car."

"Really. What's her name?"

"Kimberly Annabelle Snyder."

"Annabelle?"

"Yep."

"No wonder she's got problems." Gathering his courage, Roger added, "Was she involved in that kidnapping you were telling me about?"

He nodded. "We're pretty sure she was helping hide the kid. She and Thornton were an item. Apparently, Thornton decided she was a risk he was no longer willing to take. Paint found on the driver's side of the car you found matched the truck he was driving when he tried to kidnap a witness in Oklahoma."

"He tried to kidnap someone else?" Roger strained to stay calm as the agent nodded.

"After that, we're pretty sure he killed an elderly couple for transportation."

"That's horrible." Even if only half of this was true, the guy who had almost killed Kim was an enormous brute of a man, not to mention totally deranged. *God, I aided a felon, and now she wants to get revenge on a homicidal maniac! Kim doesn't stand a chance!* Pushing back his chair, Roger extended his hand. "I've really got to get going. Between that bout with the stomach flu and this unscheduled stop, I'm way behind schedule."

"We appreciate your cooperation, Mr. Adams. If you think of anything that might be helpful, give us a call."

Roger walked out to his rig, wondering if they would follow him. Tossing the poster of Maggie Thornton on the passenger seat, his eyes constantly darted to the rearview mirror as he left town. Ten miles down the road, he pulled off the highway, circled around and headed toward Taos one more time.

· · · · ·

Kim had no idea how long she stayed under that table watching the dirty, sandal-clad feet shuffle back and forth. She had tucked herself into a tight ball, barely breathing as the minutes clicked past.

Then he started humming. Memories flooded back, making her certain it was Ricardo, the man who had first turned her on to drugs. Of the handful of people who knew about this place, he was the only one she was sure would kill anyone he caught stealing from him. Ricardo used to brag about cutting people who got too far behind on their payments. He enjoyed watching them suffer. Kim shivered, certain she would still be under his control if her grandmother hadn't found her and dragged her home.

Terrified, Kim's knuckles went white as she struggled to keep her knees tucked tightly under her chin. Finally, Ricardo shuffled out through the cardboard box, still humming as he jerked the cord on the light. The basement fell into an unearthly black void, starkly silent. Each stair creaked as he plodded upward until the door slammed in his wake. The room was as still as a graveyard, except for the pounding of Kim's heart.

Kim waited like a statue for another half hour, only moving to stretch out her numb legs when absolutely necessary. She couldn't risk being spotted by Ricardo. Having one lunatic after her was more than enough. When she could stand on steady feet again, she slipped through the box, groping her way in the darkness. Feeling like an alley cat on the prowl, she moved up each step, waiting at the top for several moments before she had the nerve to creep into the hall.

It took all her willpower not to bolt out of that horrible place. She managed to walk through the building, across the front porch, then all the way down the block before breaking into a full run.

Halfway back to the motel, it dawned on Kim that she had not only made it out alive, no one had spotted her. Still, she didn't slow her pace. It felt good to stretch her legs, to feel them burn deep inside from physical exhaustion. For too long she had neglected her body, taken it for granted. Each ragged breath made her painfully aware that it was time to pay the price. Time to start over.

Unlocking the door to the motel room, Kim rushed inside, desperately needing a drink of water. After quenching her thirst and catching her breath, she dug out a pencil and a piece of paper. At the small table, she counted the money Roger had left and made a quick list of things she needed to buy. Stuffing the bills in her pocket, she rushed out.

Just ten minutes after she left to go shopping, Roger charged into the empty room.

• • • • •

It was late afternoon when Max, Kaycee, and Stagga arrived in Cimarron, New Mexico. Checking out the freshest scents, Stagga rambled into the vacant lot beside the gas station while Max and Kaycee stretched and yawned.

"Cal must not be here yet. His helicopter stands out like a sore thumb," Max observed.

"How much more daylight is there?" Kaycee asked, her arms folded against the chill in the air.

"Maybe an hour. Why?"

"I don't think that's long enough. . ." Her voice trailed off as she studied the western sky.

"To do what?"

"To find the place where that truck pulled out in front of me. We'll have to look for it first thing tomorrow morning."

"Sounds like a good idea. You need a decent night's sleep."

"Would you mind if I try calling my sister again?"

"Not at all." He reached inside the truck and handed her Randy's cell phone.

Kaycee leaned against the cool metal, concentrating on her new-found pursuit of listening. Even though it was a quiet town, there was still an abundance of noise. She tried to peel the layers back as she looked around, but found it was easier with her eyes closed. Cutting through the sound of passing cars, the steady rhythm of the teenager drumming against the convenience store's window, and the hum of the neon sign, she was ecstatic to hear the click of Stagga's nails as he approached her from behind. The subtle changes of the wind whistling through the pine trees made her tremble as she dialed Niki's phone number. It only rang once before she heard a strange thud followed by an odd grunt that made her heart leap.

A harsh, deep voice slithered like a boa through the phone, instantly constricting her throat. The ability to breathe, to speak, to even feel, vanished, as the hammering in her chest accompanied a silent scream. *NO!*

Thornton slept all day in the nook beside Niki Miller's bed. The sudden, sharp ring of the telephone startled him awake so quickly that he jerked, knocking over the small nightstand. It crashed on top of him, the phone spilling over his broad chest. The handset landed on one side of him, the base on the other.

Muttering a string of cuss words, he groped to unite both halves of the phone. After slamming them together, he thrashed to find his gun. A glance at the clock on the opposite side of the bed confirmed he had slept much longer than planned. For a few seconds he stayed on the floor with his gun trained on the doorway, making certain he was still alone in the house. Pushing himself up, he staggered into the bathroom.

After relieving himself, he decided to stop wasting time. Moving back to the bedroom, he dug through the woman's closet. "Perfect," he muttered as he slid an old backpack off the top shelf. Absolute silence surrounded him as he lumbered toward the kitchen, arbitrarily destroying everything in his path that wasn't worthy to be dropped into the pack.

Where the hell is she! I can't wait all night!

The phone rang again, and he quickly crossed the room to silence it. Listening intently, Thornton didn't utter a word, he just smiled as he heard the panic in *her* voice. "Niki? Are you okay? Niki?"

Cradling the receiver, he jerked the phone line out of the wall, then caught sight of the Caller ID box next to the phone. Tugging her luggage tag out of his pocket, he quickly realized she wasn't calling from home. Grabbing a pencil, he jotted down Kaycee Miller's latest phone number and tucked it safely into his shirt. He had other plans for the luggage tag.

A noise behind him made him freeze, his hand tightening around the grip of the gun. Now more motivated than ever, he listened to the soft rumble of a garage door opening.

• • • • •

Max had just tossed a ball for Stagga when he noticed Kaycee suddenly change. One minute she'd been relaxed, leaning against the Trooper; the next, every trace of color had drained from her face. As though in slow motion, he watched her shoulders slump, saw the cell phone slide out of her hand, then strike the gravel near her feet.

Rushing to her side, Max gently gripped her by her upper arms. "Are you all right? What's wrong?"

At first, she simply stood there, her mouth slightly ajar, her entire body trembling.

"Kaycee! What the hell happened?"

"My sister. He's got my sister. . ."

"*Who's* got your sister?"

For the first time, her eyes met his. He instantly felt the depth of her terror. "Thornton! Max, I think Willy Thornton just answered my sister's phone!"

"Are you sure?"

Her eyes filled with uncertainty. "That voice. . .How could anyone else sound like him?"

"What did he say?"

"There was a struggle, a string of cuss words. Then the line went dead."

Pulling her close, Max tried to think rationally. "We should call the police." He hesitated, then added, "Please don't take this wrong. You've been through a lot lately. Is there any possibility you could've dialed the wrong number?"

Kaycee sighed, rubbing her aching temple. "I suppose so, but what are the odds I would accidentally dial *his* number?"

Max shook his head. If nothing else, it was easy to tell Kaycee truly believed she had heard Thornton's voice. "Let's be sure." He picked up the phone, hoping to simply read the digital display, but it was blank. "When you dropped it, it must have cleared. What's her number?"

"5-0-5 5-5-5 1-9-9-8," she said.

Max dialed, then held the phone between them so they could both hear. It rang three times before someone answered. Kaycee weakly asked, "Niki? Are you okay? Niki?"

Kaycee shot a nervous glance at Max, who took the phone from her just as it went dead.

Still shaking, Kaycee said, "We. . .we've got to do something. Call the police! It'll take us over an hour to get there. It's *him*, Max. I can feel it. . ."

"But what if it wasn't him? Then the FBI would know exactly where you are." Hesitating to weigh their options, he asked, "Is there a neighbor we could call?"

Kaycee's face lit up. "Yes! B.J. Smith's house is about a third of a mile around the bend. He could be there in no time. Plus, he's a hunting guide, so he should be able to defend himself." In a matter of moments, she got B.J.'s number from information and related the situation to him. Hanging up, she explained, "He's going to call as soon as he gets there."

The next ten minutes dragged by as they both nervously paced. Finally, the cell phone rang. "Hello, B.J.?" Kaycee snapped, holding it where Max could hear as well.

B.J. hesitated, then said, "I'm afraid you were right. There's been some sort of trouble over there."

Kaycee asked, "Is Niki all right?"

"I'm afraid she's not here, ma'am. The place has been ransacked, and there's not a sign of your sister."

"What about her wheelchair?"

"Didn't notice it."

Max asked, "Did you see anything that might help us find her?"

B.J. hesitated, obviously uneasy. "There's a note on Niki's angel."

Ignoring Max's puzzled look, Kaycee hoarsely asked, "Could you read it to me, please?"

Clearing his throat, B.J. reluctantly uttered, "It says, 'Will she die in your place? Call in the authorities and her blood will be on your hands alone. The game goes on. Your move!'"

Kaycee's voice faltered for a moment as she reeled from yet another blow. "Thanks, B.J. I know I've already asked so much, but I'd really appreciate it if you could do me one more favor. Don't call the police just yet. This is very complicated. I know it sounds strange, but I need to think for a few minutes first. Okay?"

Tears spilled down her cheeks as she buried her head in Max's chest. Even Stagga sensed their grim mood. He sat unmoving at Kaycee's feet, his head bowed.

Max warned B.J. to be careful, and thanked him. Turning his attention to Kaycee, he pulled her even closer. "Everything will be okay."

She pushed away, obviously fighting to control her emotions. "Take me there. Please."

"What?"

"I need to see that note. Maybe I'll be able to tell what he's up to, how stable he is."

Max hesitated, then nodded. "From his handwriting?"

She shrugged. "It's worth a try."

• • • • •

The drive from Cimarron was agonizing, winding up and down the mountain pass toward Angel Fire, then veering onto another steep pass into Taos. Narrow two-lane roads made it too dangerous to speed, although Max wanted to cut short Kaycee's anguish as much as humanly possible.

When he could no longer stand the silence, he offered, "I'm sure your sister will be fine. We'll find her."

Kaycee stiffened, glaring at him. "How can you say that? Thornton is a maniac. If he'd practically bury his own daughter alive, why wouldn't he hurt a defenseless paraplegic?"

After Max struggled to come up with an answer, he finally said, "Okay. You're right. But we may be able to find a way to turn this on him. Maybe we can get his scent."

It was dark outside, and Kaycee had to strain to see much at all. Turning toward the backseat, her hand finally found the dog's soft neck. "Does Stagga know how to attack?"

"Not by training, but I suspect he has enough killer instinct to make someone think twice before tangling with him."

"Good."

"Are you feeling all right, Kaycee? How's your head?"

"As hard as ever, can't you tell?" With a grin, she closed her eyes and tried to relax, stroking Stagga's coarse, warm fur. "My father always said Niki and I were both too hard headed, just like him." She sighed, then asked, "How old were you when you lost your parents?"

"Eight."

"That must have been horrible."

"I suppose. My grandparents did everything they could to make it easier. It didn't take me long to figure out that they were hurting as much as I was. For some reason, I thought that meant I had to be strong, put it behind me and go on—for them more than me. Somehow, we all survived."

"Sounds like Niki. She's pretending to be so strong, but inside I know she's still struggling without them—just like me. It's so unsettling. Half the time I wake up and pray it was just a nightmare."

"I have to admit, your moons are definitely wobbling."

"What?"

"That's what my family always says when things seem to keep going wrong. It's easier to just blame the moons, and go on with life. I deal with it all the time doing rescues."

Kaycee shifted to look at him, then bolted upright, barely catching a glimpse of the flashing yellow light that marked the intersection near her sister's house. "You need to turn on the next paved road. We're almost there."

He took her hand, squeezing it gently as they wound up the long drive, then parked. A man balancing a deer rifle over one shoulder was leaning near the front door. Max said, "Sure hope that's Niki's neighbor guarding the place. . ."

"What?" Kaycee replied, obviously distracted.

"That tall blond man in the shadow by the entryway. Is that B.J.?"

Stammering, Kaycee claimed, "I'm sorry, I. . .didn't notice him. To tell you the truth I've only met B.J. once, and that was quite a while ago."

Max opened Kaycee's door after ordering Stagga to stay. Climbing out warily, she practically hung on his arm until they were on the porch.

Extending his hand, Max offered, "I'm Max Masterson. I believe you already know Kaycee Miller. You must be B.J. Smith. We really appreciate your help."

Nodding toward the open front door, he said, "No problem. I haven't touched a thing. The door was like this when I arrived. I noticed a fresh trail leading up this way from the highway, so I followed it. I found Niki's van abandoned up in some bushes. You think you know who did this?"

Kaycee answered, "I'll know for certain as soon as I see that note."

"Like I said, I didn't touch a thing. It's still right there on the angel's halo."

Stepping inside, Kaycee gasped. The house looked as though it had been hit by a tornado—except for the granite angel that had been dragged to the center of the room. The delicate wings, no doubt snapped off to make a point, were on the floor at its side. A piece of paper rested in the hollow of the halo above the striking face, anchored there by one of her luggage tags. *Oh, God. I led him right to her!*

Max rested steady hands on her shoulders. "This can wait."

"No it can't. He came here because of me." Afraid to disturb any fingerprints, Kaycee read the note aloud without touching it. *"Will she die in your place? Call in the authorities and her blood will be on your*

J o d i e   L a r s e n

hands alone. The game goes on. Your move!" Kneeling as close as she
could to the angel, she began to study the handwriting, trying her best
to maintain enough professional distance to be objective.

Taking a deep breath, she leaned back and closed her eyes. Images
unfurled slowly at first, then streamed in flashes. In a matter of
moments, Kaycee visualized Willy Thornton's other handwriting
samples so accurately that she cringed, the same way she had the first
time she touched them.

When she opened her eyes, Max and B.J. were standing a few feet
away, openly staring at her. "It's definitely him."

Max nodded. "Can you tell anything else?"

Her hand was shaking as she pointed at the note. "Before, his anxiety, his outrage were tightly reigned in. He was at least trying to con-
form to some of society's more basic rules. But now. . ."

"Now?" B.J. anxiously asked.

She drew a ragged breath. "Now he's free, actually happy. The
world is his playground. In his mind, he's the king, the rest of us are
pawns. I'm not sure, but I think that whatever he had planned before
now seems less important to him, as if he's found something more ful-
filling. Niki's life is nothing to him. Notice how he referred to her as
'she' instead of by name? She's an object. A means to get to the desired
end."

B.J. shook his head. "Niki told me that you could tell all sorts of
things just by looking at someone's handwriting. For her sake, I hope
that this time, you're wrong. 'Cause if I understand what's going on,
you're saying this guy has totally lost it, that's he playing some kind of
kinky game with people's lives."

Kaycee replied, "That's as good a way to put it as any."

Max extended his hand to help her stand. "I'm sorry, Kaycee, but
we've got to call Agent Jones and get the FBI involved right away."

She sighed. "I know. We can give him the basics on the phone,
then meet with him late tomorrow."

"Tomorrow? He's not going to like that one bit."

"Tough. Now Niki's life is at stake, too. I think it's more important now than ever that we find the place on the road first thing in the morning when there's good light. Maybe we can pick up his trail. I'd bet my life that Thornton's taken Niki to the same place he's hiding Maggie."

Max sighed. "If this really is a game to him, I'm sure you're right. I'll go call Jones and make sure he understands how important it is that they be discreet. Would you look around, see if Thornton left anything behind that we can get his scent from?" He started to leave, then turned back. His eyes revealed the depth of his compassion as he added, "And we'll need something that has Niki's scent, too."

Kaycee nodded. Carefully choosing her footing, she made her way through the house, trying to notice if anything was missing, or if Thornton had accidentally left something behind. By the time she finished her inspection, Max was stepping back inside. In his hands were two large plastic bags. "Jones is notifying a response team that will come in undercover. Find anything?" he asked.

"Follow me." When they were in the bedroom, she pointed at the space between the bed and the wall. "I'd bet anything that he used that pillow on the floor. See how the table is ajar, and the phone is on the bed. Niki *always* keeps everything in its place."

"Perfect," Max replied as he bagged the pillow. "Now, how about something that would have Niki's scent?"

"Would her hair brush work?"

"You bet."

Kaycee led him into the bathroom. "At first, I thought a couple of things were missing, but I found most of them out in the garage. I think he dumped them when he ambushed her."

"What's out there?"

"Her jewelry box, some kitchen knives—"

"So he was waiting here when she came home. Most likely, he planned this after you escaped. Hearing you on the phone probably made his day. He thrives on terrorizing people."

"I'm sure you're right." She pointed at the Caller ID box. "It's not blinking."

"So?" Max asked.

"That red light would be blinking to indicate a new call if he hadn't checked it."

Max nodded, pushing the button with a gloved hand to reveal the last caller's number. As they expected, Randy's cell phone number appeared. "With this, he has the way to communicate with you—or more precisely, to scare the hell out of you. I hate to say it, but I'd bet he's planning to use your sister to lure you into some kind of trap. His game is heating up."

"Then we'd better hurry. We have to find the hole that snake's crawled into before he can hurt anyone else."

CHAPTER **21**

E ven with Stagga at her side, Kaycee didn't feel safe in the dismal motel room. They had decided to spend the night outside Angel Fire, so they could begin the search first thing in the morning. In her heart, she knew that somewhere in the nearby forest both Maggie and Niki were in desperate need of help.

Crawling out of bed, Kaycee grabbed both pillows and propped them on the floor beside Stagga. Leaning her head onto her knees, she tried to remember every detail of the morning she had first encountered Max and Stagga. It was easy to recall the shock of spotting them on the road directly in her path, and everything after that initial scare.

The tough part was what had led to that moment. Mostly it was a blur of white-knuckled driving through curtains of blowing snow. How far up the road had that truck splashed slush across her windshield? Was it really the same type of vehicle Thornton tried to kidnap her in or was that merely wishful thinking? Frustrated, she wished she had been more alert, more in tune with her other senses.

Curling around Stagga's warmth, she fell into a fitful sleep. For the first time in days, the nightmare returned. Total darkness trapped her inside a world that shivered and shuddered. But this time, she wasn't alone in the suffocating void. This time there were cries in the distance, voices screaming for help.

Bolting upright, Kaycee's heart pounded as her senses slowly came back to reality. Still on the floor, she looked around the dimly lit room. Stagga sat at her side, anxiously whining. "It's okay, boy. Just a bad dream." Stretching, Kaycee walked to the window and peered into the night. White crystals danced in the light just outside her room, and she realized that in the morning the fresh layer of snow would make their job even harder. Crawling into the bed, she patted a spot near her feet. "Come on up, boy. We're in for a tough day tomorrow."

Stagga hopped onto the bed, curling happily into a ball atop the worn bedspread. Kaycee tossed and turned the remainder of the night, unable to stop picturing all the tragedies that could unfold the next day.

· · · · ·

Kim unlocked the door to the motel room in Taos a little after one a.m., totally exhausted. After kicking the door closed, she flipped on the lights and gasped, shocked to see Roger in one of the beds. "What are you doing back so soon?" she asked.

Rubbing the sleep from his eyes, he leaned onto one elbow as he cleared his throat. "Waiting for you. It's late."

"What about your load?"

He shrugged. "It'll have to wait. Where have you been?"

"Your work is important. You shouldn't have come back."

Roger suppressed a yawn. "Listen, I know it isn't my business, but do you have any idea what kind of trouble you're in?"

Kim nervously paced. "How did you find out?"

"The FBI is looking for you! They had some sort of watch out for me because I reported your wreck. They thought I might have helped you escape."

"What did you tell them?" she asked, biting her thumbnail.

"Nothing. At least, not yet. They think you're involved in a kidnapping, Kim! What the hell is going on?"

Kim stiffened. "I had nothing to do with kidnapping Maggie. I wanted to help her get away! That's why he tried to kill me by running me off that road!"

"Then go to the police. Tell them where he's hiding her."

"It's not that easy, Roger. She's in an old mine, and he's got it booby trapped. If he sees anyone coming, she'll die!"

"The police have bomb squads, Kim. They'll know what to do."

"Willy's not going to let the police catch him. But I think there's a way I can stop him, then get help for Maggie."

"How?"

"There's an old trailer he sleeps in sometimes. If I can catch him there, I think I'd have a chance."

"Catch him?"

"I'm not going to kill him—" she hesitated, then added, "—unless I absolutely have to."

Roger shook his head, amazed that he was sitting there listening to a such a pretty young woman talk about murder the way most girls her age would discuss a bad date. "What did you have in mind?"

Kim's intense grey eyes locked onto his. "I have a plan, Roger. I just want to make sure he hasn't got Maggie there. If not, then when he comes back to go to sleep, I'll trap him by slashing his tires or something. That way, if Maggie is still in that mine, I'll have time to get her. She'll be safe, and he'll never know how she got away."

Roger was wary. "It's too dangerous."

"No. Leaving Willy on the loose is too dangerous."

He thought for a moment. "You've been through so much for someone so young."

"I'm older than I look."

"What? Nineteen? Twenty?"

Her stance straightened. "I'll be twenty-two next month."

"If you live that long. . ."

Ignoring him, Kim walked across the room and shrugged off her coat. Turning away to block Roger's view, she slipped the gun out of her jeans and tucked it under the jacket. When she was back at his side, she rubbed her arms and timidly asked, "Would you mind if I sleep with you? It's awfully cold outside."

Before he had a chance to answer, she peeled off her turtleneck sweater and jeans. Crawling in, her naked breasts were cold against his chest as she sensuously curled one leg across his thighs. "I'm so glad you came back."

Roger tried to decipher the look in her eyes—eyes that had seen far too much, too early in life. Moist, as if on the verge of tears, they glistened with a longing that he'd never seen before. Whatever it was, it touched him deep inside, made him forget everything. Everything except Kim.

Speechless, he could barely nod when she buried her head in the covers. Even though half his brain was screaming he had finally found heaven, he heard his own hoarse voice whisper, "You don't have to do this, Kim. I'll help you anyway."

Kim replied in the only way she'd ever known—with her tongue, her hands, her body. But the empty feeling that usually crept inside was strangely absent. For the first time in her life, she actually *wanted* to be with this man, to show him that she truly cared about him, and more importantly, about herself.

· · · · ·

Bob Palmer glanced at the two men seated across from him in CSI's elaborate conference room. All three were clearly tense in their perfectly starched shirts with impeccably knotted silk ties, even though it was barely six o'clock in the morning. Palmer drank a long swig of steaming coffee, glared at his counterparts, Brock Bauer and Frank Moore, then began. "I've called this meeting because the Thornton matter has gotten completely out of hand. I got a call last night from the FBI. Seems Thornton kidnapped Niki Miller, Kaycee Miller's paraplegic sister. Even though they offered protection to Kaycee, she's taken it upon herself to track down Thornton and catch him."

Moore tilted back in his chair and chuckled. "Sounds like we decided to offer her a job at precisely the right time. At least she's got nerve." Reacting to Palmer's unbending gaze, he shifted nervously and resumed his study of the prismatic film that swirled atop his coffee.

Palmer warned, "I don't want to lose track of Kaycee Miller at this point. I don't need to remind either of you how much we have at stake now. Besides the value of the property, the information alone in Thornton's possession could—" He was interrupted by the ringing of the telephone. Slapping the console on the credenza behind him, he barked, "Palmer, here."

Over the speaker phone, they all heard, "Mr. Palmer, this is Kaycee Miller."

After exchanging a triumphant smile with the others, he answered in a much softer voice. "I've been hoping you'd call. Have you decided to come interview?"

"Actually, I haven't had a chance to consider it yet. Willy Thornton is proving to be something straight out of a nightmare. He . . . He kidnapped my sister last night."

"Oh, my God. I'm so sorry. Listen, I know it's not much, but I'll put my top two investigators on it first thing this morning. They're the best. If anyone can find her, they can."

"Thank you, but I don't think that will be necessary. I have an idea where he may be hiding."

All three men perked up, leaning toward the speaker phone. "Really? Where?" Palmer asked.

"That's the problem. I don't know an exact location, but I think I can narrow it down to a general area in the Kit Carson National Forest in the next few hours."

"Kaycee, let us help search. I'll bring the two investigators I was telling you about. Just call us with a rendezvous location and we'll be there within minutes in the corporate helicopter."

"I will. Thank you so much."

"Kaycee, are there any official agencies involved yet?"

"The FBI knows he has my sister, but at this point they don't know where we plan to search."

"That may be for the best."

The men exchanged a glance. "Why?"

"As I told you, we're keeping very close tabs on the Thornton situation. It's possible our inside source hasn't checked in with us because it would risk blowing his cover. If the authorities barge in, he would probably be killed. We'd rather not take that risk unless it becomes absolutely necessary."

"I see." In the background, they could hear a knock at her door. "I'll be in touch with you as soon as possible."

"Be careful, Kaycee. Thornton is a cold-blooded murderer."

"Believe me, I know."

Palmer hung up, then punched a series of numbers on the face of the sophisticated phone. The digital display showed a variety of information, including the name of the hotel where the call originated.

Standing, Palmer pushed away from the desk. "Gentlemen, we've got to work to do. Meet me at the helicopter in five minutes. For now, we'll track Miller without her knowledge, see how well she operates under pressure. We can kill two birds with one stone. Observe Miller in action, and hopefully wrap up our Thornton problem."

•　•　•　•　•

Thornton woke to a growling stomach and an urge to kill. As he methodically prepared for the day, his rising tide of excitement helped him devise a series of moves he was certain would bring Kaycee Miller straight to his trap. And this time, she wouldn't get away. She would watch her sister's agony, then it would be her turn to suffer.

With a glance at his arm, he shook his head at the memory of last night. Beside the mending imprints of the first one's bite were inflamed fresh puncture wounds, made by the teeth of the feisty one who couldn't even walk. Those two deserved to rot in hell together.

The sun was barely above the horizon when Thornton knocked aside the fresh, powdery snow to pop open the trunk of the El Dorado parked next to the trailer. She was still there, in the exact place he'd tossed her last night, her legs akimbo, set at an odd angle to her torso.

If it had been that first woman, he'd have tied her up, but Thornton didn't consider this one to be much of a threat—at least not as long as he stayed away from that foul mouth of hers. Jabbing her in the side, he stepped back to be sure she wasn't going to try to attack. But something was wrong—she wasn't moving.

Nudging her shoulder with one hand, he watched for any sign of a response as he muttered, "Wake up! It's almost time to play." If she was breathing at all, he couldn't tell. The pillowcase he had loosely taped over her head didn't allow him to see her face, and her chest seemed absolutely still beneath her heavy coat.

"No! I need you alive!" he screamed, ripping the tape so he could jerk the cloth roughly over her head. Furious with himself, he watched her limp body, sure she must have either suffocated or frozen to death overnight.

Leaning close, his face was directly over hers when her eyes flew open. Before he could react, she began wildly spraying him with a can of de-icer. Thrusting away from her, his head thumped as it banged the lid of the trunk. Dazed, he almost fell on top of her as she stepped up her assault, flailing at his face and arms with an ice scraper in one hand, the can of de-icer in the other.

"Son of a bitch!" he wailed, blinded by the searing methyl alcohol. Pitching backward, he cussed, reeled painfully against the mobile home, then spun around for several moments trying to wipe the stinging liquid from his eyes. Catching a glimpse of her trying to push herself out of the trunk, he whirled around, barely managing to kick her back, before he slammed the lid closed with her safely trapped inside.

Dropping onto his knees in the snow, he plunged his head into the cold, wet powder, dragging as much of the soothing substance as he could toward his wounded face with his thrashing arms. When the burning finally eased, he leaned back on his heels and said, "You'll pay for that!"

Although her voice was muffled, he could clearly hear Niki's antagonistic reply, "So will you!"

For a brief moment he considered opening the trunk again so he could beat the hell out of her, but then he remembered. She still had that can, and he was sure she'd use it again. It took all his effort, all the willpower he possessed, not to shoot her through the metal. Staggering to his feet, he stalked back into the mobile home, screaming, "Killing you will be a pleasure!"

• • • • •

Thornton didn't hear Niki's furious reply, "If I don't get you first!" Inside the trunk, her fist still clenched the de-icer as her heart raced. Nothing made sense, nothing except keeping that creep from touching her and figuring a way to get out of this mess.

Last night, he had muttered something about a game, and just now he said it was almost time to play. But what kind of game could she play? She couldn't run, couldn't hide. . .After a few frustrating minutes, she gave up. It was hopeless. Only that psycho knew what he had in mind, and she really didn't care to find out.

Starting to relax a little, she realized that for the first time since this nightmare started, she could actually see. Without the pillowcase to block the light, there was a ray of morning sunlight pouring in from outside. Scooting closer to the rear, it was obvious that the brake light was cracked, probably in the struggle, and that part of the carpet was caught beneath the lid, keeping the compartment from sealing completely. Pushing with her strongest arm, she pressed her face against the crack to try to see the ground behind the car.

In the white world outside, there was no sign of the monster, only the impressions he'd left in the snow. Memories of childhood overwhelmed her. She'd always loved to make snow angels, while Kaycee had preferred staying warm and dry. Warm and dry. Where was Kaycee now?

I'm not going to play his game!

Scooting back, it didn't take long for her to find something she could use to escape. In a few minutes she had shifted her lower body and positioned the tire tool for maximum leverage. Using all of her upper body strength, she held her breath as she pried at the thin gap near the lock. Hearing a small pop, she fell back, watching wide-eyed as the trunk silently inched open.

Niki instinctively cringed and grabbed the can of de-icer as she was slowly exposed to the world by the promising, terrifying light of day.

Pulling the lid almost closed again, she thought, *I can't believe it actually worked. Now what? I can't run. . . Even if I could manage to drag myself into the woods, I'd leave a trail that a monkey could follow. Why can't anything be easy?*

CHAPTER 22

"**R**ise and shine! The sun's up!" Max called.

"Coming!" Kaycee hung up the phone and rushed to slide the chain off the door.

Stagga greeted Max with the enthusiasm of a playful child, his plume of a tail eagerly brushing the floor. After tousling the hair between his ears and giving him a hug, Max hurled a ball into the snow-covered parking lot for him to chase.

Watching Stagga dash off, Kaycee admitted, "He's easy to get attached to. When I woke up this morning, I was so upset about Niki that I wanted to scream. But Stagga kept following me around, nudging me. It was like he was trying to say everything would be okay."

"That's because everything *will* be okay."

Inviting Max in, Kaycee grinned. "What? No breakfast?"

Max smiled. "So I've thoroughly spoiled you already? Must be some kind of a record."

Her reply was a sly grin and a nod.

"Sorry to disappoint you so early in the day, but as far as I can tell nothing's open yet. We'll have to get something later, or make due with my survival rations." He whipped two granola bars out of one of the many pockets sewn to the outside of his khaki pants, offering one to her.

Crinkling her nose, she eyed him from head to toe then remarked, "Maybe later. Interesting attire."

"Standard rescue apparel. What I don't have on me will be in my pack. Speaking of which, do you need help packing?" he asked, scanning the room.

"Of course not. I barely have enough with me to need a bag."

Unable to contain her nervous energy, she added, "But I have some good news. I just got off the phone with Bob Palmer. He wants to help in any way he can. Apparently, he and some of the people who work at CSI can help search on a moment's notice. All we have to do is call."

"Randy and Cal are ready and waiting in Cimarron. As soon as we notify them of the exact area, they can respond in under twenty minutes. Once the SAR teams have narrowed the search, you can contact CSI for backup. Sounds like this crazy scheme is actually going to come together."

"Did you hear anything from Agent Jones?"

"I just contacted him. Not that anyone doubted you, but you were right about it being Thornton. His prints were all over Niki's house, that note on the angel, even the driver's door of the van. He did offer some encouraging news, something I don't think either of us thought of last night."

"What?" she asked, following him to the Trooper.

"There wasn't any blood at Niki's house, or near the van. She must have gone without a struggle."

"She's practically paralyzed from the waist down! Of course she went without a struggle. I'm glad she did, too. He's so far gone he might remember too late that he needs her."

"What do you think his prime objective is now?"

"I'd guess he's pulled between getting Maggie out of state and finding me. That's assuming he went straight to my sister's place without stopping to get Maggie first."

"Either way, his scent should be fresh enough for Stagga to recognize. Randy's dog, Smokey, is an excellent air sniffer, too. If Thornton's anywhere in the area, between the two of them we'll find him."

"Or them."

"You mean Maggie and Niki?"

She shook her head. "No, I mean the inside man from CSI. Palmer told me that he didn't want the authorities in on this since it might endanger his life."

"I'm not sure I agree with that logic. Their man may not have a chance *without* the authorities."

"Either way, I wouldn't want to be in his shoes," Kaycee countered, trying to keep her teeth from chattering. Even though she was wearing two layers of long underwear beneath an insulated one-piece black ski suit, she felt her flesh crawl. But the chill she fought wasn't from the brisk mountain weather, it emanated solely from a bitter, growing fear of the day ahead.

Crawling inside the Trooper, Kaycee closed the door and watched Max toss the ball a few more times before opening the back door for Stagga to leap inside.

After knocking the snow from his rugged boots, Max climbed behind the wheel. "Ready?"

She nodded. "As ready as I can be."

"Then we're off!" With a shrewd grin he pulled onto the highway as he commented, "Oh, by the way, you weren't supposed to let Stagga sleep up on the bed. He's gotta stay tough. Remember?"

Shocked, Kaycee demanded, "How'd you know?"

"He tells me everything."

After eyeing Max, then Stagga, she closed her eyes to remember every detail of the morning, quickly recalling Max's lingering gaze at the unmade bed in her room. Glaring at Stagga, she commanded, "Next time, don't shed on the bedspread. Okay?"

Stagga ignored her, making three small circles before curling into a tight ball in the middle of the back seat.

"Excellent deductive reasoning."

Kaycee shifted her gaze to Max. "Is that a compliment?"

"Of course."

"Then, thank you. By the way, you should be ashamed of yourself. Stagga would never betray a secret."

"Maybe not on purpose."

"What's that supposed to mean?"

"It means that people, and dogs, can only do so much."

Kaycee felt, more than heard, the change in the tone of his voice. Before, he'd been playful, but now he was so serious it made her flinch. Gooseflesh crawled up her arms as she realized that Ellen had been right—her hearing was becoming more instinctive, more sensitive. With a sigh, she leaned back and said, "Okay, I'm ready. Let's have the lecture."

He took her hand. "Sometimes, no matter how hard we try, certain things just aren't meant to be. Bad things happen. That doesn't mean they're our fault, or that if we'd done something else, the end result would be any different."

She pushed back his sleeve to touch his bracelet. "I know what you're trying to prepare me for, and I really do appreciate your concern."

"I'm worried about you, Kaycee."

"Well, then, I guess we're even, because I'm terrified that just because you met me, something horrible is going to happen to you."

"That's exactly the attitude I'm warning you about! You don't control my decisions, and it was *my* choice to come with you, to help you."

Squeezing his hand, she leaned over to gently place a kiss on his cheek. "Do you know how much it means to me that you were willing to bring me here? To risk so much for me, for a little girl you don't even know, and now, for my sister?"

He nodded, putting his arm around her. They rode in silence for a few minutes before he softly said, "We first met about five miles down this road. Just tell me when you want me to slow down, and remember we can always turn back if we miss the spot the first time."

Kaycee tried to match the blurred memories of that day with the brittle white forest that surrounded them. Searching the left side of the road, she pointed and said, "We need to watch for places where a road comes in over there."

He nodded, slowing down to twenty-five miles per hour. It wasn't long before he said, "This is where Stagga and I took a leap of faith."

"Already?" she gasped, disheartened.

"It's okay. I'll turn around and we can try again. With the fresh snow, actually seeing a road may be impossible. Can you remember anything else? A landmark?"

She shrugged, fighting one more time to remember as he reversed their path. When they were heading in the right direction again, she suddenly bolted upright, pointing at a large yellow and black sign that indicated a sharp S turn ahead. "That's it! That road sign! I had just looked at it when a truck appeared out of nowhere and threw slush across the windshield!"

Max stopped, thankful there wasn't any oncoming traffic. About twenty yards past the sign was a gap in the trees barely large enough for a vehicle to pass through. With a wary look, he warned, "Hold on. This looks like it's going to be a bumpy ride."

· · · · ·

Roger watched Kim inhale her third McDonald's bacon, egg, and cheese biscuit as they drove, wondering how such a petite woman could eat so much. Brushing a crumb from the corner of her mouth, his finger grazed the bruise on her cheek, a silent reminder that she had barely started to heal. "Are you sure you're up to the hike? I really think you should stay in the semi. Just draw me a map, then I'll find the place, check it out and come back to you."

Shaking her head, Kim downed the last few drops of her second orange juice. "You'd never find it alone. We'll have to park the rig at a scenic overlook on the main road, then circle in from behind. I've only been there twice, and never from the back, so we might not spot it right away. Don't worry about me, I'll be all right since we'll have to go really slow."

Reacting to the distant look in her eyes, he asked, "Mind telling me why?"

"Willy probably has wired the woods. You know, set lines that will sound an alarm if they're triggered, maybe even worse. I know he's done it to the mine, and he's certainly crazy enough not to care who or what he hurts."

"Sounds like we're in for a fun day."

"Believe me, anything that involves Willy is *not* fun."

.   .   .   .   .   .

Niki shifted her weight, scanning the area on each side of the car from her limited viewpoint inside the trunk. Toward the rising sun was a small, open yard area bordered by a line of pine trees so tightly packed that she was certain it was the edge of a forest. Only two feet from the other side of the car was the end of an old, white mobile home. Straight ahead, a battered metal farm gate blocked the narrow dirt road.

She couldn't help but be relieved when she realized that the occasional muffled shouts she'd been hearing were from a radio talk show seeping through the thin walls. Gathering her nerve, Niki nudged the trunk lid farther up, thankful to see only one small, opaque window on the nearby wall of the trailer house.

Knowing she would hit the ground hard, she still pushed and pulled until her torso dangled far enough over the bumper that the dead weight of her legs finally followed with a thud. Frozen in a contorted heap, she listened, praying he hadn't heard. Only the sharp ring of laughter from the radio floated on the wind.

Niki fell into the chaos of unsettled snow where Thornton had writhed after her attack, gasping from the pain that shot through her twisted shoulder. Pivoting back toward the car, it took all her upper body strength to push herself up onto the bumper to reach the lid. Balancing on one trembling arm, she barely managed to pull the top slowly down until the latch finally caught hold.

Again, she tumbled into the snow, breathing hard and fast. Scooting like a seal, Niki inched her way under the car, then rested long enough to plan her next move. Twisting her head back to check the trail she'd left, she could only hope that the creep wouldn't notice the difference.

Now what? she wondered, *If he comes out, he'll either run over me or spot me in his rearview mirror as he pulls away.* With a sigh, she shifted back around, her gaze going past, then back to the shabby metal skirt of the mobile home. Niki gathered her strength again and pushed toward a seam in the metal. Even though her goal was only two feet away, it took several minutes for her to carefully maneuver her body so that she was at an angle that would work. Before she could squeeze inside, she had to bend back the sheet metal.

She carefully pried the seam open, thankful that it wasn't bolted or welded closed. The metal whined as it slowly bent upward, leaving barely enough space for her to squeeze inside. Penetrating the dark, damp underbelly of the trailer, Niki meticulously pulled herself along, trying not to make a sound. Without the wind, she could clearly hear the radio announcer's deep voice.

Suddenly, the entire floor above her head groaned, yielding to step after heavy step. His movement renewed her will, reminding her that every second, every breath was precious. There was one last thing she had to do. Circling around, Niki extended her arms to carefully smooth snow over the path she'd left. Satisfied he wouldn't immediately notice the slight changes, she wearily started to bend the metal skirt back into place.

The screen door banged, rocking her entire world.

Niki froze.

Oh, God! He's coming! In that instant, she realized she should have brought the tire tool, the can of de-icer, *anything*. She was completely, utterly defenseless.

CHAPTER **23**

D ue to the dense foliage, the closest spot for Cal to land was almost a half mile away from the point Kaycee had identified. Since there were no fresh tire tracks to follow, they had all agreed that it would be safest to bring in Randy and Smokey, then narrow down the area on foot.

From beneath the whirling blades, Randy jumped to the ground first, then turned back to lift out Smokey. Cal immediately took off, eager to scrutinize the landscape from above.

Max greeted Randy with a firm handshake and a rough pat on the back. "Thanks again for coming."

"Wouldn't have missed this for the world. I've got everything we need to go over, but I'll warn you up front, the weather doesn't look good for the next few hours."

Max nodded, leading the way to the Trooper as he explained to Kaycee, "Randy has the latest forecast information and topographical maps of this mountain. Wind speed, direction, and surface irregularities all factor into how we approach the area. We try to search into the wind whenever possible, taking into account what pattern the scent plumes will follow. The maps will help us lay out how to cover the area and avoid interfering with each other."

Randy chimed in, "Smokey and Stagga have worked so many rescues together that it usually isn't a problem. Today we've got a bigger obstacle."

Max frowned. "Which is?"

"They're forecasting increased wind speed until after 2 p.m., with gusts over 40 mph. Even though the trees will block a lot of it, there's still going to be some deceptive alternating currents to deal with. It's almost ten-thirty now. I think we might be better off waiting a couple of hours." He unfolded the map and pointed, "We'll begin along these ridges where we'll have the benefit of the daytime updrafts."

Kaycee nervously asked, "What happens when we run out of daylight?"

Max replied, "Search dog teams are quite effective at night, especially in areas like this. There's no convection from the heat of the sun, and on cold, calm nights the chilled air usually downslopes, pushing the scent closer to the ground. Handler safety is the only reason to delay, and I think both Randy and I are willing to work as long as it takes. If the dogs rest now, they'll be in good shape for this afternoon and evening."

"And Thornton might not expect to be surprised at night," she added.

"Exactly."

. . . . .

Thornton stormed down the steps of the mobile home, stomping toward the car. As he passed the rear end, he smashed his fist into the trunk so hard that it left a dent. "Game time!" he shouted, then climbed inside.

The engine groaned before dying the first time he tried to start it. Muttering under his breath, he twisted the key in the ignition, pumped the gas pedal, and waited until the motor roared to life. Slamming it into drive, he took off so quickly his back tires slid from side to side as he circled over the small yard up to the gate.

Leaving the car to idle, he stopped long enough to open the gate, pull through, then fasten the padlock once again. Almost as an afterthought, he reached into his shoulder holster and withdrew the gun. At the side of the trunk, he roared, "When we get there, I'm going to open this trunk again." He fired two rounds into the dirt beside the back tire. "If you even *think* of pulling any cute stunts like you did this morning, the next shot will be right between your eyes."

Without waiting for a response, he climbed back behind the wheel and sped away.

• • • • •

Trudging through the woods, Kim and Roger stopped dead in their tracks at the distant sound of gunfire.

Wide-eyed, Kim asked, "Was that what I think it was?"

Roger shrugged. "Don't panic. It could just be rangers setting off avalanche charges, or hunters. In the mountains, sounds can be really deceiving."

Kim didn't believe him. Roger didn't know Willy, didn't understand his sick, twisted logic, or his need to manipulate the world around him. Only days ago she had believed Willy's lies—now the thought of him made her skin crawl. Stepping up the pace, she explained, "It's not too much farther. There should be a frozen pond over the next rise, then the trailer is just down the path from it. Once we get past the pond, we need to start watching for traps. Before you step between two trees, make sure there isn't a clear string."

Roger shook his head, unable to believe someone would actually do the things she described. "How do you know about this path?" he asked.

"Willy likes to hike, and he always insisted I go with him. The trailer actually belongs to some man who only uses it in the summer. Willy comes here as a last resort."

Roger suppressed a groan. "Nice to know we're only going to find him if he's desperate."

"Willy grew up near here, so he knows every inch of these woods. That's how he found the mine—hiking when he was a kid. He stacked rocks in front of it, even planted bushes to help hide it so no one else would stumble across the place. A few years ago, right before he went to jail, he ripped off some rich guy and hid the stuff in there. For some reason, part of the main shaft collapsed while he was in prison. He never told me why he suddenly needed Maggie, but I think it's because she was small enough to crawl in and bring out his stash."

"That's disgusting."

"That's Willy. I told you, he's seriously deranged."

"Is that the pond?"

Kim followed the direction Roger pointed. "Yes!"

"I don't suppose you'd agree to stay here while I go check the place out?"

"No way!"

"Then at least promise me you won't try anything stupid."

Kim stopped, whirling back to face him. Fury burned in her eyes as she snapped, "I didn't ask for your help, Roger. I don't even need it. Don't you ever call me stupid again. I've made up my mind. No one is going to run my life! No one!"

Roger took a step back, flattening his hands and raising them like a shield. "Kim, I just don't want you to let your emotions get you into trouble. If he's there, promise me you'll do what we agreed. I'll slice his tires, then we'll go help the kid."

She sighed, turning away with a shrug. Plowing through the deep bank of snow along the edge of the pond, one hand softly stroked the grip of the small gun tucked into the front of her jeans. When they were near the last ridge, she motioned for Roger to get down as she pointed out a clear trip line. They both inched cautiously forward, moving from tree to tree.

Working up her nerve, Kim peeked around an immense pine, holding her breath. As she expected, the trailer was off to one side of the small valley, its shabby white metal looking dirty and old against the pristine snow.

"Well?" Roger whispered.

"He's not there. But he's been here. Look at the fresh tire tracks going out the gate."

"So we go back to the motel?"

Kim shook her head. "We wait."

"Wait? How long?"

"As long as it takes."

"What if he doesn't show up?"

"He'll be back. Then we'll know if he has Maggie."

Roger was quiet for a long time as they crouched behind the cover of several tall pines. Finally, as his feet were going numb he softly said, "She could be in there, you know."

"Maggie?"

He nodded.

Kim bit her lip. She hadn't considered that Willy might leave Maggie here. Before, he'd been too worried that she could be spotted, that whoever actually owned the place would show up unexpectedly. But now, anything was possible. "Guess we'd better check," Kim said, moving through the trees.

Roger caught her arm, spinning her around. "That wasn't what I was going for."

Twisting free of his grip, she snapped, "If Maggie is in there, we can end this right now. Wouldn't that be the easiest thing for all of us?"

Giving in, Roger nodded.

Kim scrambled within the cover offered by the trees, weaving in and out until she was directly behind the trailer house. "If he comes home now, he won't be able to see our tracks. You'd better go watch for his car while I check the windows."

Roger reluctantly agreed, taking a position where he could see down the weaving dirt road.

Kim broke off a small pine branch and scurried down the slope, swishing the needles behind her to help cover her tracks. She was glad the wind had picked up, since the blowing snow would make it harder for Willy to tell anyone had been there.

The back side of the mobile home had no door, only four large windows. With her heart pounding so hard she thought it would break out of her chest, she stood on her tiptoes to peer inside the bedroom window. The rumpled bed, the clothes strewn about the open closet, all seemed to be waiting like scenery backstage—once essential, now abandoned. Kim watched for several moments, but detected no movement, and more importantly, no child.

Shifting down, she slowly confronted the double windows of the living area. Again, no activity inside, only a dead television, an empty sofa, a large pair of boots by the door, a box of Band-Aids strewn on the kitchen table, and a slip of paper with a phone number scrawled across it.

With every nerve on edge, she stopped to listen. She thought she'd heard a scraping noise, something near, something peculiar. Cocking her head, she waited, mumbling, "Stupid wind." Glancing over her shoulder, she could see Roger hovering in the trees. Pushing on, she gathered her courage to look in the last window. It held no new secrets, just another bedroom, this one stacked with boxes. The trailer really was abandoned, at least for now.

Kim's stomach began churning. She could feel her time running out. Starting to turn, she abruptly stopped again. This time it was the hem of her overalls that had caught on something. Looking down Kim almost screamed, barely stopping the shriek before it gushed out.

Long, pale fingers desperately tugged Kim's pant leg one last time before they shuddered and drew back into the shadows.

· · · · ·

Kaycee, Max, Randy, Cal, Stagga, and Smokey were squeezed into Cal's hotel room in Cimarron. Only the dogs didn't mind how slowly the minutes seemed to tick by. Stagga was softly snoring on the rug beside the bed, while Smokey had stretched out for a nap directly in front of the door. Nervous energy filled the air. Finally Cal broke the silence, asking, "Why don't you help us kill some time, Kaycee?"

She tilted her head, narrowing her eyes, "What'd you have in mind?"

"I thought it might be interesting to learn our deep, dark secrets."

Kaycee shook her head. "And here I am without my crystal ball . . ."

"Max tells us you don't need one. Would you analyze my handwriting? I'd like to know if there's a good reason they call me Crazy Cal."

Glancing first at Max, then Randy, she asked, "Anyone else brave enough to have their innermost passions revealed?"

"Sure," Randy replied. "What do we do?"

"It's really pretty simple. Just copy a paragraph from something and don't put your name on the page. That way, my judgement isn't clouded by the outer personality traits of the individual." Beaming a sly smile to Max, she asked, "Aren't you going to play along?"

He shook his head.

"What's wrong? Afraid I'll see something you'd rather I not know?"

Max sighed. "You realize this is a no-win situation for me."

"Why?"

"Because everyone has bad traits. Everyone."

"And you don't want me to discover yours?"

"Not really. It's kind of like announcing on the first date that you snore like a freight train. Unnecessary information too early in a relationship can destroy a good thing."

She raised her eyebrows. "I see. Latent paranoia. Interesting."

Cal stuffed a piece of paper into Max's hand. "Come on. We've got to make this a challenge. At least give her a little to work with."

Max begrudgingly jotted down a few words, then Cal carried all three samples to Kaycee.

Suddenly, Max jumped up, his eyes sparkling. "I have one other sample we can throw in with the others to make this really interesting. It's in the Trooper. I'll be right back."

Max called Stagga and the two of them slipped outside. Kaycee placed the three samples face down on the table. Without turning them over, she studied each one for a few moments, her fingers caressing the back of the paper, feeling the ridges, the pressure of each man's penmanship. Trying something new, she closed her eyes, seeing if there was any more she could tell by touch alone. To her surprise, she could detect a minute difference.

Max rushed back in, breathless. Tossing Stagga a treat, he asked, "Did I miss anything?"

Cal joked, "Only her mysterious clairvoyant routine. You know, I hadn't noticed it before, but she has the coloring of a gypsy."

Randy raised one finger to his lips. "Shhhh! If you break her concentration she'll decide we're all perverts."

Max laughed. "Actually, that sounds pretty accurate to me. We'd have to be perverted to do what we do." Adding another slip of paper face down with the others, he commented, "Here's the last sample."

As she'd done with the others, she ran her fingers over the paper. Concentrating, she couldn't detect any sign of pressure. With a puzzled glance at Max, she asked, "Are you sure this is a good sample?"

He nodded, then shrugged. "Precisely what would be considered a *bad* sample?"

Scrunching her nose at him, she submitted, "In this case, something computer generated."

"I guarantee you that was not done by a machine."

Kaycee cleared her throat. "Before we start, I think I'd better explain a few basic concepts. First, handwriting samples reflect the person's state of mind *at the time* the sample is written. Unlike our posture and body language which are usually unconscious actions, writing is a conscious effort to convey a message. Even so, the expressive nature of the vulnerable, hidden self shines through."

Cal asked, "What kinds of things do you look for?"

"I consider zones, line slope, slant, pressure, size, spacing, rhythm, letter formation, lead-ins and ending strokes. For instance. . ."

She picked up a pencil and drew four shapes—a square, a cross, a triangle and an X. "Squares are our defense, our security. They symbolize firmness, practicality, stability and logic, although they're frigid, stiff, earthbound and materialistic. Crosses are identified with types of wisdom—spiritual, moral, even idealistic. People who use crosses communicate conceptually as well as concretely." Pointing at the triangle, she continued, "Triangles connect our mental and physical planes, both aggressively and energetically. The direction the triangle points identifies which experiences of the person's life are implicated, such as a desire for recognition, or their physical, emotional, and personal nature.

"Last comes the use of an X in letters other than X. For instance, sometimes lower case g's and y's are X'ed instead of looped. X's are identified with death and endings. Usually they're signs of trouble, since they mark an intense, strong reaction in a negative aspect of life. Thornton's writing was a classic example of full pressure lower zone X's and misplaced capital letters."

"Which means?" Cal asked.

"Violent, over-reactive nature and self-destructive behavior."

Kaycee sensed the tension in the room. Trying to lighten up, she grinned and added, "Now that I've confused everyone, shall we begin?" She was greeted by a round of nervous frowns. "Okay, what's wrong?"

Cal shrugged. "I didn't expect this to be so—"

"So serious?" Kaycee asked. "Are you attentive when you're buzzing around in a helicopter?"

"Damn right I am."

"I take the same pride in my work. Handwriting analysis is not like reading Tarot cards. Every day it becomes more of a science than an art." Flipping over the first sample, she carefully studied it, then announced, "We'll start with this one."

The three men eyed each other, shifting like school kids trying a little too hard to be cool.

After a dramatic pause, Kaycee touched each of the six rightward pointing triangles in the sample then offered, "This person is very ambitious, loves action. He's aggressive in all aspects of his life but finds it frustrating that others don't live up to his high expectations. Professional plans and goals are important to him, so much so that his personal life usually suffers. In general, he appears pessimistic, but on a deeper level he longs for the world to fly right." Nailing Cal with a gleaming smile, she asked, "Well, how'd I do?"

Cal's eyebrows flew up. "What makes you so sure that's my sample?"

"It has the attitude of a pilot. You know—that take charge, always in control, kiss my ass thing you've got going."

Randy and Max cracked up as Cal slowly shook his head. "Very impressive."

Basking in the changed mood of the room, Kaycee flipped over the next sample. "Let's see . . . See the upward triangular strokes in his *m*'s and *d*'s? This person has a probing mind. He searches to find answers, to justify existence in a world filled with inexplicable things. Significance is placed on ability to reason and deduce insightful solutions to problems. He's mentally aggressive, yet prides himself on physical control." She pointed at the left margin, which widened with each line. "He's eager to move on, impatient and optimistic about something major in the near future."

This time she smiled at Max. "I see you know how to keep the skeletons in your closet well hidden."

He winked. "Trust me, they're there."

Her eyes never left his. "I know."

Randy sighed. "Enough! The suspense is killing me!"

"Okay!" Flipping over the third of the four sheets, she burst out laughing. On it was a muddy paw print. Turning her attention to Stagga, she said, "According to this, you have the patience of a saint and the heart of a lion."

Stagga whined, shaking his head so hard his ears flapped.

While everyone else laughed at Stagga's reaction, Randy impatiently flipped over his sample. In spite of his eagerness, Kaycee took her time. As she worked through the sample, first her smile faded, then the line of her jaw hardened. Drawing a deep breath, she began, "Randy's writing is threaded toward the end of each word. See how these letters are less defined? That's an indication of someone who's sensitive and highly impressionable. It's a strong sign of a negotiator and diplomat. If two people are having a problem communicating, Randy wouldn't hesitate to jump right in. He keeps most of his own personality hidden, exerting his energy toward discerning the thoughts and feelings of those around him. High intelligence is indicated, and—"

Randy moved closer, "And what?"

She looked at him, her finger placed beneath the last letter of the final word he had written—*leaving*. "This is the only time you formed a lower zone X. Is this particular '*g*' formed how you normally write, or just a quirk?"

"Far as I know it's a quirk."

She smiled. "Good."

Through a narrow gaze Randy asked, "Why is that good?"

"Don't worry about it. I'm sure it was a fluke. Most people tense up when they know they're about to be analyzed. It's better to have samples taken from daily life." Sensing he wasn't convinced, she smiled. "Listen, I just told you that you were brilliant. What more could you want?"

"The X is the death stroke, isn't it?"

"Randy, handwriting doesn't work that way. There is no such thing as a *death stroke!* All that one little X probably means is that you're nervous about tonight, worried about your safety, as well as everyone else's. I swear."

Shaking his head, Randy walked away muttering, "Leave it to me to draw the death stroke . . ."

CHAPTER 24

Cal and Randy began playing a game of Sequence, both pretending not to listen as Max and Kaycee discussed the plans for the rest of the day. When Kaycee excused herself to go to the bathroom, Max softly said to the other two men, "I sure could use Joan's help."

Randy shot him an amused look. "What's wrong? Kaycee predicting death and destruction for you, too?"

Max sighed, "No. If Joan were here, maybe she could talk some sense into Kaycee. She just doesn't get it. She'd be virtually useless on the search, yet invaluable at the base."

Cal chimed in, "From what I've heard, you're wasting your time. She isn't going to be happy unless she's *in medias res.*"

"Cut the Latin crapola, Cal. Speak English," Randy mumbled.

Cal grinned. "It means she wants to be in the middle of things just like the rest of us. You two are a match made in heaven, or is it hell? Why do bull-headed, strong-willed people attract each other like moths to a lantern? God, if the two of you hit it off, you'll end up just like Joan and Randy."

Randy kicked Cal under the table just as Kaycee emerged from the bathroom. "Funny, Sequence didn't used to be a contact sport," she noted.

Rubbing his leg, Cal snapped, "Guess that depends on how cutthroat your competition is." Without missing a beat, he added, "When I checked out the mountain this morning, I noticed we're probably in for the same kind of radio trouble we had outside Denver. The terrain here is so diverse that we may have to tag the base to relay messages between teams."

Max and Randy both tensed, then nodded as if seriously considering Cal's statement. Max turned to look out the window as Randy said, "Since we don't have anyone to man the base, maybe we should delay the search until Joan can get here."

The three men exchanged profound looks, until Kaycee finally declared, "Have you all gone nuts? We can't afford to wait a second longer than absolutely necessary! That poor little girl may be starving to death right now, and God only knows what he's done to my sister."

Cal empathized, "I know you've never been involved in a rescue before, but there are a few basic tenets we live by. And I do mean *live by*. The first is that we never purposely endanger the lives of the team members—either human or canine." He nodded for her to come closer so he could show her the map. "Let me explain what can happen. Let's say I drop Randy and Smokey on the west end of the search area, and Max and Stagga on the eastern edge. See this peak between them?"

Kaycee's frustration manifested itself in a nervous tapping of one toe. She managed a curt nod.

"There's a good chance it will block their two-way radios. If it does, and there's no one at base—" his finger landed on a mid-point several miles south of the other two, "—then they can't help each other." Cal's eyes met hers, his gaze dead serious. "Last year outside of Denver, we were hunting an escaped con. He clobbered Randy on the head, then left him for dead."

Randy unconsciously rubbed the back of his neck, his eyes glued to the floor.

Cal continued, "Because of the mountains, no one knew he was down. We didn't know he was gone until we all met at the predetermined point. If Randy didn't have such a hard head, he probably would've died."

Kaycee nodded and turned to Randy. "Wow. Lying there unconscious for God knows how long, then waking up all alone except for Smokey. You must have been absolutely terrified."

"Well. . ."

"And having a person at a base would've made a difference. They'd have found you so much faster. . .Right?"

"Of course."

"But Cal said you were unconscious. Does Smokey know how to call for help? How to give the location of a downed man?"

Max was biting his lip, trying not to laugh while the other two sheepishly grinned.

"Okay. The men win. I'll stay at the base. But only because Cal made up such an elaborate story to try to keep me out of the field. Cal, you really should take acting classes. Now if you'll excuse me, I think I'll go for a walk." High stepping, she added, "The crap's getting pretty deep in here."

Max asked, "Mind if I tag along?"

"Are you going to try to convince me to go back to Tulsa and sit in an FBI safe house until they find Thornton?"

He quickly shook his head.

"Then you can come."

After bundling up, they gently nudged Smokey, who half-heartedly lifted his eyelids before resuming his nap. As they stepped into the wind, Max pulled the hotel door shut, then wrapped his arms around Kaycee's waist. "Don't be mad at them. They're only trying to help."

"I know. And I know they're right. I have no business running around out there in the dark. I really am pretty useless."

Max moved directly in her path, his face just inches from hers. "You are far from useless. But there's a time and a place for everything. For the search, you'd be in the way—one more scent for the dogs to filter. Tension always runs high at times like these, and every one of us knows that this is far from a routine search. Even though we're looking for victims, it's just as likely we'll stumble across Thornton instead."

"And if you do?"

"We'll backtrack, radio his position to the authorities, and confront him only if necessary."

"Will you and Randy be armed?"

"We both carry survival knives, have pistols in our backpacks, and you have first hand experience with how protective a SAR K-9 can be. By the way, how'd you know Cal was trying to pull one over on you with that story about Denver?"

"The way you turned away, and the flash of doubt in Randy's eyes. I can see why they play Sequence instead of poker."

"Part of what Cal said is true. Rough terrain really can interfere with radio reception."

"I'm sure it can." For several minutes they walked in silence, the wind plastering their clothes against them one moment, only to shift directions the next. Kaycee was quickly learning to hate the wind. When it howled through the trees, it drowned all the beautiful noises she was finally growing to appreciate.

Taking a deep breath, she tugged on Max's jacket. He moved in front of her, so his body took most of the wind's impact. Reaching up, she stroked his cheek. "There's something I need to tell you."

He simply nodded, pulling her a little closer.

"This isn't easy for me. I haven't—" The phone in Max's pocket rang. With wide eyes, she asked, "Do you think it's him?"

Max shrugged, quickly pulling the cell phone out and flipping it open. "You'd better answer," he said, holding it between them as he did his best to block the wind.

Kaycee's voice was fragile, hesitant. "Hello. . ."

"Ready to play?"

As if staggered by a bolt of lightning, every nerve in her body reacted to his voice. White-hot anger flowed from deep within as she hissed, "Where's my sister?"

"She's waiting for you." He laughed, a repulsive, deep-throated noise. "In fact, she's dying to see you!"

Through gritted teeth, Kaycee demanded, "Where is she?"

"That depends. Where are you?"

Max violently shook his head. Lying, Kaycee quickly snapped, "I'm in Angel Fire. Where's Niki? I need to talk to her."

There was a long hesitation, so long Kaycee snatched the phone from Max's hand so she could press it firmly to her ear. Fighting the wind, she heard a blunt noise, followed by a string of muffled cuss words. Her heart was pounding as she cried, "Hello! Are you there? Let me talk to Niki!"

"Later! Part of the game is wondering how long she can wait for you to save her."

The line went dead. Kaycee stared at it for a few seconds until Max took the phone from her hand and pulled her close. "Why did he hang up?" he asked.

"Something's wrong, Max. His voice, it—" she wavered, shaking her head.

"It what?" he urged.

Their eyes met. "It changed. Dramatically. Something caught him off guard, made him alter his plans on the spot."

"Do you think he was going to arrange to meet you somewhere?"

She nodded, shivering. "It's like I he's reaching out for me, trying to wrap around me."

Stroking her shoulders, he whispered, "You're safe."

"But Niki isn't. Max, at first his words carried the same degree of threat, but then the pitch was suddenly so different, so strained. Something happened to Niki. I can feel it."

With a sideways glance he asked, "Are you sure you only analyze handwriting?"

If I tell him I have RP now, he'll insist I stay out of this! Turning away, Kaycee started back toward the motel. "Max, I'm not a mind reader. It's really very complicated, but I've started working with a woman named Ellen. She's teaching me to be more aware of my surroundings. How to develop my senses, use them more efficiently."

"Sounds like a fascinating class."

"It's not exactly a class. . ." With renewed urgency she replied, "Don't ask me to explain it, because I can't right now. All I know is that if Thornton was mad before, now he's downright furious."

"Which means?"

"We'd better hurry. I think we just ran out of time."

As they rushed back to the hotel, neither Kaycee nor Max gave the two men sitting in a parked car across the street a second thought.

•   •   •   •   •

"Maggie?" Kim gasped, reluctantly bending closer to the ground. "Is that you?"

The voice was muffled, barely audible. "I. . .need help."

Dropping to her knees, Kim's cheek grazed the snow as she bent back the metal skirt, squinting to see into the dark void. A face hovered in the depth of the shadow, looming eerily behind two outstretched, quivering hands.

"Who are you?" Kim asked. "Why are you under there?"

"Please. . .help me. . .So cold. . ."

"I will. Did Willy do this to you?"

She could barely see the woman's uncertain shrug. "It was a. . .big man. He's crazy. Please. . .I can't walk."

"Hold on. We'll help you."

"Hurry! He'll be back. . .he has. . .a gun!"

Even though the woman's voice was weak, it carried such urgency that Kim cringed. With a moan, she replied, "I know."

Standing, Kim waved for Roger to come help. In a few seconds he was at her side. "Is it her?" he asked.

Kim whispered, "It's not Maggie. But we've got to get that woman out of here. She's must be hurt really bad. She says she can't walk."

Roger leaned down, trying not to let the depth of his concern show on his face as he bent the entire section of sheet metal out of their way. With a thin smile he asked, "Can we pull you out by your arms?"

"Yes! Hurry!"

Together, Roger and Kim each took a wrist and dragged Niki's limp, cold body out. Both were so shocked, they didn't know what to say. It was apparent the woman had been through hell. Her entire body was covered with dirt, numerous cuts dotted her face and arms.

When they tried to help her stand, her legs wobbled uselessly.

Barely able to hold her head up, she sighed, "I can't walk."

Roger soothed, "It's okay. We'll help you—"

"—Niki."

"Okay, Niki. Just relax and let us do all the work." It was obvious that her long struggle had left her too weak to help them. At first, they tried balancing her weight between them, but it was too hard on Kim's diminutive frame. After a few yards Roger bent low, coming up with Niki's body drooped over his shoulder, fireman style. As they crossed the first incline, a bone-chilling blast of wind almost knocked them over.

Roger staggered, then stopped. Adjusting Niki's body weight, he sternly said, "Kim, you'd better go smooth our tracks. Step where I've been when you come back up so we'll only leave one trail."

Kim nodded, silently slipping over the ridge. In only a second, she frantically returned. "Hurry! I saw a car turn down the road! He's coming!"

Roger knew it was impossible to run with his burden. Moving as quickly as he could, he said in a low, calm voice, "Kim, get the keys out of my pocket and follow our original path back to my rig. We need it warm, ready to go as soon as we get there. Do you know how to start it?"

She nodded. "I think so. I drove one once, but wasn't very good at it."

Etched on her face was a degree of terror Roger had never before witnessed—it sent chills through him, kicking in primal survival instincts. He quickly reviewed how to start the rig's motor and operate the gears, then ordered, "You go on ahead. We'll veer off across the pond to create a different path. That way he won't know which one to follow. We'll be a few minutes behind you. Keep the doors locked until you see us."

Kim hesitated.

"Go!" Roger roared.

She left with a frightened, "Be careful."

Roger watched Kim bolt halfway around the frozen pond before she stopped in her tracks. Reversing her steps, she ran back to him. "You might need this," she said as she placed a small gun in the palm of his hand.

Taking the weapon, he planted a quick kiss on her forehead and pushed her away. "Hurry!"

—

C H A P T E R **25**

B y the time Thornton arrived back at the mobile home, his arrogant confidence had returned. Sure, the crippled one had managed to throw him a curve, but in the end what did it matter? There was no way she could drag her useless body far enough to escape. No way. Besides, what did he care if she froze to death in a snow bank, or took a bullet between the eyes? Dead is dead.

As he parked in the same spot as before, he decided that playing mind games with her might be fun. But this time, when he crawled out of the car, his gun was drawn. This woman was a lot like the other, and he had no intention of letting her get away alive.

He hardly noticed the blowing snow pelting his face as he walked slowly around the car, searching for her trail. At first, Thornton wasn't sure exactly what to look for, so he merely scanned the area. On the second pass, something caught his eye. The weathered metal skirting bowed slightly out at a seam, flipping up right before it touched the ground.

Thornton was sure it wasn't like that before. A knowing smile crept across his face as he thought, *The scared little rabbit ran into a hole. Guess I'll just have to flush her out.*

Crossing to the front porch steps, he knocked the snow off his boots and stepped inside. Flipping open the cooler, he grabbed a beer and snapped it open. After a long, satisfying gulp, he plopped down onto the sofa to devise a plan.

Although he hadn't noticed it before, his head was aching. Leaning back, he closed his eyes to think of ways to convince a rabbit to come to the wolf. A kaleidoscope of images spun in his mind— visions of death, some fast, most slow. Narrowing his choices, he would only settle for ways he could witness her suffering. After all, it was *her* fault he hadn't taken more food and water to Maggie.

He hadn't thought about Maggie for quite a while. Tonight he'd get her, bring her with him to play. The rabbit wouldn't be able to resist helping a poor little kid, and neither would Kaycee Miller.

Thornton's eyes flew open, his energy restored. Standing, he stretched, turned to walk toward the bathroom, then stopped, doing a double take as he passed the picture window. Staring outside, he stepped closer to study the ground, wiping away the fog from his breath for a better look. A freshly broken pine branch was lying just a few feet away, covered only by a powder-thin layer of blowing snow.

Could the wind have snapped it off, carried it there?

Maybe, but the wind sure as hell didn't scatter two sets of heavy, wet footprints over the crest of the ridge.

•   •   •   •   •

Kaycee clutched the handset of the radio, nervously waiting. It was almost one o'clock, and twelve minutes had passed since Cal had taken off to drop the teams at their designated sites. Max had promised to check in as soon as he and Stagga were ready to begin.

The Trooper was parked on the wide shoulder of the road, a quarter mile past the "S" curve sign. The plan was simple—both teams would work the outer perimeter of the search area, heading toward Kaycee's position. If they found something, Cal would return immediately, covering them from the air.

If the first pass proved futile, they would break at the Trooper long enough to eat and replenish their supplies, then attack the center region at dusk when the dogs had their best chance of catching a scent.

"Kaycee? We're set. Everything okay at base?" Max's voice carried an edge of restless excitement.

"Yes."

"Randy? Are you reading me?"

"I'm getting some static, but I can read you."

"Okay. Be careful. Don't take any chances."

"Roger," Randy replied.

Kaycee shivered, slumping down in the seat as a black sedan whooshed past. Max had explained that they didn't use the radios unless communication was absolutely necessary, so she knew that it might be a long time before anyone called back.

The wind was easing up, making the silence in the Trooper almost unbearable. Opening the door, Kaycee savored the cold, crisp air as she studied the breathtaking landscape. A shallow, crystal clear stream snaked along the side of the road. Sunlight sparkled like scattered diamonds atop the blanket of snow. It was hard to believe anything bad could happen in the midst of such beauty. Leaning back, she closed her eyes, planning to rest for only a moment.

If she had listened more carefully, she might have wondered why the sound of a car passing from the other direction was identical to the one that had so recently gone by.

·   ·   ·   ·   ·

Thornton flew out of the trailer at a full run, rounding the corner at breakneck speed. Rushing toward the back of the trailer he slid to a stop where the sheet metal had been haphazardly crimped. Fresh dirt dusted the snow. *Maybe she can walk after all! Not a single one of them can be trusted!*

Stooping, he touched each set of tracks, one large, one small. His eyes followed the strange impressions in the snow. First there were two sets side by side with a peculiar scraping in the middle, then a few yards up the rise, they all seemed to merge into one deep set.

Drawing his gun, he carefully scaled the hill. Taking cover behind a tree, he eased over the lip until he could see. There was no one in sight, only one set of tracks leading toward the pond.

Thornton smiled. No one knew these woods as well as he did. No one.

·   ·   ·   ·   ·

Plodding across the frozen pond with Niki over his shoulder took all of Roger's agility and strength. They were a few yards inside the cover of dense trees when Niki's hand tightened on his jacket. In a panicked voice she warned, "Hide!"

Roger instantly ducked behind a huge pine tree, whispering, "What is it?"

"He's following us!"

After struggling to catch a deep breath Roger asked, "Okay, just stay calm. Do you think he saw us?"

"No. He was looking down."

"Good. Then if we stay still, he may choose the other path."

For a moment, neither of them dared to breathe. After what seemed like an eternity, Roger gathered enough nerve to peek around the side of the tree. Taking off, he whispered, "Hold on! We can't wait any longer!"

· · · · ·

Thornton had been in no hurry as he followed the tracks. Ten minutes into his hike he stopped at the lip of the pond, studying two distinct paths. The trails had split. One set went straight across the ice, the other skirted a quarter of the edge then veered off into the woods.

His gut instinct told him to follow the set across the pond. But lately, his gut had been wrong. It suddenly dawned on him—*she* had come to help her sister. Somehow *she* had found his hiding place. *I should have cracked her skull the first time I laid eyes on her!*

Thornton's heart pounded, his outrage bringing fire to his eyes. He had no intention of letting both of them escape again. Following neither of the paths, Thornton veered left, jogging toward the highway.

They think they're so smart! I'll show them!

Panting, he didn't slow until he was standing in the middle of the highway. *Which way?* he wondered, then heard the roar of a semi approaching from behind. Turning around, his mouth gaped open.

The truck was barreling down on him much faster than he expected. He started to simply get off the road, then realized that the driver was steering directly toward him. Raising his gun he took aim, targeting the driver's forehead as he squeezed off several rounds.

But the truck didn't stop, it raced on in spite of the shattered windshield. It was only a few yards from him when he gasped, unable to believe his eyes.

He'd seen that petrified face before, but this time it radiated such sheer determination and hatred he was certain Kim had come from beyond the grave to haunt him.

·   ·   ·   ·   ·

Randy crouched beside Smokey, scratching his neck. "Good boy!" he praised, tossing a handful of treats. Opening the deep pocket on his jacket, he reached in to get the radio, but it wasn't there. After patting every pocket on his pants he sighed. "Looks like I lost the radio when I tumbled down that bluff a while back. Why didn't you tell me?"

Smokey's tail wagged anxiously as he fidgeted. It was obvious he wanted to follow the scent he'd found. Randy checked his watch, carefully weighing his options. He'd be late if he veered off track now, but Smokey's eager whine made his decision easy. They'd follow the lead, then double back to find the radio.

Under normal circumstances, he would have let Smokey continue as usual without a leash, but instinct told him to take it slow and easy this time. Digging into his pocket, he pulled out the sealed plastic bag that protected the miniature doll. Opening the bag, he held it under Smokey's nose, refreshing Maggie's scent. At his signal to search, Smokey tried to bolt in the direction of the scent, but Randy reined him in. "Sorry, old pal. I know it's hard, but you're going to have to go at my pace for a while."

Smokey was electrified as he worked, a sure sign he was onto something. For almost a quarter of a mile, he headed due west, toward the inner boundary that divided their area from Max and

Stagga's search zone. It occurred to him that Smokey might be tracking their scent, but the wind was still holding steady at their backs, which made that unlikely. For quite some time they wound through the heavy brush on the forest floor, until Roger could see the bright beams of sunlight from a break in the trees and bushes ahead.

Moving toward the light, Smokey alertly tugged and strained, eager to advance into the small clearing. A sheer precipice lay beyond the open land, its lower portion lined with bushes and small pine trees. Nothing seemed out of the ordinary—there were no tracks in the glittering snow, but Randy still commanded Smokey to stop.

No such thing as the death stroke, my ass, he thought. Being overly cautious, he settled into the trees for cover, waiting and watching while he struggled to hold Smokey back. The small field was the perfect place to ambush someone—plenty of hiding places surrounding an open stretch where they'd be trapped. After a few minutes of careful scrutiny, Roger felt it was reasonably safe to let Smokey attack the area.

Unfastening the leash, he commanded Smokey to search. With absolute certainty, Smokey charged straight toward the small chain of trees. Randy watched in awe as the dog stuck his wet nose into a row of tightly packed pine limbs. Next his head disappeared, followed by half his body, then he was gone. One of the limbs fell forward, the white of its sawed off bottom poking out of the snow-covered dirt as a cascade of brittle needles fell to the ground.

"Well, I'll be damned," Randy muttered as he rushed forward. Unbuttoning one of the pockets on his pant leg, he pulled out his flashlight and snapped it on. Pushing aside the limbs, he ordered Smokey to sit, then clamped the nylon leash to his collar. Smokey softly whimpered as Randy climbed inside, trying to leave the hidden entrance as undisturbed as possible. Directing the beam of light around the musty threshold, he hugged the dog and praised, "Good job! You found it, boy!"

Randy had encountered the stench of death more times than he cared to admit. He felt the repulsive touch of its long fingers in this dreary place, making his stomach tighten, his throat close. A vivid mental picture of little Maggie popped into his head, and he choked back a wave of stinging tears. Totally disheartened, he was certain they were too late.

Smokey barked, driven by the heavy scent of Maggie in the mine. "Quiet!" Randy commanded, pulling the dog even closer to his side. "I know you're excited, pal, but this could be dangerous. We've got to get backup first."

Whining, Smokey strained against the lead, but yielded to his master's stern look.

Randy stood, wishing he could let Smokey go, but knowing it would be foolish. As he turned to leave, his flashlight danced across something metallic off to one side. Jerking the beam back, it illuminated a large box. *Could it be? Max will do a double back flip when he hears I found his light line and generator!*

Rushing toward the equipment, Roger's excitement grew. Smokey abruptly alerted, stopping in his tracks so fast that his paws skidded on the loose dirt. But it was too late. A searing white flash lit the entrance as Randy's foot landed on the booby trap's trigger.

CHAPTER 26

T he sound of Max's voice jolted Kaycee awake.

She couldn't believe she'd slept for almost two hours.

"Kaycee? Everything okay at base?" Max asked, his voice scratchy over the radio.

She groggily replied, "Yes, I'm here. Go ahead."

"Just checking in. Randy? What's your ETA?"

Silence.

"Randy?" After thirty seconds, Max asked, "Kaycee, would you try contacting Randy from the base radio? I'm working at the foot of a crag that might be blocking my signal."

"Okay. Randy? It's Kaycee. Please check in."

Dead silence.

"Randy? Check in, please!" Slightly rocking back and forth, Kaycee tried not to panic. "Max, he isn't answering."

"It's okay. There are lots of reasons teams don't respond as planned. Most likely his batteries went dead, or he's blocked."

"But we just checked all the equipment. . ."

"Kaycee, Randy and Smokey are the best there are. You can't second guess what's going on in the field, so for now, try to relax."

With a resigned sigh, she asked, "Okay, then what can I do to help?"

"Call him every five minutes. If he's just blocked by landscape, as he moves closer he should be able to pick up your signal. If he doesn't reply after twenty minutes, call Cal on the cell phone. He'll sweep Randy's area looking for an emergency beacon, or any kind of trouble."

Kaycee tried not to let fear bleed into her voice. "I'll handle it, Max. Promise you'll be careful."

"You, too. Kaycee?"

"Yes?"

"Are you in the car with the doors locked?" he asked.

She pulled the door closed and pushed down the lock button. "I am now."

"Promise you'll stay that way."

"Sure."

"I'll check back in soon. I expect to be at your location in less than an hour."

"Okay." Kaycee spent the next four minutes watching each second flash by on her digital watch. She almost jumped out of the seat when the cell phone rang. Grabbing it, she prayed it was Cal. "Cal?"

"No dear. That your boyfriend's name?"

Liquid lightning flowed in her veins, charging her with such rage that she began to tremble. She exhaled, "Thornton."

"Your sister says she'd love to see you again. Maggie, too."

Kaycee's jaw was tight, her words sharp and clipped. "Then let me talk to one of them."

"No way. We play by my rules, or not at all."

Responding on impulse, she sarcastically snapped, "Oh, that's fair! What the hell do you want?"

"To finish what I should have taken care of in the first place. I'm afraid you're a liability I just can't afford any longer."

Kaycee clenched her fists, trying to hear anything in the background, or in his voice, that might help. Then it dawned on her—in the same way she had used his anger against him the first time, possibly this time she could use his own insecurities as bait. If he started doubting himself, he might falter, might drop his guard long enough for her slip inside his head. All she had to do was focus on the vulnerable self driving the outer destructive behavior. *Maybe it's not too late after all!*

"Talk!"

"What do you want me to say?"

"Say you'll play." He chuckled, "You got away once, maybe you'll survive again. Or maybe not."

Kaycee closed her eyes, visualizing the note he left on Niki's angel. Calmly, coldly, she stated, "I know you, Thornton. I know what you're running from. . ."

"You don't know me, lady."

Keep it smooth, cool. "You're wrong. We're connected now. Subconsciously, you opened yourself to me, leaving me more than enough room to move in. I'm in your head, just as sure as if I were a part of you. Breath by breath, it becomes easier for me to see into your soul." Kaycee waited to hear his voice catch before he replied, the signal that she was winning the latest mind game.

Two seconds passed before he snapped, "You've really lost it!"

A triumphant smile lit her eyes. "Have I? Or am I so close that you can feel me drawing the life out of you? Feel me, Thornton. I'm there with you. Feel me lifting your thoughts, peeling them back like the bubble of a blister to slice into your pathetic past."

"Shut up! You're nuts!"

She suddenly remembered her other lie. "I'm not nuts, I just don't have long to live. Remember, I have AIDS. It's an amazing thing that happens, Willy. Just when your life is almost over, your mind opens incredible doors to a higher plane. You start becoming one with the universe. That's why I *know* you, I *am* you!"

"Bull!"

"If I'm not telling the truth, then how do I know exactly what you're feeling? You wake up enraged, your mind racing through all the plans you have for the future. But stupid outsiders keep throwing you off, making your perfect plans go awry. It's so unbalancing, so *frustrating*! Life is nothing more than something to struggle through, eliminating anyone who gets in your way. People are like mosquitoes, aren't they? They're just buzzing, whining, irritating insects that are easier to crush than to tolerate.

"I can help you Thornton. I can help you bring it all back together. You're a master manipulator, a man who deserves respect. You feel detached from the world because no one else can keep up with you. But I understand, Willy. No one else has a thousand ideas hitting them at once. Your parents never had a clue, did they? They couldn't comprehend the levels of your personality, much less deal with them. You may feel alone, but you're not. I'm right here with you."

Hearing him exhale, Kaycee waited a heartbeat, then added, "What you need, Willy, is guidance from someone who truly understands. I feel your brilliance, it's just been misdirected. Surely by now you've realized that we didn't meet by chance. We were brought together for a reason. If not, why do our paths keep crossing?"

This time, his words were much smoother, his voice carrying a thread of underlying control. "You're right about one thing."

"What's that?"

"You're destined to play my game."

"And if I do, what happens to my sister, and to Maggie?"

"That's up to you. If you win, then I'll be dead. They live and so do you. Seems fair enough. Besides, what have you got to lose? That is, if you weren't making up that crap about having AIDS. . ."

Kaycee's confidence sank. Even with his anger tempered, he was still deranged. "Okay. I'll play your twisted game if you'll let me talk to Niki."

"Sorry, she's temporarily indisposed."

Kaycee tried her best to match his unemotional, subdued manner as she asked, "Then how do I know you haven't killed her already?"

In an even calmer tone, he spoke his last words. "The game starts at midnight. Come alone, no police or they both die. I'll call later to tell you where to be."

The phone clicked as he hung up. Again Kaycee found herself staring into space, her mind racing through a million lousy options. But this time, she knew she had knocked a chip in his armor. He *was* vulnerable, she just had to keep digging to find the precise secrets that would bring him down.

·   ·   ·   ·   ·

Thornton hung up the phone, baffled. On one hand, he was proud of his brilliant bluff—Kaycee Miller had no idea her sister had escaped. Yet her words slithered across his mind like unleashed serpents. At first their novelty aroused and captured his attention, but then the inherent danger became all too evident.

As usual, the calm didn't last long. A hornet's nest of rapid-fire images began to buzz through his mind, bombarding him with memories of people he once thought were friends, his worthless father, the endless liars who crossed his path day by day, and finally, the game at hand.

Thornton's eyes were malignant red circles from his morning encounter with the de-icer. Shaking his head to stop the maddening rush of ideas, he rubbed his aching, bruised shoulder. *Did that witch give me the willies, or do I feel like screaming because for the last week everything I've touched has gone sour?*

Less than an hour ago a semi had almost made him part of the pavement. He thought of the truck that had tried to run him down, wondering if it could actually have been Kim behind the wheel. But how? He'd watched that crash, heard her screams.

No, Kim was dead as a hammer. The face he saw must have been a little trick his mind had flashed to keep him on his toes. His brain worked that way sometimes, throwing in twists when he least expected it to make the challenges a little tougher. *She was right about that, too. No one understands me.*

Another thought jolted him, refusing to be ignored. How had that crippled woman disappeared? The tracks were unmistakable—she had definitely had help. But he could tell by her sister's reaction that she hadn't been the one to help her escape. Kaycee Miller still thought he was in control, holding all the aces. Stalking her tonight would be a pleasure.

But who else could've found the trailer? The obvious answer was Kim. She had been there a few times, hiked all over the place with him. In a pinch, she could probably have found the back way in from the highway. *But dead people don't leave tracks.*

A cell mate once told him that the waitress he murdered would haunt his soul, slowly bite chunks from it until there was nothing left. He'd almost ripped the guy's tongue out on the spot because he'd chomped and smacked his lips. Now, Thornton wondered if he might be right. Five people were dead at his hands—the waitress, Levi, Kim, that old couple. A mental image of them chewing, teeth gnashing and gnawing, made him laugh.

Bolting up, Thornton carried the cooler of beer to the car and tossed it into the trunk. He almost slammed it closed, then stopped, wrapping one hand around the can of de-icer that had practically blinded him. Winding up like a professional pitcher, he flung the can with all his might into the forest. It flew end over end, landing softly in the woods that had always been the only place he could escape. The flash of sorrow Thornton felt was quickly replaced by bitterness. Because of those two sisters, he'd never be able to come back here again.

There was no time to linger. Whoever dragged Niki Miller's pathetic ass out of the woods was probably already on their way to squeal to the police. Tossing the rest of his things into the backseat of the car, he started the engine.

Glancing at his watch, he realized he only had a few hours to make his plan come together, and there were a thousand things to be done. The timing would have to be perfect. Once darkness settled on the mountain, he'd retrieve his daughter from the mine along with the rest of his stash. She'd make excellent bait—after all, what woman could stand the tears of a child?

And just in case Kim's ghost tried to help Maggie escape again, he'd blow the mine to kingdom come, then wire the kid with dynamite.

Tonight, even the spirit world would stand up and notice Willy Thornton.

· · · · ·

"Bauer, what's your location?" Bob Palmer barked into the radio.

Pacing outside the helicopter that was hidden in a small meadow off the road a few miles from the action, he impatiently waited for a reply.

"I'm in a tree about a hundred yards north of her, Moore's off to the southwest, keeping an eye out from there."

"What's Miller doing?"

"Nothing new. She's still sitting in the Trooper. For a while, she would get out and stretch her legs, but now she's locked the doors and is hanging tight. Had a phone call a few minutes ago that seemed to freak her out."

Palmer felt the vibration of his cell phone in his pocket before he heard its shrill ring. Answering it, his secretary announced, "Kaycee Miller is on the line. Shall I patch her through?"

"Yes!" Exchanging the radio for the cell phone, he answered, "Kaycee! I'm so glad you called."

"I'm afraid I'm going to have to take you up on your offer, Bob. I need your help. Things have really gotten out of hand."

"Just name it. All our assets are at your disposal."

"I need everything you can find on Thornton. His background, medical history, what prison terms he served and where. More writing samples would help, but we really don't have much time."

Palmer's finger traced Thornton's name on the narrow brown file that had been carelessly tossed onto the front seat. "Actually, we have a complete dossier ready on him. I believe it has a few writing samples other than those you've already seen. I'd be more than happy to let you use it. When do you need it?"

She paused, "That's the problem. If I don't have it by sundown today, it'll be too late."

"Then I'll personally guarantee you'll have it. Just tell me where you are, and the file will be there as fast as humanly possible."

"But. . .How?"

"Most of the time I pay our pilot to sit around killing time on the Internet. Trust me, bringing the file to you will be a welcome break. Where are you?"

Kaycee quickly explained where the Trooper was located, then added, "Thank you so much!"

"We'll be there in thirty minutes, forty-five tops."

"I can't tell you how much this means to me."

"Trust me, you don't have to." Palmer hung up the phone and grabbed the radio. "Moore and Bauer, return immediately. Miller finally took the bait. . ."

CHAPTER **27**

Roger pulled the semi into the crowded truck stop, purposely choosing a slot in the middle of a dozen other similar rigs. Kim was so close he could feel the warmth of her body, while Niki, wrapped in a heavy wool blanket, huddled against the passenger door. Casting a dazed glance toward Kim, he turned off the key and sighed. "I can't believe this is happening."

Kim lowered weary eyes, softly shaking her head. "I shouldn't have pulled you into my nightmare. Seems like everyone who's nice to me gets hurt."

"I'm not hurt," he whispered.

"It's not over."

"What you did back there was incredible. Darn good driving. Too bad he jumped out of the way."

Kim's tone was flat. "Yeah. Just once I wish I'd get a break."

"You were mine," Niki coughed.

Leaning forward, Roger asked, "Are you feeling okay?"

She nodded. For the first time since they'd found her, Niki's words didn't rush out between chattering teeth. "Are you sure he didn't follow us?"

"Positive. Even if he did, I know most of these truckers. They'd be more than happy to help. Showdowns are the stuff trucking legends are made of. I still think we should get you to a hospital."

Niki shook her head, suddenly remembering her sister's recent misfortune. *Could all this be connected? Is he the man who attacked Kaycee in that motel?*

"Niki, are you okay?"

Pushing away the crazy idea, Niki nodded. "The coffee and blankets helped a lot. I can't thank the two of you enough."

Kim asked, "Can you tell us what's going on now?"

Niki shrugged, drawing a deep breath. "When I came home yesterday, that man was waiting. He attacked me in my garage, drove my van to where his car was parked, stuck a pillowcase over my head and tossed me in the back like a sack of potatoes. This morning when he opened the trunk, I sprayed him with a can of de-icer. He went ballistic and slammed the lid. When he went off to clean his wounds, I pried the trunk open and hid under the mobile home. You know the rest."

Kim shook her head, casting her a troubled gaze. "But *why* did he take you? Do you know him?"

"Absolutely not. And believe me, he's not the type of person I could ever forget."

Roger took Kim's hand, his eyes meeting hers. "What's wrong?"

She shrugged, obviously puzzled. "This doesn't make sense. Willy isn't the type to just randomly choose his victims. He strikes *specific* people for his own twisted reasons. Believe me, if he has a motive for targeting you, he won't give up until he finishes whatever he came for."

Niki shivered. "Which is why I can't go home. He knows where I live. Maybe you should just take me to the police. . ."

Kim stiffened. "Please, I'm only asking you to wait a few hours. You could stay in our motel room until this is over."

For a moment, Niki considered the option, then shook her head. "Without a wheelchair I'm pretty much a fish out of water. I have a friend I met at rehab. Could you take me to her place? It's not very far and I know she's got a spare wheelchair."

"Sure. We want you to be safe," Roger replied.

They were halfway there when Niki suddenly gasped. "I almost forgot! He said I had to play some game tonight. Does that mean anything to you?"

Kim groaned. "Oh, God. Maggie!"

"Who's Maggie?" Niki asked.

"His daughter." Kim turned to Roger. "I've got to go back. I have to help her."

Roger shook his head. "No way. I'm sure he got a good look at you when you almost ran him down."

"Maybe he realized it was me, maybe not. So what?"

"So he already tried to kill you once!"

"Which is exactly why we have to stop him. That little girl didn't do any thing to anyone. Even if she is his kid, we have to help her."

Niki asked, "Do you know where she is?"

Kim mumbled, "I think so."

"Then why don't you call the police?" Her voice was strong now, full of spirit.

"Like I said before, it's complicated." After shooting a worried look at Roger, Kim added, "Okay. . .We don't want to call the police because they'll charge me as an accessory."

"Were you an accessory?"

"No!"

"Then wouldn't being charged be better than letting him hurt an innocent kid? I'll testify how you helped me. I'm sure that'll count for something."

Kim's jaw tightened as determination hardened her profile. "Calling in the police may just get her killed. Willy always said he wired the mine so that all the evidence would be buried forever if the authorities ever got close."

"Do you believe he actually has the technology to do such a thing?"

Kim almost laughed. "Technology? We're not talking about using plastic explosives. He told me he has a line of old-fashioned dynamite wired to a remote detonator—a pager."

Roger's brows raised. "A pager?"

"He learned about it in prison. All he has to do is dial the pager's phone number. When it tries to beep, the pulse of electricity will complete the circuit and . . . Boom."

Niki moaned. "Someone has to stop him!"

"Only I can get Maggie out of there."

"I'm not letting you go in there alone. It's suicide."

"I appreciate everything you've done for me, Roger, I really do. But even if you made it past the booby traps at the entrance, and were small enough to fit through the collapsed part of the mine, Maggie won't trust you. She knows me, knows I tried to help her escape once. I've got to try, and I have to do it alone."

Roger slammed his fist against the oversized steering wheel. "Damn it, Kim. He knows you're alive. He'll be waiting for you."

Her hand automatically stroked the small gun tucked inside the waist of her jeans. "No. This time *I'll* be the one who laughs in *his* face."

•　•　•　•　•

Kaycee unlocked the car door and rushed toward Max as soon as she saw Stagga break out through the underbrush. When Max was close enough to be heard without shouting, he called, "Any word?"

"No, Cal's flying over the area now. He said to have you contact him as soon as you got here."

Max nodded. Ordering Stagga to sit, he knelt at his side to praise and hug him. He tossed a stick of rawhide, and Stagga leaped to catch it in mid-air. Standing, Max opened the back door of the Trooper and commanded, "Rest, Stagga."

Quick to obey, the dog jumped onto the floorboard and curled into a ball to enjoy his delicacy. As Max watched him settle in, he called Cal on the radio. "Cal, it's Max. Having any luck up there?"

"Not yet. I'm working the roughest terrain first. Luckily the wind has died down. It's a hell of a lot easier to spot movement in still trees now."

"You could swing by and pick me up. Two sets of eyes are better than one." Catching a peripheral glimpse of Kaycee, Max noticed her stiffen. In a surge of emotion, the troubled feeling he'd fought all afternoon returned.

"Will do, but it'll take me a few minutes. I'll do a slow sweep between here and there, in case he's headed for base."

"Okay. I'll be ready."

Max tucked the radio back in his pocket, turning his attention to Kaycee. With an open stare, he scrutinized her from head to toe.

Shrinking under his glare, she asked, "Did I grow another head or something?"

"What's wrong?" he calmly asked.

She shrugged, turning away. "What *isn't* wrong?"

Wrapping strong arms around her from behind, his lips grazed her hair. "If it's Randy you're worried about, I'm sure he'll be fine. Besides, if Cal doesn't spot him, Stagga could follow their scent blindfolded. Randy's feet alone put off enough scent to lead an army of K-9's."

Kaycee smiled and nodded, enjoying the feel of being in his arms for a few moments before her grim disposition returned. Stiffening, she said, "Max, he called again."

"Thornton?"

With a abrupt nod she stepped away. "Bob Palmer is bringing his file for me to review. I think if I can talk to him about his past, I can distract him so he'll make a mistake."

"But—"

"But nothing!" She planted her feet. Standing with crossed arms, she rattled, "I know you think I've got no business being here, but you're wrong! The more I learn about Thornton's mental state, the more we'll know how he thinks, what he feels. The man is a psychotic pendulum. He's not a split personality, he merely swings from being violently out of control to periods of reason where he is capable of repressing those impulses. I may be able to ease him down with the right information."

"Kaycee, he's a homicidal maniac."

"One that *must* be stopped. Do you have a better plan?"

With a sigh, Max shook his head.

Stunned to have won so easily, Kaycee's mouth snapped closed. "You. . .you agree?"

He nodded. "You're right. For whatever reason, he's latched onto you, and you're the only one who can pull us all together. What exactly does Thornton want you to do?"

The anger he had diffused flamed back on. "He wants me to play a game for Niki and Maggie's lives. Winner take all."

Max started to voice his opinion, barely catching himself before words he was sure she'd find offensive tumbled out. After careful consideration, he asked, "Did he give you a time? A place?"

"He's calling back to say where, but Thornton declared that the game will start at midnight. Midnight, damn it!"

"You can't seriously be thinking of going. We'll have to call in the FBI, Kaycee."

Pacing, she snapped, "No, we won't call the FBI. If we do, and Willy finds out, he'll kill them and leave. That much I'm sure of."

"So what do you have in mind?"

"That's the problem. I'd go if I could figure out a way."

"Which means?" Max urged.

Tears threatened to spill. "Max, I can't do it at midnight! I won't be able to see a thing!"

Puzzled, Max took her in his arms, stroking her hair. "Calm down. What are you talking about?"

"I know I should have told you right away. I just couldn't."

He took her face in his hands. "Tell me what?"

"That I'm going blind. When the sun goes down, I can hardly see a thing. Only big shapes, huge globs of nothing." She watched him slowly nod. "You knew, didn't you?"

"No. I've known there was something eating away at you ever since we met. Is this what you were going to tell me outside the hotel this morning just before Thornton called?"

She nodded.

Hugging her tightly, he sighed. "In a way, I'm relieved. I'd decided you were pushing me away because you were going to die."

Kaycee pulled back, raw emotions boiling to the surface. "Is that supposed to make me feel better? Max, I'm going *blind!*"

"I know. But you can handle it. *We* can handle it."

"You haven't even known me a week! There is no *we*! This is something I have to face alone."

"You're not the first person to lose your sight, and you won't be the last. I guess you were right about being hard-headed. If you honestly think I'd run away from you just because you're going blind, then you don't know me at all."

"Why shouldn't you run away? Damn it, I wish *I* could run away!"

"But *you* can't, and *I* won't!"

She took a ragged breath, shaking her head.

"Think about it Kaycee."

One glance at him defused the remnants of her anger. "I'm sorry. I didn't mean to lash out at you like that."

"I just wish you'd told me sooner."

"At first I honestly didn't believe it was going to happen. I thought the doctor had made a mistake, that it was something they could cure. I suppose I was in denial. Last Friday, I went to a specialist. He confirmed the prognosis. That's when I met Ellen, the woman I've been telling you about. She explained that being blind isn't something everyone wants to announce to the world right away. She said most people treat you differently once they know."

"So Ellen's blind. . ."

Kaycee nodded. "It's funny. I only spent a few hours with her, but I feel we're going to be really good friends."

"She sounds like a very special woman."

"I can't imagine living through this without someone who knows exactly what I'm going through. She showed me that I still have a future, it's just going to be different than I expected. I know I should apologize for not telling you right away. I thought there was something special between us, and I didn't want you to—"

"To feel sorry for you? How could I feel sorry for the bravest woman I've ever met?"

She shook her head, swiping away brimming tears with the back of her hands. "I'm not brave."

"Nonsense. Look where you are. You came to save the life of a little girl you've only met for a few moments. And even though an insane criminal has kidnapped your sister to get to you, you're *still* willing to confront him. Kaycee, you can handle this. You're strong, deep inside where it counts."

"Then why do I feel so helpless? My sight is my life. How will I analyze handwriting? How will I see the truth in people's eyes, in their gestures? Pretty soon, I won't be able to drive even in broad daylight."

"Have they told you how long?"

She shook her head. "No one knows. It progresses differently for each person. Could be a few months, could be years. Max, I'm so afraid."

"I know you are. I am, too."

Her breath caught. "You are?"

"Kaycee, until I met you I can honestly say there wasn't much I truly feared besides being too late when it really mattered in a search. You've changed all that. Now I'm afraid of losing you." His hand gently cradled her cheek as he kissed away a tear. "Close your eyes." When she did, he took her in his arms to whisper, "Without seeing me, can you still sense how much I care about you?"

She sighed, "Yes."

"We'll get through tonight together, then take each day as it comes. Deal?"

Kaycee nodded, then looked him straight in the eye. "Deal."

"Great. Now, let's find Niki and Maggie."

Cal's voice crackled on the radio in Max's hand, "Max! I've spotted Smokey. Looks like he's hurt."

"What about Randy?"

"Negative. Smokey's alone."

CHAPTER 28

Kaycee and Max exchanged an anguished look as Max asked, "Anywhere you can land?"

"Negative. I only caught a glimpse of him in the trees because he's dragging his fluorescent orange lead. Max, he's not moving very fast. I think if I drop you near this location, you'll be able to find him."

Max fully understood the gravity of the situation. Smokey would never have left Randy's side except to go for help. "I'll have Stagga ready."

Kaycee asked, "What should I do?"

Biting his lower lip, Max shoved all the spare emergency medical supplies into a pack. "I don't like it, but I think you'd better come along. If Smokey is alone and hurt, Randy is down, too. We may need your help to rescue them, and I don't like the idea of you staying here alone."

Relieved that she wouldn't be kept away from the action again, Kaycee nodded. "Do I need to bring anything along?"

He handed her a utility belt dangling lengths of looped rope. "Wear this. We may not need it, but it's better to be safe than sorry."

Snapping it on, she drew a ragged breath as her eye caught the cell phone on the passenger seat of the car. Slipping it into the pocket of her overalls, she asked, "Are you as afraid as I am?"

"Nope. It always hits me later. Right now, I'm too busy trying to make sure we have all the tools to handle every possible situation." Hearing the distant whisper of a helicopter, Max said, "That was fast. Smokey must be closer to base than Cal thought."

A much larger helicopter came into sight. Shouting, Kaycee said,

"That must be Bob Palmer from CSI."

Max nodded, watching the aircraft hover just above the tree line. From the passenger side Palmer waved, then dropped a package to the ground. Rushing to pick it up, Max carried it back to Kaycee. On the outside of the narrow brown file was a note:

We have to find a place to land. If you hand signal the radio frequency you're using, we'll be glad to assist in any way we can.

Max quickly used his fingers to indicate which frequency they should tune to, and before the wake of the helicopter died, Palmer's voice filled the air. "Do you read me?"

"Loud and clear," Max responded. "This is Max Masterson. I'm leading a K-9 search and rescue effort. Kaycee and I both appreciate your bringing the information."

"Glad to help. What else can we do?"

"We may have a man down. If so, we could use your help transporting him to the closest hospital. Could your pilot stand by for an exact location?"

"Absolutely. Do you need my men to help search?"

"Not yet. Discretion is absolutely necessary. Anything we do to draw attention to our location could further jeopardize the lives of the victims."

"We understand. Is Thornton responsible for injuring the man?"

"At this point, all we know is that a member of our K-9 team has been separated from his dog. We can only assume he's hurt."

The edge in Palmer's voice clearly showed he wasn't used to taking orders from anyone. "Mr. Masterson, are you fully aware of exactly who you're up against?"

Max's response was equally cold. "Yes, I am, and I have to go now. Please maintain radio silence on this frequency until you hear from one of our team."

"Will do."

Tucking away the radio, Max fastened Stagga into his harness. "Cal will hover pretty low. Do you think you'll be able to climb aboard?"

"Of course."

"Then you'd better get ready. You'll go first, then Stagga. I'll bring up the rear."

She nodded, zipping the file inside her jacket as she watched Cal maneuver the helicopter directly above them. With a knot in her stomach, she caught the line and began the short ascent to the helicopter. Seconds later, she was pushing herself inside.

"You did great!" Cal shouted. "Put on that safety harness, then get ready to help Stagga in. You'll have to unfasten the tether line once he's inside. Hurry! Every second counts."

She nodded, watching with fear and amazement as Stagga left the ground and floated toward her. Working as fast as she could, she lifted him over the edge and unsnapped the line. In no time, Max was at her side. Her stomach did a back flip as Cal executed a hard, fast turn then leveled to skim the fragrant air just above the tree tops at lightning speed.

Max wrapped one hand around hers, giving it a gentle but confident squeeze. Without a word, the expression of hope in his eyes told her to relax, that everything would work out.

Doing an abrupt circle in mid-air, Cal's voice boomed, "There he is!"

They all looked down. Kaycee's hand flew to her mouth as she gasped. Smokey was dragging himself on two legs, barely inching along. When she glanced back up Max was already in position to be lowered, the pack of extra medical supplies on his back. With a quick nod from Cal, he was gone.

Cal immediately said, "Kaycee, get Stagga set. Once he's down Max will use his sling to send Smokey up."

Kaycee snapped the tether onto Stagga and waited for Cal to tell her what to do next. Instead of speaking, he held out a headset. When she put it on, she could hear Max's steady voice as he tried to soothe the dog. "He's lost a lot of blood through a bad wound on his front leg. . .Stay, Smokey. . . He's so weak he can barely move. . .Lie still, boy. . .Cal, I'm afraid all I can do is apply a pressure bandage. By the time you lower Stagga, I'll have Smokey ready to come up. Give Kaycee a choice—she can either help you get Smokey to a vet, or stay here and search for Randy with me."

Cal shot her an inquisitive look. Kaycee didn't miss a beat as she firmly pointed down in reply.

Over the radio Cal replied, "Max, looks like you and Stagga will have company. Are you sure you want me to leave the area? Randy may not be far."

"Smokey's in bad shape. I don't think he'll make it if he doesn't get medical help immediately. CSI has a jet helicopter standing by. If you're not back by the time we locate Randy, they can assist."

"Roger. Heads up, Max. Stagga's in flight."

Watching the way Max gently cared for the injured dog brought tears to Kaycee's eyes. *What have I gotten them into?* she thought as she lifted Smokey's limp, bloody body on board. Only Cal's authoritative voice in her headset kept her from totally losing focus.

"Kaycee, you'll have to get Smokey out of the sling so you can take it back down with you. Once you've worked it off of him, fasten him in with the back safety harness. There's a blanket in the side storage compartment. Cover Smokey, then descend as fast as you can. Okay?"

Even though she wanted to scream, No!, she nodded and followed his directions.

Cal expertly kept the aircraft hovering as he reached under his seat, groping until he found a short, leather-sheathed knife. Just as Kaycee was about to leave, he thrust it into the palm of her hand. "Tuck this in the sock above your boot. There's a button on the side that pops out a razor-edged blade." Kaycee had never seen a more serious expression on any person's face as he added, "Be careful down there."

A thin smile accompanied her quick nod and she tried not to think about the task at hand. Looking down, her heart raced as she realized how far it was to the ground, and how fast she needed to be there. Max and Stagga were waiting, both of them anxious to find Randy.

Gathering her courage, she coiled strong fingers around the line and closed her eyes. The instant Kaycee set foot on the ground below, Cal saluted, then whisked Smokey away.

A raw silence fell over the forest. Max looked Kaycee in the eye. "I wish you'd gone with Cal where you'd be safe. I know you're determined to help, but this is a very volatile situation. Please promise not to try anything heroic. If we're going to survive, we have to work as a team. Agreed?"

She nodded. "Of course."

"Then let's go find Randy." Max ordered Stagga to begin the search. As the dog anxiously led, he added, "By the way, that was some pretty good heli-repelling for an amateur."

For a brief moment a flash of pride made Kaycee forget the horrors that lay ahead.

· · · · ·

Palmer slammed his fist against the side of the helicopter, hard enough to make him wince. "Damn it! I hate just sitting around."

"You didn't have a choice," Bauer said, running one hand over his balding head while he pointed at the screen of the laptop computer with the other. "According to the database, Masterson's team has been cited several times for heroism. He's not the kind of guy who's going to just sit back and let you call the shots."

Palmer nodded. "Okay. We can utilize this time to formulate a plan. Even if Thornton isn't directly responsible for the disappearance of their friend, you can bet we're near his lair. Levi's last report said that Thornton mentioned a place he'd kept secret since he was a kid. He grew up near here, so we must be getting close."

Frank Moore, the pilot, agreed. "We're close, all right. I can feel it."

Palmer unsnapped his shoulder holster and checked his weapon. "Everyone have extra ammo?"

They both nodded.

"Remember, shoot to kill," Palmer said.

• • • • •

Max cast a glance over his shoulder, making certain Kaycee was still on his heels. Both the tracks and Smokey's broken trail of blood were so fresh that Stagga was working at breakneck speed, dragging Max along on an extended lead. "You holding up all right?" he asked without slowing down.

"Stop worrying about me. I'll be fine."

A hundred yards later, Max pushed back a branch just in time to see Stagga almost break into a clearing. Keeping his voice hushed, he demanded, "Stagga, halt!"

With an *are-you-crazy-I'm-almost-there!* glare, Stagga hesitated, then indecisively sat down, stood up to inch forward, then sat down again with an impatient whimper.

Stopping just behind Max, Kaycee asked, "What's wrong? Did you see something?"

Max held a finger to his lips and motioned for her to get down. Pointing at the snowy tracks that disappeared into what appeared to be a rock bluff, they could clearly see where one sawed-off pine limb had fallen forward, leaving a guarded glimpse into the darkness beyond.

Squatting at her side, he handed her Stagga's lead as he dug a flashlight out of his pocket. The entire time, he never stopped surveying the area. A thin line of sweat on his brow betrayed his outward composure. "I'm going to circle around in the trees, then peek inside. Keep Stagga reined in tight."

Whispering, Kaycee asked, "Shouldn't you take him for protection?"

Max shook his head. "Not until I find out what Randy and Smokey ran into in there. Only release him if you hear me call his name or I wave that it's clear."

"Okay."

Unzipping an inside pocket, Max withdrew a piece of electronic equipment, smaller than most cell phones. Turning it on, he punched a few buttons and handed it to Kaycee. "This is a GPS – Global

Positioning System. It'll only take a couple of minutes to lock onto a few satellites and triangulate our exact location. If anything happens, you'll need the coordinates it gives to call for help."

"Do I just leave it on?"

"Yes." Touching the dog's black nose, Max sternly commanded, "Stagga, stay!" Then to Kaycee he added, "*Both of you keep out of sight and be quiet!*"

She nodded, nervously wrapping Stagga's leash around her hand as she watched Max leave. The dog whined, but stopped when Max shot him a disapproving glower over his shoulder.

Kaycee whispered in Stagga's ear, "I know you aren't any happier than I am, but he'll be all right."

Settling in, both watched and waited.

· · · · ·

Max crept along the side of the bluff, searching for any movement, any sign of danger. At the barricaded entrance, he stood to one side for several seconds, merely listening. At first, he thought his mind was playing tricks on him. A low moan floated past, like the eerie strain of tall pines swaying on a windy night. He waited until he was sure the sound was real, and that it was coming from inside the wall of rock. Pressing forward, he knelt in front of the small opening and gazed into the murky shadows.

With his powerful flashlight illuminating the entrance to the mine, he inched inside. Moving the beam methodically up and down, Max quietly called, "Randy?"

In a hoarse whisper, Randy cried, "Max, stop! The place is booby trapped."

"How?"

"I stepped on a trigger wire. . .discharged a couple of shotgun shells. Smokey caught one. . .He's hurt, too. . ."

Scrutinizing every inch of dirt with the flashlight before he dared to step, Max worked toward Randy as he said, "Smokey's going to be okay. Cal's flying him to the closest vet right now."

Randy nodded, growing weaker by the minute.

"What about you? How bad is it?"

"Feels like it blew off my leg. . .Hope it's still there. . .Can't feel a thing now. . .Made a tourniquet out of my belt. . .Slowed down the bleeding. . ."

Max was at his side, propping the flashlight so he could open the first aid pack. "Any sign of Thornton?"

Randy shook his head.

"Good. Let's just get you out of here."

Randy was fading fast as Max splinted his mangled leg. "Max, she's. . .here. Little Maggie. . ."

"We'll get her soon, I promise. I'm going to radio for a helicopter to evac you. Stay still, okay?"

Retracing his exact steps, Max emerged into the light. He took out his radio as he signaled for Kaycee and Stagga that it was safe to approach. "Palmer, CSI, do you read? We have an emergency."

"We're here. Go ahead."

"The victim has been seriously injured by a shotgun blast. He needs immediate transport to a hospital. Our exact location is—" grabbing the GPS from Kaycee he read their coordinates.

"We're on our way."

"There's a clearing here. I think there's barely room to land. Be careful."

Turning to Kaycee he said, "Stay out here and flag them down. Don't come inside. The place is wired with explosives. I'm going to move Randy to the opening."

"I'll clear away the branches."

"Good idea."

When Max's light illuminated Randy's pale, listless face, he almost panicked. As he knelt to feel for a pulse, for the first time Max noticed the foul stench carried on the slight movement of air running through the tunnel. *Randy was right. Maggie's here, maybe Niki, too. But we're too late.*

Touching Randy's cool, clammy skin with unsteady fingers, Max felt a weak but rhythmic heartbeat and sighed. "Hang in there, old buddy. I'm going to move you as carefully as I can." Grabbing him under the shoulders, Max hauled Randy slowly toward the growing stream of light where Kaycee was clearing away the limbs.

"Hurts. . ." Randy muttered.

"Good. That means you're going to make it."

"Did you. . .see it?"

"See what?"

Randy raised one arm, barely able to point at a dark hole deeper in the mine. Max stopped long enough to aim the flashlight. "Randy! You found my light line!"

"Hey. . .What are. . .friends for?"

Kaycee was waiting at the entrance when Max finally pulled Randy into the warm sunlight. Dropping to his side, she took his hand. "I'm so sorry, Randy."

Even though his eyes were closed, Randy managed a weak grin as he mumbled, "Guess that. . .death stroke. . .isn't such nonsense after all. . ."

C H A P T E R **29**

Palmer and Bauer jumped out of the helicopter the second it landed in the clearing. As all three men joined to carry Randy aboard, Max asked, "Can you hear me, buddy?"

He nodded.

"Was the snow in the clearing disturbed when you found the entrance?"

He shook his head, squinting his eyes open long enough to groggily wonder, "Where's Cal?"

"Remember, Cal's flying Smokey to a vet. CSI offered to help. You just relax and save your strength, okay?"

Another feeble nod and he was securely strapped in. Max quickly asked, "Do you have any fuel I can use to crank up a generator?"

Moore nodded, pointing at a storage compartment. Inside it was a red plastic container. Giving a thumbs up, Max shouted, "Thanks! Take good care of him!"

As soon as the helicopter disappeared over the trees, Palmer asked, "How'd it happen?"

Max motioned toward the mine. "It's booby trapped."

"Did you find the girl? Or Kaycee's sister?"

"Not yet. That's next."

"Just tell us how we can help."

"There's airflow coming from somewhere deep in the mine. That means there could be another entrance. We have to assume since the snow was undisturbed when Randy arrived, that Thornton hasn't come in this way for at least two days. That could mean lots of things—maybe he's entering from another site, or could be he's been preoccupied and hasn't checked back here lately. Randy said Smokey alerted on Maggie's scent, so I'll use the light line to take Stagga in. We'll have to go very slowly because of the booby traps."

"Light line?"

"Thornton stole my latest rescue equipment last week. It's a generator that powers a clear line of lights—red, white, and green. Red leads away from safety, green shows the way home. The lights are bright enough to be seen through thick smoke. In most cases it illuminates the area so well you don't need a flashlight. In this case, if there are branches off the main mine shaft, it will show which way Stagga and I went in case there's trouble."

"How can we help?" Palmer asked.

"If one of you can climb this bluff and search for another hidden entrance to the north, that would be great. I'd like the other to stay here at the entrance with Kaycee in case we run into some kind of problem." His gaze fell on Kaycee. "Can you look through Thornton's file while I work inside the mine?"

She glanced at the rapidly falling sun, then replied, "Yes. Do you have an extra flashlight?"

Max nodded, handing one to her. "I kept Randy's equipment."

Palmer snapped, "I'm an experienced climber. I'd be happy to search north of here."

Bauer added, "I've had training in weapons disarmament. I can help look for booby traps, then disable them."

"Perfect."

Kaycee asked, "What kind of traps are they?"

Bauer replied, "From what he's described, they're very basic. A trigger line runs to a rat trap rigged to a brick. Inside the hole of the brick is a shotgun shell. When the line is pulled, the trap snaps closed, firing the shell. What your friend triggered was a double whammy. There were traps on *both* sides, so he took the brunt of one while the dog took the other. They're not very sophisticated, but they usually manage to stop intruders."

"That is truly repulsive," Kaycee grumbled.

"Which is exactly what Thornton was going for, ma'am," Bauer replied. "He wanted to be sure that if anyone found this mine, they'd be too scared, or too hurt, to venture very far inside."

. . . . . .

Thornton turned off the main road into the forest just as the low-flying helicopter zoomed overhead. For a moment he merely thought how odd it was—in all his years roaming this land he'd never seen a helicopter buzz the treetops. Then the sinking feeling hit. *My God, they've found Maggie!*

Driving as fast as he dared, he took a different route than usual and parked well away from the mine's entrance. By the time he hiked through the woods, he was huffing and puffing. Stopping a hundred yards away, he silently crawled up a tree that had once been his favorite place to hunt deer and elk. High above the ground, he climbed onto the old seat he had nailed there years ago.

His heart pounded as he trained his binoculars on the entrance to the mine. The first thing he noticed was the glowing red light on the generator just outside the entrance. From it, a strange rope of light led into the belly of the mine. *Damn it! They'll find Maggie for sure!*

Next, his eyes focused on the man. He didn't appear to be much of a threat—medium height, athletic build, probably a wuss. For a moment he slipped into the mine, then walked out carrying several bricks and rat traps. *He's disarming my booby traps!*

Last, Thornton saw *her*. He would recognize that long, dark hair anywhere as she sat on her ass reading, without a care in the world. *I should have known that underhanded witch wouldn't play by the rules! The game starts NOW!*

. . . . .

Kaycee opened the file, shuddering as she picked up the same handwriting samples she'd handled at the interview less than a week ago. Touching each piece of paper in turn, she delved deeper, trying to *feel* the soul, the pulse of a monster. As she worked, the basic conclusions she'd first gleaned held true, but now the writing revealed a new perspective, one enhanced by hearing, seeing, and witnessing the inhuman spirit of the man behind the pen.

A rush of rising optimism made her anxious to view the rest of his file. With every exposure to him, she was beginning to see his life as he did, to feel his dead reaction to the world. For now she knew that was all life was to him—a series of cold, meaningless steps leading from one hell to another. People were merely diversions along the inevitable string of events that would result in his death, a death he expected to be brutal.

Glancing up, she realized she would soon be out of daylight, so she quickly scanned the remaining pages in the file. Kaycee was surprised to find a vast array of documents she was certain were confidential—medical records, military service history, prison logs, psychiatric evaluations, even the report of the parole board. *Has Palmer abused his power on the parole board to gain access to such things?* she wondered.

With the generator purring softly in the background, Kaycee delved into the parole board's findings. Thornton had been released within days of first being eligible for parole. *Why? How could they ignore every warning signal?* It seemed clear enough. The evaluations of the last psychiatrist were completely inaccurate. Every test appeared to have been interpreted wrong. It was almost as if someone had *wanted* Thornton to be released as soon as possible.

Startled, she practically jumped out of her skin when the cell phone in her pocket rang. *No! I need more time!* Purposely slow to answer, she waited five rings, taking several moments to brace herself to deal with his turbulent thoughts.

"Hello Kaycee."

"Yes, Mr. Thornton." Glancing up, she answered Bauer's questioning gaze by mouthing *it's him*, as she motioned for silence. Bauer nodded, moving to her side so he could eavesdrop.

"I'm afraid that due to extenuating circumstances, our game time has changed."

She tried to seem unfazed, even though the hair on the back of her neck began to crawl from intuitive fear. "That's interesting, although not very fair. Why?"

"Because I said so."

"Sorry. I forgot for a moment that you're a control freak. Please excuse me." Kaycee had to fight to ignore the *are-you-insane?!* glare Bauer pinned her with each time she uttered a word. Keeping her voice steady, she closed her eyes to concentrate as she asked, "So, when do you want to begin this little game you've planned for so long?"

An unreal echo suddenly pierced the mountain air, followed by the *wham!* of a high velocity impact. Kaycee's eyes flew open. By the time she realized it was a gunshot, Bauer had been propelled against the rock wall by a bullet in his forehead. His shocked eyes stared straight ahead as he slumped to the ground, then fell face first into the snow at her feet. "Oh, my God!" Kaycee gasped, unable to take her eyes off the gaping hole that used to be the back of Bauer's head.

Thornton emerged from the nearby line of trees, smiling widely. When she finally dragged her eyes away from the gruesome sight, he was walking toward her, a cell phone in one hand, the gun in the other. His reply hit her in grisly stereo—over the phone and across the closing gap of snow covered meadow:

"The game starts now."

•   •   •   •   •

Deep inside the mine, the stench of death soaked the air so completely that Max found it hard to keep from retching. He hadn't encountered a booby trap since just past the entrance, but he walked with the caution of a man who knew each step might be his last. His insurance policy, a stick with a shoestring tied to the end, led the way. If there were a trigger line in the path, the shoestring would lightly catch, revealing the danger before man or beast came to harm.

The tunnel ahead sharply narrowed where the support beams on one side had completely collapsed. Although Stagga could still stand upright, Max was forced to crawl, inching the light line and the stick along ahead of him. It wasn't long before Stagga alerted. They had found the source of the foul odor.

Fighting back a wave of nausea, Max edged past the decaying corpse without trying to identify it. There would be plenty of time for that later. When he and Stagga were well on the other side of the body, he stopped to rest and catch a breath of refreshing air. Relief washed over him as he realized two things. Although the tunnel was closing ahead, the down draft was stronger—they were getting close to the source of fresh air. But more importantly, this air was clear—it no longer carried tidings of death. *Maggie might still be alive!*

Working faster, he started crawling. There wasn't enough room for Stagga at his side, so he told him to stay. Pressing forward another twenty yards, he could no longer squeeze through. Using his flashlight, he aimed it toward the end of the tunnel, spotting an opening.

"Maggie! Are you in there?" he called.

Silence.

Pushing the light line through the narrow tunnel, he watched as the open area ahead was slowly illuminated. "Maggie! My name is Max and I've come to take you home. Please answer me if you can. That glowing rope is called a light line. We can follow it out together."

The silence was broken by a muffled sneeze.

"Maggie! Is that you?"

Suddenly Stagga rushed forward, barking frantically and tugging at the hem of his pants. Scooting back to where he could sit up, Max tried to control him. "It's all right, boy. I know she's in there. She may be too afraid to answer. Or maybe she's hurt. Crawl to her, boy. Search."

For the first time Max could remember, Stagga disobeyed his order. The dog ran in the opposite direction, stopping a few yards away to thunderously bark his warning—which disturbed the unstable ground overhead enough to free fresh showers of dirt.

Before Max followed Stagga, he called, "Maggie, I'm going for help. We'll have you out of here in no time. I promise!"

Leaving the light line in place, Max crawled, then ran as fast as he could behind Stagga. Several times he shouted, "Stagga, halt!", but the dog merely waited for him to almost catch up, barked his defiance, then took off again.

Max trusted Stagga's instincts as much as he trusted his own. Something terrible had happened at the entrance to the mine. *Please, let me make it in time!*

· · · · ·

A fine mist of Bauer's blood rained on Kaycee's shoulders, even on the folder she held. Time seemed to hold its breath, waiting for the horror to end. But it didn't. Mind-numbing terror demanded she move, but she couldn't. Her muscles seemed frozen, her ears ringing as if it were *her* brains scattered in the snow.

The purest form of survival instinct kicked Kaycee out of her stupor. Her slack jaw snapped closed when she heard a noise ahead, forcing her to break contact from the repulsive sight at her feet. Thornton was storming across the open field, totally unafraid of anyone or anything.

Raw anger surged through her veins with each of Thornton's advancing steps. Trying not to be obvious, she reached down for the gun that protruded from the dead man's holster.

Thornton merely laughed. "Surely you're smart enough to know what I'll do if you touch that."

Kaycee stopped. A dead person couldn't help Niki or Maggie, *or keep Thornton from killing Max!* Suddenly, she thought of Max and Stagga hearing the gunshot, rushing to help her, and walking right into Thornton's trap. She had to get Thornton away from the mine. Fast!

Standing, Kaycee straightened her shoulders. "Okay, so you've killed another innocent man. What now?"

"You come with me."

"Fine. Lead the way."

Her unexpected cooperation made him wary. Suspicious, he said,

"That's it? You're just going to do what I say?"

With narrow eyes, she pretended to hear something in the distance, then challenged, "Put down the gun and we'll see if you're such a big man. I believe I won the first round."

"Which is exactly why I don't trust you." Straining, Thornton listened and watched the sky. "They're coming back, aren't they?"

"They?" she asked innocently.

"I saw the helicopter!" Shoving her forward he screamed, "Now quit stalling and move!"

Kaycee didn't look back. Walking as fast as she could without breaking into a run, she headed into the forest, thankful he couldn't see the look of triumph on her face, and that at least for now, he didn't seem to realize they weren't alone.

"Follow that trail," he ordered, shoving her down a narrow path that showed only the fresh tracks of several deer.

"Where are we going?"

"To a safe place to watch."

"Watch what?"

"You'll see. Just shut up and move!"

Kaycee did as she was told, but the terrain was steadily becoming steep and rocky. Hardly any snow had survived the afternoon sun in this barren area, which meant they wouldn't be leaving an easy trail to follow. Glancing at her watch, she guessed they were already a quarter of a mile from the mine.

Grabbing the back of her coveralls, Thornton held her steady as he declared, "This'll do."

Looking around, she didn't know what to think. There were few places to hide, they could easily be spotted from the air, and running would be almost impossible. "*This* is where you want to play the game?"

"Hell, no!" He pulled out his cell phone and dialed. "This place has the best reception." Just before he punched the last number, a wide grin lit his face. "Bombs away!" he laughed.

At first Kaycee didn't understand. Then she felt the slight tremor of the earth, a ripple in time that slashed her heart out of her chest as it slowly rumbled past. Wide-eyed, she shook her head, denying what she feared more than anything. Her voice was hoarse, barely even audible. "The mine?"

He shrugged. "Gone."

"But. . .your own daughter? My s. . .sister?"

Thornton shrugged, shoving her toward the tree line as he jabbed the gun into her ribs. Still, she refused to walk.

Tears streaked her face, and her legs no longer seemed to be part of her body. They felt as heavy as lead, yet were quivering like Jell-O. Collapsing, the rocks painfully chewed at her knees and she felt light-headed.

She didn't care what Thornton did to her. She prayed he would just kill her quickly. It wasn't only Niki and Maggie in the mine. Max and Stagga were there, too. *They're all dead. . .*

In the background Kaycee could hear Thornton's string of threatening cuss words, feel his hatred, but she didn't care. Holding her head in her hands, she was overwhelmed with such grief that she longed for each breath to be her last.

S tagga rushed out of the mine first, even though Max was still shouting orders for him to halt. Ignoring his master, the dog barked frantically as he slid to a stop next to Bauer's lifeless body.

Max slowed to a hesitant walk, afraid to step into the sunlight where he would be an easy target. Although he couldn't see much from inside the entrance, the blood splattered snow told him all he needed to know. In a low voice, he called, "Kaycee? Bauer?"

His question seemed to be answered by a deafening blast that started deep in the belly of the mine. Like a tsunami, the impact rolled toward him, riding atop tons of collapsing dirt. "Run, Stagga! Run!" he screamed.

Max made it a few yards outside the mine's entrance before diving to elude the wall of energy plowing into his back. Still, the shockwave rolled both he and Stagga like tumbleweeds halfway across the snowy meadow. Before the last clumps of dirt hit the ground, Max was on his knees searching for Kaycee.

When he could focus again, he knew Kaycee was gone, that the blood had been Bauer's. *Thornton has her again!* he thought, clenching his teeth.

Enraged and determined, he crawled toward Stagga. "It's okay, boy," he whispered, burying his face in the dog's soft fur. Stagga tried to raise his head, but only managed to whine. Pushing himself up, Max discovered a long, black sliver of a mining beam was protruding from Stagga's hindquarter. Ignoring the sharp pain in his own shoulder and the ringing in his ears, Max shrugged off the backpack and took out the medical supplies. "We've got to find her, Stagga. You're gonna be okay. I'll make this as fast and painless as I can."

As if he understood, Stagga laid perfectly still, releasing only a small yelp when Max jerked out the offending shrapnel.

"Sorry, boy. This is going to sting, too," he warned as he dumped a generous amount of hydrogen peroxide on the wound, patted it dry, then wrapped it tightly with clean gauze.

"Can you walk?" Max asked, as if speaking to a human.

Stagga raised up on his front paws, then pushed up on his uninjured hind leg. Although he was wobbly at first, by the time he followed Max to Bauer's body he was balancing pretty well on three legs.

Max rolled Bauer over, grimacing at the bullet hole in his head as he felt for a pulse that had long ago ceased. Surveying the rest of the area, he noticed the bloody trail of footprints that led away from the body. It was all too easy to imagine what had happened, and the image served to push him to a new level of rage.

Seeing that the generator had been blown over by the blast, Max realized the light line was no longer connected. Unwilling to give up hope, he struggled to upright the equipment, refilled the gas, and prayed that the line would still work. When the generator started purring softly on the first try, he sighed and reconnected the line. As it glowed to life, he said to Stagga, "If Maggie's still alive in there, maybe the light will give her hope."

Just as Max picked up the utility belt of ropes that Kaycee had been wearing, Stagga alerted. Declaring approaching danger with a deep, low growl, the hair on the back of his neck stood on end. Max felt every muscle in his body tense as he prepared to take evasive action. Carefully, he turned to look over his shoulder.

Working his way down the ridge, Palmer shouted, "What the hell happened? First I heard a shot, then it felt like there was an earthquake."

Max relaxed, patting Stagga. "Easy boy. He's on our side." To Palmer, he called, "Apparently Thornton killed Bauer, took Kaycee, then detonated enough explosive to collapse the mine."

Palmer's breath caught when he saw Bauer. Turning away, he staggered for a moment, then gagged. When he'd recovered, he turned back. "Is it too late? Should we be doing CPR?"

Max shook his head. "He's dead. I'm sorry, but there's nothing we can do."

Turning away, Palmer fumed, "Thornton will pay for this."

"Fine. Let's just stop him before he kills Kaycee, too. She has my cell phone. Can you call the police on yours?"

Palmer hesitated, then nodded. Pulling out his cell phone, he punched a button, then dialed 9-1-1. Giving a detailed account of where they were, and the gravity of the situation, he requested help from both the local agencies as well as the FBI. His last words were, "Approach with extreme caution. Thornton has another hostage and is armed and dangerous."

•   •   •   •   •

Maggie had been in her hiding place when the explosion rolled through the mine. A few of the carefully stacked rocks had fallen, but her invisible friend, Jeremy, had promised he would help her fix them.

When the food ran out last night, she saved the final box of juice for breakfast. That was hours ago, and her stomach ached and grumbled. Tired and hungry, she rocked back and forth, twisting the chain of the gold cross around her finger. Jeremy wanted her to look out, to see what had happened, to find out what had made that big noise. But Maggie didn't care. All she wanted was to listen to the pretty music in her head.

Squeezing her eyes tightly closed, she hummed *Jesus Loves Me* as she waited for the angels to come take her someplace she was sure Daddy would never, ever find her.

•   •   •   •   •

Kim and Roger trudged toward the mine in the silence of the last few moments of daylight. Halfway there, Roger muttered, "I still think this is crazy."

"Don't start nagging me again. I only agreed to let you come because I'm going to need help carrying Maggie out of that hellhole."

"*If* she's even in there. You said yourself she was in the car with him last time you saw her."

"She's in there. She wasn't in the mobile home, and we know he's still in the area. Besides, Niki said that this morning he talked about playing a game. That's what he told Maggie—hiding in the mine was all a game."

"Assuming we find her, what are we going to do with her?"

"Take her home to Liberal, Kansas."

"Just like that. We don't call the police. She just appears on her mother's doorstep."

Kim nodded.

"And what happens to you?"

"I start over. Kimberly Annabelle Snyder is dead. She died in a car wreck last week."

"What about your grandmother?"

"She's better off without Kim. Kim was nothing but trouble."

"And Thornton just goes on killing people."

Kim stopped, holding up a hand. "Shhhh. Did you hear that?"

"You mean the dog barking?"

"What's a dog doing out here?"

"Probably a stray."

Both froze when a voice a few yards ahead of them called, "Stop right there and nobody gets hurt." A tall blond man stepped into their path, an immense handgun trained directly on Roger as he barked, "Who are you and what are you doing here?"

Neither spoke for a moment, then Roger asked, "Are you a forest ranger, FBI or what?"

"No. Just an interested citizen."

Another man with a dog came up behind him. The dog's hind quarter was newly bandaged, yet bright red spots of fresh blood had already begun seeping through the gauze. Roger took one look at the injured dog and nervously rattled, "What is going on here?"

Flaunting the gun, Palmer demanded, "First you tell us why you're here."

Kim snapped, "We really don't have time to play twenty questions. There's a little girl not far from here who needs our help."

Recognition spread across Max's face. "You're Kim! From the motel. Do you know where Thornton's hiding Maggie?"

Wide-eyed, Kim nodded, "In an abandoned mine. We're here to get her out of there."

Max sighed. "If she's in the mine, we may be too late. Thornton set off an explosion that collapsed the entrance. Is there another way in?"

After shooting Roger an *I-told-you-so* glare, for a moment Kim was silent, then she shook her head. "I should have come sooner." Suddenly, a sparkle lit her eyes. "Maggie was in a natural cave at the far end of a branch of tunnel that had already partially fallen. He told me only the front part was wired to explode."

Max nodded. "If that's true we may be in luck. The energy of a blast near the entry might not have carried all the way through. Plus, the impact to the area where she's hidden was probably minimized by the constricted passage."

"At the top of where she is there's an opening! It's less than a foot wide and only about two feet long, but it's enough to let in air and sunshine. If we find it, I'm sure we can get to her with those ropes."

Max pushed aside one of the ropes, reaching for his radio. The half-empty pocket reminded him that Kaycee still had his GPS and cell phone. "Damn it! Cal should have been back by now." Ignoring the others, he keyed the radio and asked, "Cal, do you read?"

The answer was barely audible over the heavy static. "Almost there. Ran into some trouble in town. ETA eight to ten minutes. Did you find Randy?"

"Affirmative. Randy was injured by a booby trap, but he's in good hands now. I don't have a fix on our exact location, so when you get close I'll light a signal flare. On your approach, keep an eye out for any activity or light source on the ground. Cal, Thornton has Kaycee."

"We'll find her, Max."

"I know." For a moment Max was obviously torn. Casting a harsh look at Palmer he said, "We can only work one lead at a time. Looks like we can find Maggie quickly, then resume the search for Kaycee."

Palmer nodded.

Turning to the others, Max said, "Follow me. We'll go back to the clearing by the mine where Cal can land the helicopter. Stagga and I'll go with Cal while the three of you search on foot for Maggie. If I'm right, if the chamber didn't collapse, it will be well lit. Hopefully, we'll be able to spot it from the air. It can't be too far."

Puzzled, Kim asked as she plodded along, "Did you give Maggie a flashlight?"

"Not exactly. I fed an illuminated rope into the area where she is. As long as its generator is running, it should be working. It's designed like Christmas tree lights—if the blast knocked out one piece, the rest should still work. Listen." He paused, then added, "That's it. We're almost there."

When they approached the clearing, Kim whispered, "Thornton planned some game for tonight. We'd better be careful."

Max's breath caught. "You know about the game?"

She nodded. "First Maggie told me, then this morning we found a crippled woman he'd kidnapped. She heard him say it was tonight."

"Niki? You found Niki?" he asked excitedly.

Kim beamed. "She's safe. We left her with her friend about an hour ago."

Max sighed. "Thank God. Now if we can only save Kaycee."

Pulling out a gun she offered it to Max. "Take this. It may save her life." "I already have one. Besides you may need it. Thorton could be anywhere."

Kim shook her head, dead serious as she replied, "I don't need a gun anymore. If I get half a chance, I'll kill him with my bare hands."

·   ·   ·   ·   ·

In a matter of minutes, Cal spotted the flare in the meadow and landed. After a quick round of introductions, Palmer agreed to stay in radio contact as he led the others to the top of the hill to wait for further instructions.

Max gently carried Stagga on board, cradling him in his lap as he buckled up. Cal maneuvered the helicopter, tossing Max a headset as he shouted, "How bad is he?"

Max stroked the dog's neck. "Stagga's a warrior. He'll make it. Take us slowly east, then north. If that doesn't work, we can try a zigzag pattern back toward the entrance."

"Still looking for a light source?" Cal asked.

"It's down there. I can feel it."

Only thirty seconds later, Cal excitedly reported, "Bingo! There it is!"

Max leaned as far as he could, but saw only the gloomy, barren land below. In a flash of memory, he recalled Kaycee's fear of the dark and longed for yet another miracle. "Sorry, Cal. I didn't see a thing. Where should I look?"

"I'm coming around again. It's only visible from straight overhead because of the brush. Looks like you two better gear up. It's a calm night. Are you going down together?"

"Yes. Once we're down, you'd better swing back and show our friends the easiest way with the spotlight." Putting the sling around Stagga, he strapped their safety harnesses together and took off the headgear. With a thumbs up, he signaled they were ready to descend.

Although the terrain was too rough to land, Cal hovered within ten feet of the ground, making the drop-off easy. After helping Stagga out of the sling, Max carefully tested the ground near the opening to be certain his weight wouldn't cause it to collapse. Crawling slowly toward it, he leaned in far enough to see.

The tunnel where he had been just prior to the explosion had completely disintegrated. Two feet of light line seemed to be growing out of the new wall of dirt. To his dismay, the chamber appeared to be empty except for a large box on one end, a pile of rocks on the other, and a small pile of trash.

"Maggie? Are you in there? I came back to help, just like I promised."

Dead silence. Max thought he might explode, certain every second brought Kaycee closer to death. *I should have tracked her first. . .* "Maggie? Please answer if you can!"

Still, not a sound. Taking out the doll with Maggie's scent, he commanded, "Stagga, search!"

This time Stagga's job was almost too easy. He instantly came to full alert. Hanging his nose over the lip of the entry, he whined and barked, scratching the dirt as the sound echoed through the chamber below. Max grabbed his radio. "Palmer. Do you read?"

"Yes. Did you find her?"

"I think so. I'm going to lower Stagga to be sure, but then I'll need your help to get her out. Cal will light the way. We're running out of time, so hurry!"

Max wrapped the sling around Stagga once again, then carefully tied a rope to his harness. After anchoring to a nearby pine, he slowly eased him down, trying to ignore the fiery pain in his injured shoulder.

As soon as the dog's paws touched the dirt, he crawled out of his sling to scurry toward the pile of rocks. Instead of barking, he let out a soft yap, as if he knew better than to frighten the child. With his tail wagging wildly, his head and upper body disappeared from sight.

Tears jumped to Max's eyes as the dog slowly backed up, delicately towing the little girl out of her hiding place. Her face, and small , bound hands were buried in Stagga's soft, brown fur.

When Stagga's eyes met his, Max would've sworn he was crying, too.

CHAPTER 31

"Are you ready?" Palmer asked, amazed at the strength the little girl showed in spite of all she'd been through in the last week. When she nodded, he called, "Okay, hoist her up!"

Maggie sat in Stagga's sling, humming softly as Max and Roger steadily pulled her up and into Kim's waiting arms. Next, Max impatiently rushed Palmer through the steps to get Stagga ready to ascend. As soon as the dog was safely up, Palmer grabbed the dangling rope and gracefully climbed to the surface. A smug, confident smile lit his face.

After Max made certain Kim, Roger, and Maggie were securely strapped in and Stagga was in his sling ready to be lowered, he joined Cal and Palmer standing a few yards away from the helicopter.

Turning to Cal, Max asked, "How soon do you think you can be back?"

"Roughly fifteen minutes."

Palmer glanced at his watch and volunteered, "I expect Moore to be in the area in our helicopter any time now."

"We've got to be careful. If Thornton sees helicopters buzzing all over this mountain, he's sure to try to get away. Cal, once you drop us off, you'd better go due north to minimize the chances that he'll hear you. Palmer, will Moore contact you before getting too close?"

"Without further instruction, he'll return to the area near where the Trooper was parked, south of the mine."

"We'd better call him off for now. Thornton was taking Kaycee southwest when we left his trail. Do you know how to *heli tac?*"

Palmer's face fell. "It's been a while since I've ridden the skids of a 'copter. I have to admit it's not my favorite mode of transportation."

Max positioned himself on a skid. "We don't have time for training. Kaycee's waiting. If you're not up to it, then stay here. We'll be back."

Giving Cal the thumbs up he yelled, "Let's go. Drop me as close as you can to where we left the trail."

At the last moment, Palmer jumped onto the passenger side skid, casting a wary look over his shoulder as he glanced at his watch.

Maneuvering a few feet above the tree tops, Cal flew them over the crest of the mountain, then eased as low as he could to drop them off at Max's signal. When Stagga had safely joined Max and Palmer on the ground, Cal whisked the others away.

Palmer cringed as a hush fell over the forest. "God, I *hate* heli tac! It's like being a bug on a friggin' windshield."

Max agreed, "But the time we gained may save Kaycee's life." Digging deep into his pack, he found something he had hoped he would never need—the ball he had playfully rubbed on Kaycee to get her scent. Holding it under Stagga's nose, he ordered, "Search, Stagga. Find her for me, boy. Find her fast."

•   •   •   •   •

For the fifth time in as many minutes Kaycee stumbled, unable to negotiate the path's rocks and stumps in the darkness. The light of a crescent moon helped, but not enough.

"Quit stalling! Who do you think's gonna help you? I blew your boyfriend's brains out, remember?"

Kaycee shuddered, praying those words weren't true. As they hiked, the events of the week seemed to uncurl before her, and her inner pain gradually turned to an even deeper loathing of the man lumbering on her heels. *I have to be strong. It's up to me to stop him!*

She knew the situation wasn't totally hopeless. The razor knife was still tucked in her sock. Bob Palmer was on the mountain somewhere, and he'd probably already called in help. Plus Cal would be searching the area soon.

As if her prayers had been answered, Kaycee's heart skipped a beat at the distant whisper of a helicopter. Instantaneously, she realized the threat that simple sound presented. Coughing loudly, she pretended to choke for several seconds, hoping to drown out the noise. Finally, she hoarsely whispered, "Sorry. Must have. . .inhaled a bug."

When Thornton brutally shoved her forward, she realized the noise was gone, and that he must not have heard it. Ellen had been right—knowing how to listen could save your life.

Over the next rise she spotted something gleaming in the moonlight ahead. A few steps closer sent her spirits plummeting. *A car! If we leave here, I don't have a prayer. I've got to keep him talking.* Desperate to distract him, Kaycee abruptly asked, "Who was Levi?"

Thornton stopped. "How'd you find out about Levi?"

"That's the guy's name they were paying to snitch on you."

"Then he got exactly what he deserved."

She leaned against the front bumper, hoping he wouldn't force her to get in. "Why would they do that? Why would they plant someone in your prison cell, then have you followed when you got out? What makes you so special?"

He laughed. "I've never been special to *anybody.*"

"You're wrong." With a defiant cock of her head, she added, "I can prove it if you like."

"How?"

"Remember that file I stuffed inside my jacket? It spells it all out."

"Sure it does. Your little scheme isn't going to work."

"This isn't a scheme. Haven't you wondered how I found this place? It's all in the file."

He raised the gun in warning. "Take it out slowly, very slowly."

She did as she was told, easing out the file, then spreading it open on the hood of the car. Gaining his confidence by playing to his ego, she pulled out several of his writing samples. "Did you know they had these?"

"Those sons-of-bitches! So my letters never got mailed."

"Apparently not. You know, you have the most complex handwriting I've ever analyzed." Even though she could barely see to pick up a piece of paper, she found one and continued, "If you'll shine a light on this I'll show you what I mean."

His curiosity piqued, he snapped on the flashlight.

She began by pointing out the letter formations that showed his few actual strengths, using every buzz word she could think of to try to drag out time. "You have strong-willed zonal characteristics, although they're frequently overridden by your unconscious intellectual drives. You make your capital I's backwards, don't you?"

"What do you mean?"

"I mean you start at the bottom and curve up."

He nodded.

"That can be an expression of genius." She left out that it was more likely a sign of perversion, of a person who resents authority. "And see the reclined slant? The past pulls at you, dragging you back when you should be looking forward."

"What are you, a psychic? People don't actually pay you to do this, do they?"

"Yes. Handwriting is the window to the soul."

"More like the door to the outhouse."

"Think about it, Thornton. All human thought, action, even desire, stems from one place—our brain. When the mind controls the pen, all the other impulses that effect us come out on that page. Even when you try to hide something, you can't."

"Why are you telling me all this? I'm not hiding anything."

"If you're not worried about hiding, than what about me? Why didn't you just forget about me and go on?"

"Had to cover my ass. Prison isn't where I care to spend my leisure time."

"Then why did you kidnap Maggie? Surely you knew they'd look for you first."

"I needed her."

"We both know it's not that simple. You could've used any child, but you wanted to show your power over your own." Kaycee shook her head as she took a deep breath. She felt like a lawyer fighting for the life of a client with mere words, except this time it was *her* life hanging in the balance. Slowly, she gathered the courage to face him eye to eye. "When I first touched your handwriting, I was almost overwhelmed. You are highly intelligent, so much so that you can fool most of the people who have tested you. It was easy in prison, wasn't it? After the first few exams, you knew exactly what the new shrink wanted to hear."

"So?"

The lies flowed more naturally the longer she spoke. Like a ravenous bird waiting for another handful of bread crumbs, Thornton hung on her words. "So most men don't aim for their target that aggressively. Most couldn't even figure it out if they tried. You were born with the intellectual capacity to do whatever you dream, yet your existence is utterly focused toward self-destruction. That's why you kidnapped Maggie. You knew they'd come after you. It's what you wanted." She touched his hand. "Remember this morning when I said our paths were destined to cross? I think I'm supposed to stop you."

There was a glint of humor behind his self-assured stare, "Stop me from killing you?"

She shook her head. "No. Stop you from killing yourself."

· · · · ·

In spite of his injured hind quarter Stagga was easily tracking Kaycee's scent. Max rubbed his aching shoulder as he glanced back toward Palmer to softly say, "By the way, thanks for volunteering to rappel into the chamber back there. My shoulder's not in the best shape right now."

Palmer's voice was equally hushed. "My pleasure. I'll never forget the look on that little girl's face. Although I'm not sure she'd have been very eager if it hadn't been for Stagga."

"It's the best part of working rescues. Dogs can break down emotional barriers people don't even know exist. How do you suppose the police are handling our situation?"

Palmer hesitated before commenting, "Hopefully, they'll do as I asked and be discreet. I'd bet we won't even know they're around until it's all over."

Stagga suddenly froze. Turning north, he cocked his head, perked his ears and growled. A millisecond later Max understood. A thunder-like rumble accompanied a slight tremor underfoot. "I'm glad we rescued Maggie first," Max breathed.

Palmer nodded. "I'll bet Thornton just remotely detonated another charge. That's what he did in the Army, you know, munitions expert. Our source said he had trip lines all over this mountain, some booby trapped, others that set off silent alarms. That may be our message that he knows we're coming."

Max muttered, "Great."

Stagga led them up several steep inclines, then back down again. When they were about to crest another, Max could tell by Stagga's intensity that they were close. Very close. Holding the dog back, he motioned for Palmer to stay down as he peeked over the top. At the base of the ridge a hundred yards ahead, he spotted them. Although it was too dark to tell for sure, it looked like they were using a flash-light to study something on the hood of a car.

Scooting back, Max whispered, "They're up ahead."

Palmer instantly took charge. "I'll circle around. Are you armed?"

Max nodded. Slipping off his backpack, he bit his lip, fighting back the urge to remind Palmer who was leading this mission.

"A lot of good it would've done you in there," Palmer quipped.

Max took a deep breath, ignoring Palmer's attitude. This wasn't the time or place for a confrontation. "It's not something I normally need for directing rescues."

"Do you even know how to use it?"

Fed up, Max glowered. "I won't hit you, if that's what you're wondering."

Palmer nodded toward Stagga, who kept impatiently sniffing the air. "Is he going to give us away?"

"He'll keep quiet."

"Good. Give me three minutes to get into position. If you get a clear shot, take it."

"Shouldn't we give him a chance to surrender first?"

"That depends."

"On what?" Max whispered.

"On whether you're willing to gamble with Kaycee's life."

Kaycee was confident her plan was working. In the last few minutes Thornton had become noticeably less agitated. "Where'd you get this stuff?" he asked.

She lied, "From the F.B.I."

"Why would they have it?"

"I guess because you're a wanted man. They do extensive profiles on kidnappers."

"You can't kidnap your own kid."

Ignoring his twisted logic, she asked, "What about my sister? What do you call that?"

He smiled and lightly shrugged. "Okay, so I'm a kidnapper. But some of this isn't true." He pointed to the parole report. "This says I never got busted in prison. I practically killed one guy for smackin' his lips at me." With a degree of pride he added, "Got solitary for six months for that stunt."

It was her turn to be intrigued, "See anything else?"

"Says here I stole jewelry from a warehouse." He laughed as if the very idea were preposterous.

"So what *did* you take?"

"Platinum from a guy's house."

"Platinum? Why platinum?"

"The stock market is one of my hobbies. Couldn't afford to play it the *real* way, but I still kept my eye on it. I watched and waited, decided platinum was a good investment for my future."

"So you stole a little?"

"Hell, no. I stole the whole load. Pure stuff."

"Where'd you find pure platinum to steal?"

"That waitress I offed told me exactly where it would be. She'd been screwing some rich guy who bought it out of the country. Got his personal stash. Amazing what a diversion an explosion can be. Just walked in dressed like a fireman, wrapped the whole safe up in a tarp and rolled it out on a dolly."

"And later you killed her because she wanted her share?"

"Nah. My eggs were cold that day."

Even with all her psychiatric training, Kaycee was amazed at the degree of his depravity. He truly placed no value on human life. "So, you must be a very rich man."

"Nope. It's still hidden. Just can't get to it now."

Kaycee easily began piecing the puzzle together. "You hid it in the part of the mine that collapsed, didn't you? You needed Maggie to help you get it back out."

He nodded, pushing her toward the trunk. "I think maybe you really are a psychic. Maybe you should have your own 900 number."

Kaycee turned to face him as he opened the trunk, inwardly happy that he was calm enough to crack jokes. "Why haven't you tied me up?"

He flipped open an ice chest and grabbed a beer. The gun he'd kept steadily trained on her dipped slightly for only a breath as he took a long swig. "What for? You won't escape."

"I did once."

"That was before. Here, we're in my territory. There's nowhere you can hide that I won't find you. Besides, the hunt will be half the fun."

"Why kill me?" Reaching into the trunk, she picked up one of Niki's shoes. "You've already taken away everything I love. The rest of my life I'll be miserable. Isn't that enough?" As Thornton considered her words, she watched him transform. In the blink of an eye the dark side of his personality abruptly erupted again.

"That bitch! Your sister—" His voice was clipped by the crack of gunfire so close that it whistled as it passed.

Thornton wrapped one immense arm around Kaycee's neck,

using her as a human shield while he returned fire. Recoiling from the deafening noise and shower of bullets Kaycee automatically screamed, "No!" In the confusion of the moment, she thought she heard a dog's piercing bark nearby.

Kaycee was dragged backward while Thornton fired first one direction, then another. *Stop! He'll kill all of us!* she tried to scream, but couldn't. A flurry of bullets flew around them until one snapped her head back, shifting the world into slow motion. The slug sang as it grazed the edge of her right temple, then stopped with a sickening thump somewhere deep inside Thornton's massive chest. Falling back against the car, he relaxed his grip, freeing her to drop to the ground.

With repulsive accuracy four more bullets pummeled Thornton's body, each one showering her with bits of bone and blood. Their screams merged, then faded as he dropped to his knees and collapsed directly on top of her. Except for the lone flashlight that illuminated a triangle of dirt nearby, the world was dark and deadly quiet.

Kaycee no longer knew where she was or how she got there. She was trapped in thick black sludge, unable to move, just like in her nightmares. But now, seeing didn't matter. The only thing that *did* matter was the need to breathe. Yet as hard as she tried, she couldn't drag in even a trace of air.

Suddenly, the suffocating weight lifted off her chest. Fresh air replenished her body's needs, slowly bringing back the horrible reality of the moment. In spite of the sensory assault of spent gunpowder and spilled blood, she cherished every breath.

A rough, wet tongue stroked her cheek. Stunned, she opened her eyes and smiled. "Stagga," she whispered. A smile creased her face when she saw his ears perk at the sound of his name. He replied with a tender yap. Impulsively, she grabbed his neck, gleefully crying, "You're alive!"

Max finished pulling Thornton's body away and moved to her side. As if her hand would pass right through his ghostly form, she gazed in wonder. "Max? Is it really you?"

"Of course." He gently picked her up, carrying her as far as he could from the gruesome scene. "It's all over now. You're going to be all right."

"But, I thought. . .The explosion?"

"Stagga warned me just in time. Niki and Maggie are both safe, too."

"Really?"

"Really." He gently placed her on a large, flat rock. "Let's have a look at you."

Kaycee gasped as she gazed down. She was covered with blood. Touching the graze on her temple she said, "I'm fine. I'm pretty sure most of it's not mine."

"Thank God." His eyes searched hers. "Will you be okay here for a minute?"

She nodded.

Max quickly used the radio to give Cal their location and to ask him to notify the authorities. As he ignited a signal flare, Max shouted, "Palmer? Are you okay?"

"Coming," Palmer replied, emerging from the woods a few yards away.

"Are you hurt?"

"Not a scratch."

Max stepped forward, putting all his weight behind a solid suckerpunch to Palmer's jaw.

The unexpected blow sent Palmer reeling against a nearby tree. Staggering to his feet, he wiped a trickle of blood from his mouth and demanded, "What the hell was that for?"

Stagga was growling at Max's side, his teeth bared. "That was for senselessly risking Kaycee's life."

"In case you haven't noticed, she's alive."

"No thanks to you."

•　•　•　•　•

The world grew smaller as Cal expertly whisked them away from the mountain. With one hand Max squeezed Kaycee closer, with the other he stroked Stagga's neck. On the winding pass below, he saw a line of flashing lights atop speeding emergency vehicles. "Looks like the cavalry finally arrived."

"A little late," Kaycee sighed, resting her head against his chest.

Max nodded, concerned only with getting both Kaycee and Stagga medical attention.

Gingerly touching the bandage on her forehead, she asked, "What was Palmer thinking? I had Thornton under control. He didn't have to shoot him. . ."

Max shook his head. "I still can't believe you didn't get killed in the crossfire. He's either one helluva shot or you're very lucky."

Kaycee tiredly replied,"I don't think anyone on the planet would consider me lucky at this point."

"Things could always be worse."

"Let's hope not!"

. . . . .

At ten o'clock the next morning Max stood at the door of Niki's house, his eyes nervously darting about the disorderly room. "You know, you both should be resting. You've been through so much. . ."

"Which is why I want to get this done now, before I go back home to recuperate," Kaycee replied.

"Are you positive the two of you will be all right? I could stay. . ."

Kaycee shook her head and demanded, "For heaven's sake, just go! You're only going to be gone a little while. Niki and I will be fine. Give Randy and Smokey a hug for me."

"I could leave Stagga with you for protection. . ."

"If he knows how to vacuum and scrub, fine. Otherwise, he'll only be in our way, and I have enough cleaning to do without adding dog hair to the list," Niki called from the bedroom."I'll be back before Agent Jones gets here at noon. Don't forget to lock up."

Giving him a playful shove, Kaycee closed the door and locked it.

"What's his problem?" Niki asked, stopping her wheelchair at the bedroom door.

Kaycee turned around, softly shaking her head, yet smiling. "I think he's wired backwards. In a crisis he's as cool as ice, then after all the excitement is over, he starts getting paranoid."

"As handsome as he is, he can be paranoid whenever he likes. Makes no difference to me."

"Back off, sister. He's mine."

"Believe me, that's more than obvious."

"It is, isn't it?"

"When you're not watching, he looks at you like you're the only woman alive."

"Really?" Kaycee asked, closing the gap between them to give her sister a hug.

"Really. I'm happy for you. And for me."

"Which means?"

Niki grinned. "It means I don't have to live the rest of my life feeling guilty."

Kaycee raised her brows, obviously puzzled. "I'm only operating on a few hours sleep, so I guess you're going to have to spell it out for me. Exactly what would you have felt guilty about? My never finding a man?"

"Of course not! You moving back here. Your life is in Tulsa. Don't you see? You can't throw it all away just because you feel sorry for your little sister. I keep telling you, I'm doing great! I really will get out of this wheelchair. It's just going to take a little time."

"You certainly have the determination."

Niki smiled. "We both do."

"Then why are you just sitting there? Clean!"

Rolling into the bathroom, Niki resumed her scrubbing as she asked, "Can you believe we both kicked that Thornton dude's ass?"

Following her, Kaycee started sweeping up the remnants of the broken lamp. "That's it! Our new profession!"

"Sorry, I'd rather not scrub bathrooms for a living."

"No! Once you're out of that wheelchair we can become a pro-wrestling team. I can see it now, the Mighty Miller Sisters in matching purple body suits."

"Hold on, I look like crap in purple."

"Okay, then black. We'll wear black. It's always flattering," Kaycee offered.

"On you, maybe."

"Oh, I almost forgot. I hope you don't mind what I did last night."

"If it was with that sexy hunk, I not only don't mind, I wish you'd give me all the juicy details!"

"Niki! No, seriously, I know I should have asked you first, but there just wasn't time. At the hospital, I had a chance to talk to Maggie, the little girl who'd been trapped in the mine. She was wearing Mother's antique gold cross. She wouldn't even let the nurse take it off when they admitted her. I told her to keep it. Are you mad?"

"Of course not. And I'll bet Mom is up there smiling right now."

"As long as I live, I'll never forget the look on Maggie's mother's eyes when she saw her daughter for the first time. It was more than just love, it was a mixture of disbelief, gratitude and pure joy that was so strong that everyone in the room was in tears. Now I truly understand why Max is addicted to rescues."

The doorbell rang. Kaycee asked, "Are you expecting anyone?"

"Not a soul. B.J. already came by to check on me."

"Just in case Max's instincts are right, stay in here and keep quiet. Okay?"

"Good grief. You two deserve each other. You're both nuts."

"Coming!" Kaycee called, rushing across the room after throwing a warning glare at Niki. Through the peephole she recognized Bob Palmer. Pulling open the door, she asked, "How in the world did you find me here?"

"Agent Jones said he was meeting you at this address later. I hope you don't mind my dropping in. It's just, I—" he pulled a dozen long-stem pink and white roses from behind his back "—I really wanted to apologize for last night. I would never purposely endanger anyone's life. I must have gotten caught up in the moment."

Taking the flowers, Kaycee stepped back so he could come inside. "You didn't have to do this. Believe me, I'm quite aware how differently people react under stress."

"I'll bet you're an expert on it," Palmer agreed. "Last night was unbelievable. You certainly held your own. For a few minutes toward the end, it looked like you had him eating out of your hand."

If you were close enough to see that, why did you fire? she wondered, but simply nodded. "I did. Which reminds me—" she picked up Thornton's file and handed it to him, "This is yours. To put it mildly it was quite interesting."

"We have excellent sources."

"Apparently that's an understatement. There are things in that file that are quite confidential. Like the parole board information. . ."

"It helps that I'm on the board."

Kaycee nodded. "I see. . ."

"You're not complaining about CSI's methods, are you? Looked to me like that information saved your life. By the way, how'd you do it? How'd you calm him down like that?"

Ignoring the growing feeling of discomfort deep in her gut, she said, "Actually, I just diverted his attention using his own background to earn his trust. Strangely enough, he claimed some of it wasn't accurate." She sensed, more than saw, Palmer stiffen.

"Like what?"

"Nothing major. I didn't mean to imply CSI does second-rate work."

His voice took on a placating tone. "Kaycee, I employ over seventy people. If our company hopes to keep its edge, we have to make sure our quality surpasses our client's expectations. Without it, we're history."

"I understand."

He was growing impatient. "Then please tell me what Thornton said so I can determine who's not doing their job."

Kaycee shifted uncomfortably. "Well, I don't remember it all. Seems like he had a problem with the police report on what he stole."

"The jewelry?"

"Exactly. He said it wasn't jewelry at all, that it was pure platinum."

"Interesting. What else?"

"He was surprised that Levi was hired to follow him. By the way, why was CSI so interested in Thornton's whereabouts?"

"We were hired by the family of the waitress he murdered."

With a faraway gaze, Kaycee muttered, "Because his eggs were cold. . ."

"What?"

She shook her head and tried to smile. "Nothing. I'm just worn out."

"It has been a long, hard week. I guess it's time to pick ourselves up, dust off, and go on with life."

"You sound like you've had your share of hard times," she commented.

He nodded. "Three years ago today a gas leak blew up one end of my house. Killed my wife and baby. I suppose you could say I've got first hand experience with tragedy. And now, poor Brock Bauer. He was my loyal employee for fifteen years. He deserved better than a bullet through the head."

Kaycee closed her eyes, fighting back yesterday's untouched memories. The pain they carried was still too fresh to confront. "He seemed like a nice man. And I'm sorry for your loss. Every anniversary must be hard."

"You learn to focus on other things. Are you here alone?"

Something about the way his eyes darted across the room made Kaycee leery. Fully aware that Niki had probably been hanging on every word, she said, "Yes. Max went to the hospital to check on Randy, so I thought I'd straighten up Niki's house before she came back. She's so frail. I don't think she should see it like this."

"And Cal?"

"He flew home to Tulsa to pick up Randy's wife, Joan. Why?"

"Just curious. Did Thornton mention where he hid the platinum?"

"In the mine. I suppose the authorities will recover it."

"I doubt that," Palmer snapped. "The explosions effectively buried everything."

"That's odd, too."

"What?"

"I watched Willy detonate the first charge. I could tell he was surprised when there was another blast."

"Probably a misfire of some sort. I'm sure black market explosives aren't the most reliable in the world."

Kaycee shrugged, then sucked in a deep breath. "I know this isn't the best time to tell you, but I'm afraid I've decided not to move back to New Mexico. I'll still be available for consultation, but I won't be coming to work for CSI."

Palmer simply stared at her for a moment, then slowly pulled a gun out of a shoulder holster hidden beneath his jacket. "Actually, Kaycee, you won't be going to work for anyone at all. Thornton told you, didn't he?"

Her heart leaped in her chest, not only for her own sake, but for Niki's. "Bob. . .I. . .I don't know what you're talking about. Put that gun down!"

With a sneer, Palmer stepped forward. "Sorry. I can see it in your eyes. You know the truth."

CHAPTER **33**

Niki's hands were so sweaty she could scarcely get the wheelchair to roll. Afraid the floor would squeak, she only dared to move an inch at a time as she worked her way toward the phone on the far side of the bed. Barely past the end of the bed, she stopped. Raw wires dangled where the phone jack had been ripped out of the wall.

Scanning the room, she searched for anything she could use as a weapon. A broken wedge of lamp caught her eye. It would do in a pinch, but not very well. Spotting Kaycee's purse on the bed, she hoped that her sister was better prepared for a crisis. Inside she found a wallet, cosmetics, and at the very bottom a leather sheath.

Niki peeled back the leather and slipped out the surprisingly savage weapon. Pushing a button on the side, a gleaming blade shot out, locking into place.

Tucking the knife carefully under her thigh, she wiped her hands dry, then rolled toward the door.

• • • • •

Kaycee clasped her hands, unable to believe the twisted chain that linked Thornton to Palmer. "Oh, God! It was your house he bombed, your platinum?"

"I always knew you were smart."

"Thornton killed your wife and baby?"

"Yes. It was a pleasure blowing him away last night."

"But you were cheating on your wife. The waitress. . ."

"Bullseye. So you do know all the dirty details. Guess I'm still a good judge of character."

"And I suppose I should be grateful that you didn't shoot me last night when you had the chance."

"True. I'm an excellent marksman." He gently caressed the bandage on her temple with his index finger. "I did miss once last night. This shot was a little off center."

"You *meant* to kill me?"

"Only if I could make it look like an accident. That's why the first shots didn't take him out. I knew that coward would use you as a shield. But you moved at the wrong moment."

"And that second blast at the mine?"

"After I helped Maggie out, I planted a homing device on the platinum to be sure I'd be the only one who knew where to dig, then I set a digital timer on a small charge."

"You planned for every possibility, didn't you?"

"No. React and adapt are the keys to survival. Surely you've learned that by now."

Out of the corner of her eye, Kaycee saw Niki roll into the doorway of the bedroom. She knew she had to keep Palmer from turning where he could see her as well. "So you came back today to finish the job?"

"More like to test the water. I wasn't sure how much you knew. I truly hoped you'd be so busy licking your wounds that you'd just be happy to be alive."

She shook her head. "One thing escapes me. Why'd you give me the file if you knew I might piece all this together?"

"Morbid curiosity. At the time, I was certain Thornton would never let you out of there alive. Regardless of what you think of my tactics, the man was a cold-blooded killer. Obviously, I underestimated your people skills. It's too bad. You'd have been a hell of a feather in CSI's cap."

With a pathetic grin, Kaycee asked, "I don't suppose you'd believe me if I told you I would keep your secrets?"

"Now there's an interesting thought. How many secrets would you be keeping?"

"I know you influenced the parole board to get Thornton released early."

"True."

"If I had to guess I'd say there was some reason you had a personal stash of platinum. Money laundering, maybe?"

"My, my, you are intuitive. Thornton stole over a million dollars. To put it mildly, my other business contacts were not amused. And they're not the type of people I want to have as enemies."

"Thornton had proof of what you were doing, didn't he?"

"That he did. It was in the safe with the platinum when he stole it. Did he mention the diskette to you? In some ways, it's even more valuable than the platinum."

Niki had made it to the garage door and was opening the door. Nervous excitement made Kaycee's voice raise slightly as she lied, "As a matter of fact, he did. What's on it that's so earth shattering?"

"Details. Names, amounts, your basic set of books that the IRS can never see. Highly incriminating records. Where is it?"

"Get real, Palmer. Why would I tell you? As soon as I do, you'll blow my head off."

"If you don't, I'll blow if off anyway."

"No you won't. If that diskette finds its way to the authorities, you're dead."

"Seems we've reached an impasse."

Niki slammed the door, calling, "I'm home! Anyone here?"

By the time she turned her wheelchair around, Palmer had shifted behind Kaycee. Holding the gun behind his back, he whispered, "Make a wrong move and I'll kill her, too." Raising his voice he called, "This must be your sister, Niki. Kaycee's told me so much about you. I'm Bob Palmer, president of CSI."

Niki rolled across the room, extending her hand to greet him as she replied, "Kaycee has spoken very highly of you. Thank you for saving her life last night."

At the moment his hand gripped hers, Niki lurched forward, swinging the razor-sharp knife. Palmer's eyes went wide as the blade sunk into the soft tissue beneath his rib cage.

As he fell, Kaycee kicked the gun from his hand, shoved Niki away, and grabbed the weapon as it hit the floor.

"Are you okay?" Kaycee asked, training the gun on Palmer's head.

"Sure," Niki replied, staring at the bloody knife in her hand. "I'm glad that worked. Plan B was a lot more shaky."

"What was plan B?"

"The Mighty Miller Sisters were going to have to wrestle the gun from him."

"Better dial 911 before he decides to try," Kaycee said with a crooked smile. Tightening her grip on the gun, she felt her confidence grow. Niki really was going to be okay. And she was, too.

Hanging up the cell phone, Kaycee turned to Max. "Agent Jones says they're wrapping up the case. Palmer's still listed in serious condition, but they expect him to make a full recovery. The only loose ends are Roger and Kim. As soon as they heard she wasn't going to be formally charged, they left a note for her grandmother, then disappeared."

"They deserve a clean start. From what Jones told me, Kim has already had more than her share of hard knocks."

Max parked the Trooper in Kaycee's driveway and sighed. "You're home."

Kaycee beamed. "It's hard to believe so much happened so fast. Do you realize we've known each other less than a week?"

"Meeting you certainly added excitement to my life," he laughed. "I can't wait to see what's going to happen next."

"Oh, no! I'm spending the next month doing as little as possible. Unlike you crazy search and rescue guys, my body can't take this kind of abuse." When Stagga whined in the back seat, both of them laughed. "See, he wants some rest, too."

"Which he greatly deserves."

"I'm glad Randy is going to be okay. It's sad about Smokey, though."

"Just because Smokey won't be doing SAR work anymore doesn't mean he won't have a long, happy life. Besides, training a new dog will give Randy something to do while he goes through his physical therapy."

"It's still sad. Smokey was such a good SAR dog."

"The hardest thing about working with dogs is that their life expectancy doesn't match ours. You get so attached, then have to start from scratch again. But we all know up front that it comes with the territory." Touching her cheek, he smiled. "Can I at least talk you into spending the day with me tomorrow?"

"Sorry. I promised Ellen we'd have lunch and catch a show."

"Then I'll settle for Thursday. We can celebrate our one week anniversary. Randy's already bugging Joan to drive him out to the ranch. He says I owe him BBQ ribs and Smokey a steak for getting them into this mess."

"Well, then technically *I'm* the one who should fix them dinner." Kaycee opened the car door and jumped out. "Before we go in, I've got some business to take care of." Walking across the front lawn, she pulled the *FOR SALE* sign out of the ground. "I definitely won't be needing this anymore."

Max wrapped his arms around her from behind, kissing her softly on the nape of her neck. "Are you sure?"

"I'm not moving."

"Well, at least not to New Mexico. I was hoping you'd consider relocating, though. I know of a spacious ranch house that could use a feminine touch. . ."

Dropping the sign, she turned into his arms to return his kiss. "Not very patient, are you?"

"Maybe it's just that I believe in love at first sight. Don't you?"

Her smile widened as she playfully shrugged. "Guess we'll just have to wait and see. . ."

SPECIAL THANKS TO:

Ellen Jones—*who answered every prying question with honesty, sincerity and humor.*

The Tulsa Police Department's finest—*Dennis Larsen, Dave Been, R.T. Jones & D. Davis*

The Tulsa City County Librarians, *especially those at the Helmerich Library*

Jim Stovall, Pat & Larry Larsen, Joan Rhine, Bill & Kirsten Bernhardt

My running buddies—*Ben, Joy, Chester, Brent & Julie and my family*—*Mark, Amanda & Jonathan*